LEGACY OF RA

BLOOD OF RA BOOK THREE

M. SASINOWSKI

KINGSMILL PRESS

ISBN 978-1-7324467-5-5

ISBN 978-1-7324467-4-8 (ebook)

This is a work of fiction. Names, characters, and incidents are the product of the author's imagination, except in the case of historical figures and events, which are used fictitiously.

To my parents, Barbara and Ryszard.
Thank you for your legacy.

Alyssa Morgan—Daughter of Horus and Anja. Moved to Cairo at age ten after her mother's death. Raised by Kade Morgan, an archaeologist.

Bes—A reptilian Rathadi and first among the Council of Elders. Mentor to Dharr.

Claudia Tibaldi—Respected geologist and senior member of the Society, a group of ultra-rich individuals and followers of psychic Edgar Cayce.

Clay Obono—Technology whiz and bioinformatics intern at the World Health Organization (WHO). Best friend of Paul Matthews. Helped Alyssa and Paul by designing a VR apparatus to access Horus's memories stored in the crystal recovered by Kade Morgan from the Hall of Records.

Dharr—A reptilian Rathadi. Commander in the Rathadi military. Led mission to rescue Alyssa and Tasha from Nephthys in the mountains of Nepal. Boyfriend of Tef.

George Renley IV—Eccentric British nobleman and wealthy collector of antiquities. Great-grandson of George Renley who, in 1913, discovered the entrance to the Hall of Records.

Heru-pa—Son of Horus, in line to receive Horus's consciousness and become the next Horus.

Horus—Leader of the Rathadi. Reincarnated for millennia via transfer of consciousness. Grandson of Thoth, half-brother of Nephthys, and father of Alyssa.

Jawad—A canine Rathadi and twin brother to Vol. Mechanic and soldier in the Rathadi military. Participated in mission to rescue Alyssa and Tasha from Nephthys in the mountains of Nepal.

Kade Morgan—Maverick archaeologist who rediscovered the Hall of Records and recovered the crystal that contained Horus's memories. Husband of Anja Morgan.

Kamal Khanna—Director of the Genetics Institute in Cairo, Egypt. Friend of Kade Morgan and Alyssa Morgan.

Maxwell Torin—Head of security of the Society megayacht, the *Valediction*.

Minister of Antiquities—Flamboyant Egyptian archaeologist and television personality.

Nel—A feline Rathadi. Medic and soldier in the Rathadi military. Participated in mission to rescue Alyssa and Tasha from Nephthys in the mountains of Nepal.

Nephthys—Born as a half-Rathadi to Horus's mother. Leader of the Pureans, enemy of the Rathadi. Reincarnated for millennia via transfer of consciousness.

Paul Matthews—Student at Oxford University. Met Alyssa during his internship at the World Health Organization (WHO). Best friend of Clay Obono. Captured by Nephthys after her attack on the Rathadi home in Hong Kong.

Sia—A feline Rathadi. Member of the Council of Elders.

Tasha Renley (Mendeva)—Born in St. Petersburg, Russia. Rescued and adopted by Lord George Renley when she was nine. Former girlfriend of William Drake. Used by Nephthys to infect the Rathadi by carrying a virus inside her body into their Hong Kong home. Captured by Nephthys after her attack on the Rathadi home in Hong Kong.

Tef—A serpentine Rathadi. Pilot and soldier in the Rathadi military. Participated in mission to rescue Alyssa and Tasha from Nephthys in the mountains of Nepal. Girlfriend of Dharr.

Thoth—Grandfather of Horus. Scribe to the gods. Creator of the memory capture technology and the ancient bioweapon found in the Hall of Records.

Vol—A canine Rathadi and twin brother to Jawad. Pilot and soldier in the Rathadi military. Participated in mission to rescue Alyssa and Tasha from Nephthys in the mountains of Nepal.

Wen—A Rathadi boy. Befriended Alyssa when they met at the Rathadi home in Hong Kong.

William Drake (deceased)—For a brief time, the leader of the Society, a group of ultra-rich individuals and followers of psychic Edgar Cayce. Masterminded the plan to steal the memory crystal from the Hall of Records. Alter personality of Edward Wallace, former student of Kade Morgan.

Xander Hart—Inventor and friend of Lord George Renley.

Xin—An avian Rathadi. Member of the Council of Elders.

PART 1

DISCORD

THE FRIGID WIND slipped through Alyssa's thermal gear and bit into her skin. She drew the heated parka tighter around her and used a gloved hand to wipe the snow from her visor for the tenth time.

Who knew doing surveillance was like being stuck in the armpit of some frost giant?

She scanned the white expanse that stretched before her, then shifted her pupils down and blinked, activating the optics in her visor. The landscape zoomed in, and a square building rose out of the snow: their target.

A soft chirp in her headset alerted her to movement in the perimeter. She switched her focus to the head-up display inside her helmet. Three red dots skimmed across the terrain map, converging on the square that represented the building in front of her.

Her mouth twitched.

The patrol is back. Earlier than anticipated.

She shimmied deeper into the powder, the all-white

chameleon suit blending into the snow, concealing her almost completely. Moments later, the throaty purr of snowmobile engines rang over the flat terrain.

Three vehicles, each with a single rider, came to a stop in front of the building. The tall figures dismounted and removed their helmets, their dark skins in stark contrast to the white snow surrounding them. Two of them slipped inside, the third pulled a knit cap over his shaved head and remained at the door.

A hand squeezed her left shoulder. She turned. Dharr's gaze beckoned from behind his visor, the thin black slits inside bright yellow irises gleaming with anticipation. Only four weeks ago, she had met the Rathadi for the first time when Dharr's team rescued her and Tasha from Nephthys in the mountains of Nepal. Now, four weeks later, the same sense of awe filled her every time she peered into his reptilian eyes, set deep inside the scaly skin of his face.

Four weeks without Paul and Tasha…

"Three more than we had anticipated," Dharr's voice rang in her headset, snapping her back into the present.

"Wh-What?" Alyssa stammered.

Dharr blinked. "Three more Purean soldiers," he said.

She drew in a sharp breath. *Stay focused,* she scolded herself.

A week ago, they had received information that Nephthys might be holding Paul and Tasha in this abandoned facility. After spending a week double- and triple-checking the reports and preparing this mission—and an additional two days staking out the building in the bitter cold—her focus had begun to wane.

"Perhaps we should wait…" Dharr started.

We are not turning back without Paul and Tasha.

"We may not get a second chance," she said. "More than half of the Pureans are still out, not due back for another hour."

Dharr met her gaze for several moments. "Very well," he said. "We proceed as planned." He shifted to his mic. "Vol?"

"In position and ready," Vol's voice was stern and razor-sharp, replacing the usual jovial tone he shared with his twin brother, Jawad.

Dharr glanced over his shoulder. Behind him, Tef and Nel, the two Rathadi females, lifted their left hands in unison, their thumbs and forefingers in a circle.

"We're go in fifteen seconds," Dharr said.

A countdown clock appeared in Alyssa's head-up display. She turned to their target as the numbers ticked down.

0:05

She zoomed in again, focusing on the Purean sentry.

0:02

0:01

The sentry collapsed to the snow. Alyssa leaped up and broke into a sprint, with Dharr beside her and Nel and Tef bringing up the rear. The powerful, steady breaths of the Rathadi echoed in Alyssa's headset as her feet pounded the soft snow. They slowed when they approached the Purean lying face down on the ground, a red stain spreading in the snow beneath his head.

Dharr reached inside the Purean's uniform and pulled out a keycard. He swiped it at the door, and the latch released. He cracked it open and rolled a dozen marble-sized balls into the building. A second later the balls whirred to life and lifted off the ground. They rose until they hovered just below the ceiling, then fanned out along the corridor leading deeper into the compound. Alyssa's map of the exterior of the building switched to a three-dimensional projection of the inside. The image evolved into a complex of corridors and rooms as the miniature drones mapped out the passages and transmitted the data to her helmet.

A few seconds later, two blue dots materialized in what appeared to be two separate, small rooms, several corridors into the building.

"The drones picked up a trace," Dharr said. "Their heat signatures are consistent with humans. One female, one male."

Alyssa shivered. Not from the cold, but from the anxiety that curled up like a creature inside her stomach.

Tasha.

Paul.

Timing was everything, and they would have to move fast if they wanted the rescue to succeed.

Dharr signaled to Tef and Nel. "Get Tasha." The women acknowledged, and they slipped inside the building. "You and I are on Paul," he said to Alyssa.

She paused at the door, surveying the space. An empty corridor with gray, drab walls stretched out in front of her. As Alyssa took in her surroundings, the view in her helmet was augmented by transparent arrows, leading her to one of the rooms. She and Dharr moved along, keeping low in a crouched position, hugging the walls to their left and right for cover.

They reeled to a stop when the head-up display showed two red dots approaching, crossing their path ahead from the right-hand passageway. They backed up and squeezed into a small alcove. Alyssa pressed her back against the wall and waited, keeping her eyes locked on the junction of the two passageways in front of them.

Dharr lifted his weapon as the guards neared the crossing. The sound of footsteps grew louder. Alyssa held her breath—then exhaled as the guards continued moving straight, away from them. She remained motionless and followed the dots in her display until the guards moved into a parallel hallway.

They left the alcove and continued along the corridor, turning right, then left into a narrow passageway. Alyssa's heart hammered against her chest when they stopped in front of a heavy metal door.

She pushed down on the handle.

Locked.

Dharr reached into his thigh pocket and took out a small transparent square. He kneaded it in his gloved hand for several moments and flattened it against the lock. A few seconds later a sizzling sound followed by a wisp of smoke emanated from the metal behind the material. Dharr pressed the handle, and the door swung open.

Alyssa glanced inside. She reeled at the sight before her. A prisoner lay on the floor of the cramped cell, facing the wall, his clothes disheveled and soiled. He slowly rolled over.

Paul? Alyssa fought against the burning liquid rising in the back of her throat.

His skin was ashen and his cheeks hollow. Dark circles rimmed his eyes, and a scraggly beard covered his features. Alyssa's gaze moved down to his right arm—

Her mind refused to accept the image in front of her. Paul's right arm came to a stump below his elbow, the wound covered by a filthy, blood-stained bandage.

Alyssa's hands trembled as she slipped off her helmet. She gagged at the smell of blood and human waste that invaded her nostrils.

"Paul?" she whispered, her voice almost failing her.

He looked up at her with an empty expression.

Alyssa took a steeling breath and entered the cell. "Paul, it's me. It's—"

The sound of a wounded animal ripped out of Paul's throat an instant before he leaped to his feet and charged her, his eyes gleaming wildly.

THE SCREAMING of the men echoes into the moonless night. Their clawed hands rake at their twisted shapes. I cannot bear to watch and turn away. My grandfather pulls me to him and holds me tight. I look up, seeking solace in the coarseness of his robe against my cheek and the familiar furrows of his ancient face.

His features change, they become softer, younger. The gaze shelters me. Warmth washes over me as the terror ebbs. Incomplete, the face transforms again.

No... don't leave...

Bitter cold floods me once again, culled from the night sky with its stars as hard as diamonds.

Another face, strong and sculpted. The yellow iris in his single eye reflects thousands of distant pinpoints of light.

Cold metal presses against my palm and weighs down my right hand. I lift my arm. I blink at the sight of the weapon I hold. I point at the figure and squeeze the trigger.

He reels from the impact. His features twist into a mask of

rage, and his glare burns into my skin, scorching me down to my soul. He roars and charges.

Pure terror surges through my veins. I draw back. My foot meets empty air. The darkness swallows me as I fall, a silent scream seared into my lips—

Alyssa lurched as the floor dropped from beneath her feet. Her hands reached out and gained purchase, barely keeping her upright. She took a wavering breath and shook her head, trying to clear the fog. Gradually, the walls of the cramped medical bay in the Rathadi jet came into focus, and memories fell into place.

I dozed off... standing...

She glanced down. Her hands were clamped around the grips of the medical cot. She forced herself to let go and appraised the occupant.

Dharr's eyes were closed, but he grimaced and stirred restlessly. His right hand whipped free of the silver blanket covering him and knocked the oxygen mask from his face. Alyssa grasped his arm and gently pushed it down then adjusted the mask over his mouth and nose. She pressed her palm to his forehead. His gray reptilian scales were cool under her touch, and his breathing seemed less labored than when he and Heru-pa first stormed aboard the plane after Nephthys's attack.

The attack that had turned the Rathadi home into a raging inferno.

The attack that killed Horus.

Alyssa shuddered as the memories threatened to surface. She forced them down.

Not now.

Not yet.

Dharr coughed. Tiny red dots splattered against the inside of the oxygen mask. His eyes fluttered open. He studied Alyssa for several moments, his gaze unfocused. Slowly, recognition spread through his face. He pushed himself up.

"Where are we?"

Alyssa helped him sit up and put the thin pillow behind his back. "Crossing the Celebes Sea," she replied.

He leaned against the cabin wall. "Heading to Indonesia?"

Alyssa nodded. During their flight, they had received a single command. Regroup with the other Rathadi at their safe location in Indonesia. The AI on the jet had locked in on the signal of the beacon, and their heading has not changed since. Soon they would be reunited with the other Rathadi… and Paul. Would she be able to tell him the truth about Horus? The thought of lying to him—

"Heru-pa?" Dharr asked, interrupting her thoughts.

"Still in the aft cabin."

"Has he said anything?"

Alyssa shook her head.

A soft ping broke through the silence. Dharr glanced at a display on the wall.

"We're approaching the target," he said.

Alyssa helped Dharr ease down from the cot, and they strapped into a pair of jump seats. Alyssa glanced out the small window. She could make out mountains and trees below, but it was too dark to discern any details. The jet decelerated then descended steadily as the AI guided it down to a flat rocky outcrop in the side of a mountain. A small jolt confirmed they were once again on solid ground.

The plane rolled forward, and moments later they passed

through a massive gate into what appeared to be an enormous cavern. Alyssa blinked when she recognized scores of Rathadi unloading equipment and servicing other planes. The planes seemed of similar design to their jet, but they were larger and not as sleek. *Transports?*

Dharr noticed the quizzical look. "We've kept this safe location ready in case we had to evacuate at a moment's notice," he said. The Rathadi in the cave hangar stopped what they were doing and watched the jet as it rolled to a halt, and the engines began to spin down. Dharr loosened his harness and stepped to the door. He glanced back, beckoning her, and Alyssa followed him to the rear of the plane.

They entered the aft cabin. She froze. Heru-pa's back was turned to her as he kneeled down on the floor before Horus's lifeless body. She closed her eyes, banishing the images that threatened to surface again.

Not yet...

Heru-pa slid his arms under Horus and lifted him off the floor. He swiveled around, and their gazes met. Any hope Alyssa may have harbored that the flight had eased his resentment for her evaporated when she glimpsed the hatred burning bright through his anguish.

Her shoulders sagged under his gaze and her own guilt.

He is Horus's true heir. His true Legacy. I am... nothing...

She flinched at the hiss of the ramp seals releasing. Dharr gently nudged her forward, past Heru-pa. They waited for the ramp to lower to the ground then exited the plane. Dharr swept his gaze over the parked planes. He exhaled in relief.

"All of the transports are here," he said as a crowd of Rathadi gathered around the jet. "I was—"

Dharr stopped when he spotted four young Rathadi soldiers rushing to them, breaking through the ranks of the gathering crowd. A shiver of relief passed through Alyssa as she recognized Tef's shimmering reptilian skin and Nel's sleek features and champagne blond curls. The twins, Vol and Jawad, trailed behind the two Rathadi women, toothy grins set in their shaggy, canine faces.

Tef scurried to Dharr and wrapped her arms around him, the scales of her skin glowing brightly. She turned to Alyssa and approached, arms open, but froze before she could reach her. She stared over Alyssa's shoulder. Her smile fell away like a cracked mask.

Heru-pa stepped past them and stood at the edge of the ramp, holding Horus's lifeless body in his arms. A gasp billowed through the assembled Rathadi. Alyssa's heart sank as anguish and disbelief filled the faces before her. Tef sank to her knees. Row after row, the Rathadi who had gathered around the plane kneeled down and bowed their heads.

Alyssa's vision blurred. Only a few hours ago, these Rathadi had been celebrating her as she stood on the summit of the glass pyramid in their Hong Kong home. This same throng now probed into her, their bodies ravaged by the disease Nephthys brought on them.

That we *brought on them…*

No… You and Tasha were just pawns in Nephthys's game.

A long stretch of silence filled the vast space. Tef was the first to speak. "The Legacy?" she asked Heru-pa, her voice trembling.

Heru-pa stared at her wordlessly, his lips pressed into a tight line.

Horror spread through her face. "Has it... has it been lost?"

Dharr stirred next to Alyssa. He seemed to gather his remaining strength before he spoke. "The Legacy lives on," he declared, his voice fierce.

A spark of hope shimmered through the anguish. "Heru-pa?" Tef asked.

Dharr shook his head. He faced Alyssa and sank to his knees. He lifted his hands to her, his palms forming the sacred Rathadi blessing, the triangle between his palms symbolizing the rays of the sun spreading onto the earth below, bathing it with life.

A murmur rippled through the Rathadi.

"How...? How is it possible?" Tef gasped.

"She is Alyssa, daughter of Horus and Anja," Dharr said reverently.

The murmur rose in volume. Tef stared at Alyssa as if trying to reach into her mind.

Several heartbeats later, she slowly lifted her arms in the Rathadi blessing. Behind her, Vol and Jawad repeated her gesture, then Nel. Alyssa stood frozen as more of the other Rathadi raised their arms, offering their sacred blessing to her.

"No!" Heru-pa's voice ripped Alyssa's breath away as it tore through the cavern. The Rathadi stopped in mid-motion. All voices faded, like wind falling in the wake of a sandstorm. "This girl is not Horus's Legacy! She is his bastard child!" He lifted a golden amulet above Horus's body. "I am his son! I am his true heir!"

Alyssa stared at the amulet. A cascade of images blinded her, frozen snapshots from another life flashing through her head.

My mother, peering down at me, eyes calm and full of confidence, the sacred amulet shining in her hands.

I bow my head, ready to accept it as her gift and blessing.

"Heru-pa!" Dharr's voice cut through the images, snapping her into the present. "The sacred relic is not yours to bear. How dare you remove it from Horus before the ceremony? It is to be received by the Legacy!"

"I am his Legacy!" Heru-pa roared.

"Your father made his choice."

The voices stirred through the crowd again, rising in intensity.

"He should have waited!" Heru-pa shot back, his voice breaking.

"You know there was no time," Dharr pleaded. "This is not the place for this discussion. We can—"

"She is an abomination," Heru-pa spat. He cast a withering glance at Alyssa before storming down the ramp, carrying Horus in his arms.

The Rathadi scurried to part before him as he tore through their ranks.

"Heru-pa!" Dharr shouted after him. "Do not do this!"

The gazes of the Rathadi darted between him and Alyssa standing on the ramp. The cavern fell into a sullen silence, as if the world were holding its breath. One by one the Rathadi stood and followed Heru-pa out of the cavern.

Alyssa heaved a ragged breath. Her heartbeat pounded in her temples. "I… I'm sorry…" she stammered. Her head spun. "I…" The word came out in a rasp. She stared at the thinning crowd, now keenly aware of the strangeness of the faces peering back at her.

"Paul…?" she asked. "Where is Paul?"

———

PAUL WAS BURNING UP. He stumbled again. This time his knee smashed into the hard floor, sending waves of pain through his leg. He groaned, his entire body shivering from the freezing cold and the illness that raged within him. His bound hands and the hood on his head transformed every step and wheezing breath into a perilous struggle.

A pair of strong hands jerked him roughly to his feet and pushed him along. The echoes of their footsteps bounced off the walls as he plodded along the corridor.

Where is Tasha?

His mind wandered to their capture. After he woke up in the helicopter that took him and Tasha away from the burning Rathadi building, Nephthys's Purean soldiers hooded and bound him. He gave up fighting against the restraints hours ago. It did nothing but force the sharp plastic to cut deeper into his skin.

He and his captors had been traveling for several hours. They exchanged the helicopter for a jet and stopped once. He assumed it was to refuel. After that, he fell asleep, or perhaps he had simply passed out from the pain and exhaustion. *Not that it made any difference.*

When they finally landed, and he stepped off the plane, his feet sank into snow, and the cold air chilled him to the bone in an instant. Fortunately, they entered this building after only a few steps. He hoped Tasha was still close. He had called out to her earlier, but a slap to his head discouraged him from trying again.

He was pulled to a stop and out of his thoughts. He heard the sound of a key against a metal door. *A cell?* A moment later, his hood was plucked off, and he was shoved inside. The door slammed shut behind him, followed by the sound of the lock turning. He stood frozen in place. His muscles shook with invisible tremors, and his skin felt like it was going to peel away from his body.

The fear and weakness paralyzed him even more than the frigid air. Slowly, he sank to the floor and curled up, his teeth chattering madly. He didn't fight the tears when they came and flowed freely down his cheeks, sinking into the cold floor beneath him.

———

ALYSSA PERCHED at the edge of her seat across from a long metal table in the center of the room. Heat rose behind her eyelids as she stared at Tef. The young woman's serpentine scales shimmered a bluish green in the dim light that reflected from the cavern walls. Alyssa and Dharr's team had been summoned by the elders to one of the rooms set inside the vast cave system that served as the Rathadi emergency shelter.

"Nephthys captured Paul?" Alyssa echoed Tef's words, her mind refusing to accept them.

"He was with us when we were defending the last transport," Tef continued. "I... I don't remember what happened. One moment I was fighting, then I passed out. When I came to,

I was in the escape pod—" she gave a slight quiver—"with a severed Purean arm lying on top of me."

Alyssa cringed at the image.

"Wen said that he saw Paul after the explosion," Nel offered. She looked from Alyssa to the center of the room. Three old Rathadi and Heru-pa regarded them with grim expressions from behind the council table.

"Wen?" Alyssa asked. "The boy?" Alyssa recalled the young boy's rabbit-like features and fine fur.

Nel nodded. "He said that Paul carried him to the transport. He went back for Tef when…"

"When what?" Alyssa pressed. "What happened?"

"He defeated a Purean soldier in combat and remotely launched the pod," Nel said.

"He saved us," Tef added. "There were two dozen of us in that escape pod."

Alyssa rubbed her temples, struggling to absorb the information while trying in vain to tune out the pressure building behind her eyeballs. "We have to get him away from Nephthys," she said finally.

"No." Heru-pa stood from the chair at the edge of council table. "We have much greater problems than the human boy."

"That *human boy* saved twenty Rathadi!" Alyssa shot back.

"They would not have needed saving if you and the other girl hadn't brought the infection into our home."

"You know what happened wasn't Alyssa's fault," Tef said.

Dharr stepped in. "I agree that Paul deserves our help, but the infection has taken a great toll on our people."

Alyssa blinked. "I'm going after him whether you help me or not."

"We are in no condition to mount a rescue mission right now," Dharr urged.

"I will not just sit—"

"You will do exactly as you're told," Heru-pa said.

"I am Horus's Legacy!" Alyssa cried out before she realized what she said.

Heru-pa leveled her with a scornful glare. "Until the memories reveal themselves to you—if they ever will—you are nothing but a vessel," he scoffed. "Not worthy of what has been entrusted to you."

Alyssa flinched at the sound of the chair falling behind Dharr as he leaped up and rushed Heru-pa, but Tef held him back. Heru-pa stared at him, his lips twisted into a taunting sneer.

"You will not speak to her that way!" Dharr growled, his voice low and threatening.

"Or what?" Heru-pa asked. "You will choose her over one of your own?"

"She is one of our own now," Dharr countered. "Your father entrusted me with her protection. I will do what I must to carry out his last wish."

Heru-pa moved closer to Dharr, baring his teeth.

"Enough!" a voice from the middle of the elder table broke through. An ancient-looking Rathadi held up his hand and rose slowly to his feet. His crocodilian scales were dark and rough, and his ageless reptilian eyes burned into Heru-pa and Dharr.

Bes, Alyssa recalled. *The first among the elders.*

"We shame him with our actions and our words," he said, his voice choked with grief. Heru-pa and Dharr lowered their heads like two scolded school boys, then took a step away from each other.

"We lost thirty-one of our kin," Bes continued. "Less than seven hundred remain. The Rathadi owe Paul a debt of gratitude, for without him our numbers would be even smaller." He took a labored breath. "Be that as it may, and whether we agree with it or not—" his gaze shifted from Heru-pa to Alyssa —"you have been chosen to bear the Legacy of Horus. As such, you are too valuable, and too vulnerable, to risk right now. You do not yet know how to use his powers or how to pass on the Legacy. If anything were to happen to you…"

"The Legacy would be lost forever," Dharr uttered.

The elder Rathadi lifted his scaly chin. "The infection that plagues us is our greatest threat and common enemy. We shall reflect on the wisest course of action." He swept his gaze through the room. "And you must all do as you are told, for that is our greatest chance to survive this plight." He rested his eyes on Dharr. "Horus entrusted you with keeping her safe. Now the weight of your responsibility is higher than even he could have foreseen. You must do as he commanded."

Dharr nodded somberly.

Alysa opened her mouth, ready to press her case, but Dharr shot her a glance and shook his head. She closed her mouth and paused, thinking.

"What is the status of the infection?" she asked.

"The symptoms peaked shortly after the pathogen was activated," Nel answered, "before our immune system had a chance to respond. Nephthys was aware of that and attacked us when we were most vulnerable."

"So the disease has stabilized?" Alyssa asked.

"No," Bes answered. "It continues to progress. The symptoms are sometimes more tolerable than at other times."

"Let me contact my friends," Alyssa offered. "With the resources at the WHO they could—"

"Out of the question!" Heru-pa interrupted.

"This decision is not yours to make," Dharr snapped.

Nel glanced at Dharr. "Heru-pa has a point," she offered softly. "The risk of exposing us may be too great."

Dharr threw her a sidelong glance, and Nel looked to the floor.

"But they could help…" Alyssa pleaded.

"We don't need their help," Heru-pa spat. "The council is sufficiently able to address this on our—"

"Do not presume to speak for the council, young Heru-pa," Bes said. "And do not forget that while you have been granted a seat at this table, it is only as an observer—to learn—as befits the role of Heru-pa, and not as a full member."

Heru-pa opened and closed his mouth, but remained silent.

The old Rathadi regarded him forlornly. "So much pride. It has always been your weakness." His shoulders slumped. "We are losing this battle."

"Please," Alyssa said, "let me contact them."

Bes looked to the two elders who occupied the tall chairs on either side of him. They nodded. "Very well," he said to Alyssa. "You may contact your friends."

"Thank you," Alyssa replied.

Dharr turned to the door. He hesitated and swiveled back into the room. "What about Horus's amulet? By ancient rite the sacred talisman now belongs to Alyssa."

Heru-pa scoffed. "I will not relinquish my father's amulet into her hands!"

"What are you hoping to accomplish?" Dharr asked sharply. "You are dividing the Rathadi at a time when we are weaker than we have been in millennia. We must strive for unity to stay alive." He addressed the three elders. "Our wise council, I implore you. You must intervene."

Bes returned his gaze, a rueful expression on his face. "There is no precedent. By ancient rite, the amulet belongs to Heru-pa as much as it belongs to the one to whom Horus transferred his consciousness. These two have always been one and the same Rathadi." He shook his head. "I fear there is no simple answer to this."

"But the Ceremony of Legacy! How can Alyssa go through it and claim Legacy without the amulet?"

The female Rathadi elder to the right of Bes spoke up. "Until Horus's memories begin revealing themselves to Alyssa, we cannot allow the Ceremony of Legacy to proceed." Despite the deep furrows that stretched from the corners of her teal eyes to the edges of her lips, her feline face shone with resolve. "We must have patience."

"Patience?" Dharr called out, exasperated. "Our leader lies dead along with thirty of our kin. A disease is ravaging us. We are cowering from Nephthys in caves, fearful that she may strike at any time. We must proceed with the Ceremony of Legacy and establish Alyssa as the rightful heir to Horus. Only then will we have unity and strength. Patience will not win the war against Nephthys!"

The feline elder's body grew taut as a panther stalking its pray. She slowly rose. "We understand there is a special bond between Elder Bes and you, young Commander Dharr," she hissed, an edge of threat seeping through the graceful features, "but never forget that you are addressing the Council of Elders."

Alyssa caught Heru-pa's smug look. Dharr opened his mouth, but Tef put a calming hand on his arm. Dharr closed his mouth and took a deep breath. He bowed his head to the feline elder. "I beg your forgiveness, Elder Sia," he said, then turned to the other two ancient Rathadi, "and Elders Bes and Xin. I have forgotten myself."

Elder Xin perched on the tall chair to the right of Bes. He craned his long neck and click-clacked a thin, beaklike mouth. "These are trying times indeed," he trilled, his voice pitched high. He ran a restless hand over the crown of wispy white hair on top of his speckled scalp. "Trying times for all of us. We must deliberate."

Dharr's face tightened. "I understand," he said. He bowed once again. "We thank you for your time."

He turned on his heel and left the room. Alyssa and Tef followed him. He stomped through the corridor into the first empty room. Tef closed the door behind them just before Dharr slammed his fist against the wall.

"Old fools!" he cried out. A moment later Nel stepped through the door. Dharr shot her a look. "Thanks for the support back there," he said.

Nel furrowed her brow, but kept her mouth shut.

"Maybe you've still got feelings for your former boyfriend," Dharr pushed.

Nel drew back at his words.

"Come on, Dharr," Tef said. "That's not fair."

"Boyfriend?" the question was out of Alyssa's mouth before she realized it.

Nel bristled. The expression on her face made it clear that she would rather endure the council's wrath than continue this conversation.

"We must convince the council to allow the Ceremony of Legacy to proceed," Dharr said, oblivious to the exchange. "The Rathadi will unite under one Legacy."

"The Ceremony of Legacy?" Alyssa asked.

"The council will refuse to endorse the ceremony while Heru-pa holds the amulet," Tef said, ignoring Alyssa's question.

"They need to force him to give it up," Dharr said.

"But how—" Alyssa started, her voice tight.

"You know they won't," Nel cut in. "They are afraid to press the matter."

Alyssa sighed.

"Can't they see that Heru-pa is playing them?" Dharr grumbled.

"Once the memories begin to reveal themselves to Alyssa, the council will have no choice but to accept her and allow the ceremony to proceed," Nel said.

"How will the memories—?" Alyssa tried again, forcing calmness into her voice.

Tef spoke over Alyssa. "That could take weeks, or months."

"Weeks or months we do not have," Nel said.

"Then we must start the training immediately," Dharr said.

Alyssa opened the door and slammed it shut.

The three Rathadi whirled, their expressions frozen.

"What *training*?" Alyssa cried out, her head spinning from their words. "And what ceremony? Why are you talking about me like I'm not here? I'm tired of being treated like a pawn! I... I..."

Her vision swam. Sweat sprouted on her forehead, and she staggered. Dharr and Tef rushed to her, but Alyssa lifted a palm to wave them off. She stared at her arm, as if seeing the dried blood and dirt on it for the first time. She shuddered, the emotions threatening to overwhelm her.

She took a few breaths to settle herself. "I need to get cleaned up," she said quietly.

"I will show you to the shower," Tef offered.

PAUL WOKE at the sound of the turning lock. He didn't remember falling asleep. He lifted his head off the floor. Footsteps. A pair of arms hoisted him to his feet as if he were a small child. His body ached like it was trapped in a vise. He groaned, and a coughing fit shook through him.

The tall Purean guard regarded him, the angled features of his dark-skinned face smooth and expressionless. The guard waited for the cough to subside then dragged him out of the cell. Paul wavered, struggling to keep his balance. He squinted at the bright lights that illuminated the corridor and the four steel doors on each side. The gray walls around him added to the cold and sterile feeling of the building, chilling him to the bone.

"What is this place?" he asked, his voice rasping in his throat. "Where is Tasha?"

"Quiet," the guard said and pushed him forward.

They took a turn at the end of the hallway and entered a

small room. A metal gurney fitted with leather straps stood against the far wall, a single circular light hung above it.

A cold wash swept through Paul when the guard pulled a long knife from the sheath on his leg. Paul tried to squirm away, but the guard held tight. He spun Paul roughly and cut through the plastic restraints on his wrists then pushed him onto the gurney and strapped him in.

"What do you want from me?" Paul asked, trying to sound braver than he felt.

The door opened, revealing Nephthys and another Purean. Unlike the guards, he was dressed in a simple white coat and rolled a metal cart before him as he followed her inside. Paul blanched when he spotted the collection of stainless steel instruments carefully arranged on the polished surface. The Purean brought the cart to rest a few inches from the gurney. Paul shrank away from it, as far as the straps would allow.

"What do you want from me?" Paul asked again. This time his voice came out in a whimper.

Nephthys appraised him with an amused look. She eyed the contents of the cart and nodded to the Purean who stepped forward and lifted a syringe from it.

"What is that?" Paul cried out, flighting against the restraints.

The guard grasped his right arm.

"Wait! Don't!" Paul screamed as the other Purean plunged the syringe into his arm and emptied the contents. Paul's arm grew hot, the wave of heat surging from his arm to his torso, then spreading through his entire body.

"What did you do to me?" he cried out again.

"You're no good to me dead, boy," Nephthys said and left the room.

The world spun as the guard unstrapped him and pulled him off the table. He half-dragged, half-carried Paul through the corridor and pushed him into the cell then slammed the heavy metal door shut behind him.

————

ALYSSA SET the temperature as hot as it would go and let the scalding water pound on her back. The burning pain was almost enough to numb the guilt she kept buried inside her since they fled Hong Kong, the guilt that had been threatening to break through at any moment. Steam filled the cramped metal stall as she picked up the soap and began methodically scrubbing her skin, washing off the layers of dried blood and dirt, turning the water at her feet to a muddy brown. She scrubbed even harder, as if to rub out the confusion and despair that was taking hold inside her. When the water at her feet turned clear, she moved on to the tangled mess on top of her head. She worked through it, knot by knot. She didn't know when the tears started. They flowed down her cheeks, mixing with the water and disappearing at her feet. She tugged at her hair, harder and harder, frustration building until the pain in her scalp and the scorching water overwhelmed her.

She screamed and slammed her fist into the metal wall.

The shots echoed in her head like cracks of thunder as the memories broke through.

I killed him.

I killed Horus.

I killed my father.

No. She banished the thought.

Nephthys had controlled her mind. There was nothing—

What if she could have resisted it? Fought it harder?

No.

Then why had she lied to Dharr? Why hadn't she told him the truth about Horus's death? Why was she afraid he wouldn't believe her?

The questions kept coming, flooding her mind, until she collapsed to the floor, sobbing. The water continued pounding her body as she lay in the small metal tub, curled on her side, hugging her knees to her chest.

She lost track of time when the knocking at the bathroom door pulled her back into the present. The knocking repeated, more urgently and louder.

"Alyssa?" Tef called from behind the door. "You okay in there?"

Alyssa reached up blindly, fumbling for the faucet. She managed to turn off the water. She took a deep breath and a few seconds to collect herself.

"I'm fine," she muttered. "I'll be right out."

She gained her feet and took another deep breath, letting the hot steam fill her body and help her clear her mind. She toweled off quickly and slipped into the stretchy black jumpsuit that Tef had laid out. The tight fabric clung to her damp skin as she opened the door.

Tef eyed her, concerned. "You okay?" she asked.

Alyssa nodded, paused, shook her head.

"Want to talk about it?"

Alyssa shook her head again.

Tef touched her arm. "Dharr is waiting in the comm center," she said. "Clay received the message you wanted us to send him, and he responded. He's waiting for your call."

Alyssa snatched the towel from the sink and slipped past her. "Let's go!" she called over her shoulder.

She rubbed her hair dry as they paced along one of the tunnels. Alyssa marveled at the labyrinthine cave system and the effort it must have taken to convert it into this full-fledged hidden base.

I suppose when you've been at war for millennia, you plan ahead...

They reached the end of the passage and stopped in front of a gray door. Tef pulled it open and motioned Alyssa inside. The room was small and dimly lit. The wall on the right-hand side had been carved completely smooth and held six large flat screens. A dozen computers and communications terminals lined the other three walls, surrounding a small conference table with eight chairs in the middle of the room. Dharr and two other Rathadi were hunched over the console in the far left corner. He glanced up when they entered.

"There you are," Dharr said. "How are you feeling?"

"Better," Alyssa lied.

Dharr pointed to the chair in front of the terminal, and Alyssa settled into it. She scrutinized the screen and the camera.

"We're sure this will be secure?" she asked Dharr.

"We sent Clay instructions to set up an encrypted channel after he replied to your email."

"Did you tell him anything else?" Alyssa asked. "About..." She pointed at him and the other Rathadi.

"No," Dharr replied. He moved to the side, out of the frame of the camera.

Alyssa clicked to initiate the video call. A soft chirp confirmed the outgoing signal. A few seconds later a video feed popped up, and Clay's face filled the screen.

"Alyssa!" Clay exclaimed. He leaned over his shoulder. "Lord Renley! She's on!" He turned back to the camera. "Are you okay?"

Alyssa gave him a small nod.

Clay scratched the black stubble on his chin. "We've been tearing our hair out, worried sick about the three of you. First, Paul and Tasha storm off in the middle of our conversation. Then you go dark for two days..." He stopped and moved closer to the camera. He squinted. "Are those yellow contacts?"

Two days? It felt like two months ago when she had first arrived at the Rathadi tower in Hong Kong.

Renley moved into the frame and stepped closer to the camera.

"It's a relief to see you, Miss Morgan," he said. "How are Tasha and Mr. Matthews?"

"You should both sit down," Alyssa said, her voice cooler than she had intended.

Renley's lips narrowed at her tone.

Dharr moved to the door, staying out of the picture. "I will give you some privacy," he whispered.

"No," Alyssa said, swinging around. "I'd like you to stay... please." She motioned him to her, in front of the camera.

Dharr hesitated. "Are you certain?"

"They need to know."

Dharr slowly moved into view. Renley and Clay took a collective breath and held it, their features frozen.

After several moments Clay exhaled. "Is that..." he stuttered. "Is he... what I think he is?"

Alyssa encouraged Dharr to step closer. "Lord Renley, Clay, this is Dharr, a Rathadi... a Hybrid."

Renley rubbed his temples. "Just when I thought I'd reached an age at which I have grown immune to surprises..."

"Dharr and his team saved me and Tasha after Nephthys captured us in Nepal. They brought us to their home in Hong Kong."

"A Rathadi home?" Clay carved both hands through his black curls and held tight, scratching his head, open-mouthed. He finally released his hair. "There are more?"

"Hundreds," she said. *But fewer now.* "Nephthys attacked the Rathadi—"

"Wait, attacked you in Hong Kong?" Clay broke in. "Please don't tell me you had something to do with the skyscraper fire that's been all over the news."

"Nephthys convinced Yuri Korzo to alter the ancient bioweapon from the Hall of Records to—" Alyssa started.

"Yuri Korzo?" Renley interjected. "The scientist who took over Baxter's work for the Society?"

"Nephthys used him to modify the bioweapon to make it lethal to the Hybrids. She injected it into Tasha when she took us captive."

"My god," Renley said, his face turning ashen. "Is Tasha...?"

"She seems to be immune to the virus," Alyssa said.

"Immune?"

"I don't understand it either. We thought we had escaped Nephthys, but it was part of her plan all along. She waited for the virus to infect the Hybrids and fall ill, then attacked them when they were weakest, debilitated by the infection."

Clay paled. "Why would anybody do this?"

"The Rathadi and the Pureans have been at war for millennia." Alyssa paused. "Horus... he was there."

"Horus?" Renley raised both eyebrows.

Alyssa clasped her hands together to keep them from trembling. "He... he was shot by Nephthys. Before he died, he transferred his consciousness... to me."

Clay gawked at her, slack-jawed. "You have Horus's consciousness inside you? And his memories?"

"His memories are in my head, but I don't remember them... yet. I'm told they will reveal themselves to me —in time."

Renley leaned forward. "You said Tasha was infected. Is she all right? Can I see her?"

Alyssa winced. "Lord Renley, I'm so sorry..." Dread flared in his eyes. "Nephthys captured her. She captured Tasha and Paul."

Renley stared at her silently, his body rigid.

"I'm so sorry," Alyssa repeated, her shoulders slumping.

His face hardened. "Do we know where she is? Is she hurt?"

"I don't know."

"I will find out and get her back," Renley said, his jaw set.

Dharr stepped in. "I would advise against that course of action at this time," he offered gently.

A small muscle in Renley's cheek twitched. "I am not going to sit on my hands while my daughter is suffering!" he bellowed. "After she has been used as a *bioweapon*!" he added, his nostrils flaring.

"With all due respect, Lord Renley," Dharr said, "you have no idea who you are up against. Please understand that anybody whom you should choose to dispatch after Tasha will perish."

"Then why don't you help us? Why don't you go after her and the boy?"

"The illness has taken a great toll on us. We are too weak to mount a successful rescue mission."

"This infection," Clay said, his brow wrinkling. "Tell me what happened exactly?"

"After Tasha and I arrived at the Rathadi home, it seems that the disease spread among the Rathadi, and then all of them got sick at the same time," Alyssa said. "But… for some reason Tasha didn't."

Clay scratched his ear. "Tasha was not exhibiting symptoms? But Paul was?" he asked. "And everybody got sick at the same time?"

"We can't explain it either," Alyssa pressed her lips into a tight line.

"Were you able to contain the infection?" Clay asked Dharr.

"We had some success in slowing it down, but it is a losing battle," the Rathadi replied. "It's just a question of time before it overwhelms us."

"How long?" Clay asked.

"Weeks," Dharr said. "At most."

Clay leaned forward. "Allow us to assist you. We have resources at the World Health Organization that may prove helpful."

Dharr glanced at Alyssa, and his lips curved into a narrow smile.

"What is it?" Clay asked.

"Alyssa has already convinced our elders that we should accept your help. We were going to ask for your assistance." He inclined his head. "On behalf of the Rathadi, we are most grateful for your offer. However—" he hesitated— "I'm certain that I don't have to emphasize to you how sensitive this situation is. No one other than you must know about the Rathadi."

Clay nodded solemnly. "You have my personal guarantee that this information will be handled in strictest confidence."

"Thank you," Dharr said. "I will put you in touch with our physicians and researchers."

Dharr's hand moved to disconnect the call.

"Wait," Alyssa put her palm on his arm. "Have you been able to find out anything about my... about Kade?"

"I was able to reach Kamal yesterday," Clay said. "He told me your father is safe, but he is still under arrest." He sighed. "Since he assaulted a police officer, they're playing hardball, but Kamal assures me he's receiving preferential treatment and is comfortable."

"Can I talk with him?" Alyssa asked.

Clay shook his head. "Any contact you will make with your father will be tracked and monitored. It's probably not the safest thing to do at this time."

Alyssa nodded, but the tightness in her chest grew with every breath.

"I'm sorry," Clay said. "I promise we will stay on top of it and will let you know as soon as we find out anything new."

"I know," Alyssa replied softly. "Thank you both."

She disconnected the call.

THE CELL DOOR scraped against the stone floor. Paul shivered, covered in cold sweat. The inside of his body was on fire, but his muscles spasmed uncontrollably from the icy tremors that cut through him.

How many hours have I been locked up... or has it been days?

He strained to lift his eyelids and make out the shapes at the door, but his eyes refused to focus.

A body flew into the cell and landed on the floor next to him with a soft grunt. Paul cried out with relief as he recognized Tasha's violet eyes glaring at the guard. A large purple bruise covered her right cheek.

The guard threw two military-style food rations and plastic bottles of water on the floor. "See that he eats and drinks," he barked at Tasha, keeping his hand on his rifle. "If he dies, Nephthys will be displeased."

He slammed the door shut and locked the door.

"Tasha?" Paul moaned, reaching for her in the dim light.

"I'm here," she replied. She drew near Paul and lifted his head on her lap. He closed his eyes, taking solace from the warmth of her body and the soothing touch of her hands stroking his hair.

"What's happening?" he whispered. "Where are we?"

"Sshh... Don't you worry about that now. Try to rest. You need to get better."

The tightness welled out of Paul's chest and choked his throat. "I... I don't think I will."

Tasha picked up one of the food packages and ripped it open then broke off a piece of the bar and fed it to Paul. He took a bite and chewed slowly then forced himself to swallow. He started coughing. Tasha lifted his head and pressed a bottle of water to his lips.

"Not if I have anything to say about it," she said, her voice harder than the stone beneath him.

ALYSSA ENTERED the small room that had been assigned as her living space. A narrow cot with a thin mattress and gray blanket stood against the far wall. A small dresser to her right and a simple metal desk and chair on the opposite wall completed the sparse décor. She sighed and closed the door. *I guess this is home for now.*

She plopped down on the side of the cot. She slipped off her shoes and scooted back against the wall then pulled her thighs to her chest and rested her forehead on her knees.

A knock at the door stirred her.

"Come in." She lifted her head.

Dharr entered with a smug look. "The council has agreed to let you begin with the training," he said.

"Ah... *the training*," Alyssa said. "Maybe now you can explain to me what it is you were talking about?"

Dharr pulled the chair from under the desk and straddled it. He leaned toward Alyssa, his yellow eyes crinkling with concern, but also gleaming with damnable enthusiasm. "Training to guide your mind to reveal Horus's memories to you. And to prepare you for the memories when they begin revealing themselves."

Alyssa cocked her head. "And *all* the elders want that?"

Dharr exhaled a frustrated breath. "Not exactly. The council is divided. The feline elder, Sia, still sides with Heru-pa. But Bes was able to convince Elder Xin to vote in our favor, so it's their two votes against Sia."

"Isn't Heru-pa on the council, too?"

"He is, but as an observer he is not allowed to cast a vote—which is most fortunate."

Alyssa's shoulders sagged. "The Rathadi are divided because of me."

"It's not because of you," Dharr asserted. "Heru-pa continues to insist that he is the rightful heir and that the Legacy is his. He—" Dharr paused, snapping his jaw shut noisily.

"What?" Alyssa pressed.

"He tried to convince the council to force you to transfer Horus's consciousness to him."

"Wait, what?" Alyssa perked up. "That's possible? He can have it!"

"The process would kill you," Dharr said glumly.

Alyssa slumped. "And yet he still wanted…" A lump formed in her throat. "What happens if Elder Xin changes his mind and also sides with Heru-pa? Will they force me to transfer the consciousness to him?"

"It is not in the Rathadi spirit to take an innocent life. The council would never endorse forcing you into it. But they will also not force Heru-pa to give up the amulet, to allow us to proceed with the Ceremony of Legacy."

"Why is this ceremony so important?"

"The Rathadi must come to recognize you as the true Legacy of Horus. The one who will lead us in our fight against Nephthys."

"Is that what this is all about?" Alyssa pinched her brow. "The fight against Nephthys? This war?"

"As long as Nephthys is alive, no Rathadi is safe. Horus has kept us alive for millennia."

"This is a conflict *he* created, Dharr. Is there really no other way?"

"Have you not seen the evil of which she is capable?" Dharr challenged. "Nephthys must be defeated. At all cost."

"Including Paul and Tasha?"

"The council remains united in their decision. We are too weak to attempt a rescue mission. Perhaps in due time."

"Due time?" Alyssa snapped. "What does that even mean?"

"It means that for now the most important task is to unify the Rathadi behind you. They must come to see you as Horus's rightful heir."

Alyssa dropped her head. "How can they see me as his rightful heir when I feel like a fraud?"

Dharr narrowed his eyes. "You are his daughter. In time all Rathadi will recognize that."

"What if I don't want this? What if I don't want to be this Legacy? Or have Horus's memories reveal themselves to me?"

Dharr appraised her silently, his body rigid, as if refusing to consider her questions.

"The Rathadi need a strong leader," Alyssa whispered. "Somebody like Heru-pa."

A long pause stretched as if Dharr was weighing what to say. When he spoke, his words were measured. "The Rathadi are rooted in traditions that date back ten millennia. In all that time, you are the first female offspring of Horus, brought of a union between a Rathadi and a human. This makes you different and unknown, and some Rathadi perceive this as a threat. But because you're different, you are also capable of unlocking potential no heir before you has been able to achieve. With the training you will become strong. Perhaps stronger than any heir has ever been. Worthy of leading the Rathadi."

Alyssa stared at the floor for a long time, digesting Dharr's words, their meaning waking shivers under her skin. She raised her head. "What exactly is this training?"

"Once Horus's memories begin to reveal themselves, and his consciousness begins to awaken inside you, they will threaten to overwhelm you. The training will protect you, allow your consciousness and Horus's to coexist within a single mind. Without the guidance, the memories will take over your mind, driving you into madness."

Alyssa shuddered. "Has that ever happened?"

Dharr shifted in the chair, drawing back. "Only once," he said.

"What happened to him?"

"That Legacy was challenged by his brother, who defeated him in a duel. According to the Rathadi laws, the vanquished heir was forced to give up Horus's consciousness… and his own life." Dharr's face darkened. "It was a dire day in the history of the Rathadi when one brother had to claim the life of another."

Alyssa sat in sullen silence, processing the information. "If I agree to train, will you help me convince the elders to save Paul and Tasha?"

Dharr regarded her, unblinking. "You have my word."

Alyssa swung her legs over the side of the bed and stood. "When do we start?"

———

PAUL OPENED HIS EYES SLOWLY. His mind was in a fog. He focused on the figure sitting across from him, eyes closed and back pressed against the wall, her palms resting on her legs.

Tasha.

He stirred softly, trying not to wake her. He rolled over, and a grunt escaped him.

Tasha opened her eyes. "Paul!" She dashed to him and kneeled at his side.

"Hi," he said, lifting his head. He blinked, confused, unable to identify the strange sensation, before realizing that it was the absence of pain.

Tasha helped him sit up. "How are you feeling?"

"Better, I think." He moved his arms and legs cautiously. The burning pain in his muscles and wrenching cramps in his gut had been replaced by a dull ache, like his body reminding him of the ordeal he had put it through. His stomach growled.

"Definitely better," he said. "I'm starving."

Tasha reached for one of the shrink-wrapped meals on the

floor. She tore it open. "Military rations. At least they're not letting us starve."

Paul snatched it up greedily and took a bite. He almost gagged. It was like chewing on stale cardboard. "How old is this thing?"

"I said they weren't letting us starve," Tasha said. "I didn't say it was tasty."

Paul opened a bottle of water and took a swig, washing down the mouthful. He took a second bite and forced it down with another sip.

"How long did I sleep?" he said, stuffing the last bite of the bar into his mouth and draining the rest of the bottle.

"You were in and out for a while," Tasha replied. "Assuming they come twice a day to bring us food and water"—she pointed to the stack of water bottles and discarded wrappers in the corner—"we've been here for almost three days."

"Three days?" Paul said. He blinked. His vision seemed to be returning to normal. He frowned at the fading bruise on Tasha's cheek. "Your face… Are you…?"

"I'm all right," Tasha shrugged him off. "You should see the other guy."

"Just one?"

"I did have my arms tied behind my back," she replied wryly. "And I was blindfolded."

Paul gave a thin laugh that turned into a hacking cough.

"Whoa, there," Tasha said. She handed him another bottle. "Small sips. I know you're feeling better, but take it slow."

"They injected me with something," he said.

A crease appeared on Tasha's forehead. "Maybe whatever they gave you was to help fight the infection."

"Fight it?"

"I don't think Nephthys wants us dead," Tasha said. "If she did, we would never have made it off that skyscraper."

Paul tensed at the memory.

"If Nephthys wants to use us as bargaining chips for Alyssa, we're useless to her dead," Tasha continued. "That's probably why she brought us so far away. To make sure Alyssa and the Rathadi couldn't come after us."

"Do you have any idea where we are?" Paul asked.

Tasha pursed her lips. "I have a hunch, but I can't be sure," she said. "And it may sound a bit crazy."

"Crazy is good. It'll help keep my mind off things."

"I think we're in an abandoned Soviet Arctic station," Tasha said.

"What?" Paul sat up. "How can you know that?"

"Just a hunch. We switched from the jet into a prop plane when you were out. We flew for about six hours. Nephthys doesn't strike me as one to switch into a propeller plane without a reason. Given the temperature when we got off the plane, we're pretty far north. Oh, and I could have sworn I saw a red star as they were leading me to your cell. You learn to spot them, growing up in St. Petersburg."

Paul looked at her, vexed. "Why would she bring us here?"

Tasha shrugged. "I've been trying to figure that out."

"And why would she have access to a Soviet base?"

"It's an abandoned, obsolete base from the looks of it. And it's Nephthys. She attacked a skyscraper in the middle of Hong Kong using Chinese Army helicopters. Compared to that, borrowing an old Soviet base doesn't seem that hard. I'm sure she could have used her connections to have the right people conveniently forget about the base's existence."

Paul mulled over her words. He scanned the cell, assessing the walls and ceiling. "So how do we get out of here?"

A sly smile built on Tasha's face. "I thought you'd never get to that."

ALYSSA'S KNEES were on fire, and her feet were completely numb. She cracked her right eye open. Dharr mirrored her kneeling position, their knees almost touching. His eyes were closed, his face as expressionless as it had been when they started this meditation exercise thirty minutes ago.

Thirty minutes that felt like three hours.

"Keep your eyes closed," Dharr admonished her. "Concentrate."

Alyssa snapped her eye shut. *How did he?*

"Focus on your breathing," he said. "In through your nose, out through your mouth."

Alyssa inhaled, working hard to ignore her thighs' cries for mercy.

"I need a break," she said, and opened her eyes.

Dharr met her gaze. "Very well," he said and stood up effortlessly, as if he'd just spent two minutes resting in a chair rather than kneeling on the ground for half an hour.

Alyssa moaned and fell to her side. She used her hands to

straighten her legs. Her body screamed as the blood flowed back into her tormented limbs.

"This is torture!" she whined. "How is this even supposed to help?"

"Your mind must become more disciplined. Only then will you be able to control the memories when they begin revealing themselves to you."

"But does it have to be so painful?"

"That's why it's called discipline. Forcing yourself to do something you don't want to do or that is causing you discomfort is the best way to learn discipline and master your mind. Other heirs begin training early in their childhood. You have much catching up to do. And you must have patience."

"Now you sound like Bes," Alyssa quipped.

"I am attempting to sound scholarly," Dharr replied dryly. "This is my first time teaching."

Alyssa groaned. "Patience has never been one of my strong virtues." She rubbed her knees and feet, trying to ignore the thousands of pins and needles prickling at her skin. "What am I even trying to accomplish?"

Dharr lowered himself to the ground next to her. "Before you can brave the Ceremony of Legacy, you must awaken Horus's last memory before his death."

Alyssa stopped massaging her legs. "Horus's last memory?"

"This memory will reveal itself to you first and will become your link to his consciousness, allowing you to safely delve deeper into Horus's mind. Your own consciousness will follow this trail, setting free memory after memory." He leaned forward. "Horus's last memory will serve as your anchor, allowing you to pull back to the safety of your own mind. This is the only way to ensure that his memories do not overwhelm you as they begin flooding into your mind."

Alyssa pondered his words. "Will the memories help me understand what's happening with the infection? Find a cure for it?"

"I don't know," Dharr replied. "But I do know that without them, we are lost. Infection or not."

Alyssa savored the last moment of comfort before forcing herself back onto her knees. "Okay, Master Yoda," she said, "continue we shall."

————————

TASHA WRAPPED her hand around one of the metal pipes that ran along the ceiling and gave it a firm tug. It didn't budge.

"How's it looking?" Paul grunted, holding on tightly to her ankles as she balanced on his shoulders.

Tasha tugged again, then carefully shifted her weight from Paul's shoulders to the pipe. It supported her easily. "I recognize sturdy Soviet built when I see it. It should easily be able to—"

The steps echoed through the corridor outside the cell. Tasha skipped down to the ground as Paul dashed to the far wall and lay against it. He pulled his legs to his stomach, doing his best to look miserable. Tasha slid to the ground next to him.

A moment later the small window on the metal door opened. The Purean guard scanned the room.

"Stay where you are," he said. He opened the door and took a cautious step inside. Keeping one hand on the automatic weapon, he tossed a couple more food rations and bottles of water on the floor.

He threw a glance at Paul. "How is he?"

"I think he's getting worse," Tasha said. "I keep trying to feed him, but he looks weaker." She touched Paul's forehead, and he moaned.

"And we're both freezing," she said. "Can you at least get him a blanket?"

"This isn't a hotel," the guard scoffed.

"You said yourself Nephthys wants him alive," Tasha shot back. "I think we will all be better off if we got a blanket before he freezes to death."

The guard eyed her. "I'll see what I can do." He closed the door and locked it.

A few minutes later he returned and opened the door. "Stay back." He threw a couple of blankets on the floor then slammed the door shut and locked it.

Paul lifted his head and gave her a small grin. "Brilliant start," he said. "Still, even if we make it out of this cell and this building... if you're right about where we are, we're just as likely to freeze to death as we are being shot while trying to escape."

"It's a base. There must be some kind of transportation," Tasha said. "Maybe snowcats or at least motor sleds. And there's got to be a communications station. There are cables that run along the ceiling in the hallway. They should lead us to the comms room. We can send a message. Tell them where we are."

"And hope our friends get to us before Nephthys does or before we turn into icicles?"

Tasha's expression froze for a moment before she blinked.

"What is it?" Paul asked.

"Nothing," she said, her voice flat.

"Come on," Paul pressed.

"I don't have friends," Tasha said, frowning. "I never did."

"What do you mean?" Paul asked. "I thought living with Renley you had… everything."

A bitter smile ghosted the corners of Tasha's mouth. "I owe George my life, but everything has a price. I had tutors, trainers, mentors… lovers… but never friends. With George, every day, every action had to have a purpose, but it was never my own."

"What about before George Renley?"

Tasha's lips twisted into a grim line. "It is not a time I care to remember."

"I'm sorry," Paul reached out for her arm, but hesitated and stopped short. He pulled back.

"I went from wandering the streets of St. Petersburg, looking for my next scrap of food, to living in a mansion wondering whether I'm going to become somebody's next meal." Tasha scowled. "I would give up everything George ever gave me for a chance at a normal life, to spend time with friends, or attend university to study—whatever it is that you are studying."

"Medical physics and molecular biochemistry," Paul offered quietly.

"Yes, that," Tasha gave a wry chuckle. "Ever since I can remember, I've been used in people's games, for their own purpose or profit. So, if the choice is between risking our lives to get out of here, or staying in this frigid hole to be used in Nephthys's game, it's an easy decision for me."

Paul blinked at Tasha's words and shook his head. "Why do I always get stuck with the loony ones with a death wish?"

———

EMPTINESS SURROUNDS ME. Pinpricks of light break through the darkness, glimmering like distant stars. One of them grows larger and streams toward me.

The light brightens and features emerge. A face, kind and familiar. A rush of warmth spreads through me, a curl of happiness. I reach for it. It is almost within my grasp—

A breath of cold air surrounds me, fills me.

No, don't leave… Not again…

Three loud cracks cut through the darkness. The stars around me explode, and the face shifts, snarling with fury.

I draw back. My foot steps in empty air—

Alyssa jerked up with a gasp.

She stared at Dharr, kneeling across from her. He grasped her shoulder.

"A memory?" he asked.

"Yes… no… I don't know," she stammered, still trying to get her bearings.

"What did you see?"

"A face," Alyssa said. "I think."

"A face? Whose face?" he pressed.

"I… I don't know." Alyssa shook her head, frustrated. She stood. "Every time I get close… We've been at it for a week, and I still feel like I'm doing everything wrong!"

Dharr frowned and rose to his feet. "I don't understand it. It is as if something is blocking the memory… as if…"

An icy shiver swept through Alyssa, raising goose bumps on her arms.

"You keep thinking about Paul and Tasha," Dharr said. "Is that it?"

She exhaled. "Yes," she said, too quickly. She grimaced and lowered her gaze, unable to look him in the eyes.

Dharr put his palm on her shoulder, and she flinched beneath his touch. "I know how difficult this must be for you," he said, "but you have to—"

He deserves to know what really happened that night. "Dharr," Alyssa interrupted before she realized the word was out of her mouth.

Don't do this, her inner voice warned.

Dharr stopped and regarded her expectantly.

She met his gaze. "That evening when Horus died…" She paused, not knowing how to continue. Unsure of whether to do so.

The door opened, and they both turned. Nel stepped inside, her feline eyes sparkling with excitement. Alyssa sighed and pressed her lips into a tight line.

"What is it?" Dharr asked.

"Clay just made contact. He thinks he and his collaborators found a way to slow down the disease."

Alyssa's stomach fluttered at Nel's words. "They found a cure?"

"No, not a cure," Nel said. "But he said they succeeded in isolating the antibodies from the blood samples we sent and were able to amplify them. Their tests showed that these antibodies significantly lowered the virulence of the virus."

Alyssa stared at her, confused. "Meaning?"

"Meaning they can use the antibodies to suppress the disease. And Clay believes it will no longer be infectious."

"That's wonderful!" Alyssa threw her arms around Nel.

"How long until they'll be able to deliver?" Dharr asked.

"Two days," Nel replied, breaking the embrace. "We are setting it up right now. The council has approved taking the jet to bring the treatment here as soon as possible. Vol and Jawad are coordinating the delivery."

Dharr blew out a huge breath. He sank to a chair and put his head in his hands. When he looked up again, his eyes glistened. "Thank you, Nel."

Nel gave him a nod and stepped out.

"And thank you," he said to Alyssa. "The Rathadi owe you and your friends a debt of gratitude." His lips curved into a fragile smile.

The first time he has smiled since Hong Kong.

"You were going to tell me something before Nel came in?" he asked.

Alyssa swallowed hard, choking back the memory. "That's okay," she replied, her voice sounding hollow to her own ears. "It can wait. Let's get back to the training."

ALYSSA'S FEET pounded the hard stone of the tunnel. Her heart hammered in her chest, threatening to break through her rib cage as she struggled to keep up with Dharr on their way up the steep slope.

"Your mind is preoccupied. It's fighting you," Dharr called out in an infuriatingly steady voice. "You must exhaust it."

The slope grew steeper. Alyssa grunted.

Dharr adjusted his backpack and gripped the straps tighter. "Keep up!" he said and sped up.

Alyssa bit back a curse and willed her legs to move faster. "At least the treatment is working," she mumbled between heaving breaths. Even though it had only been three days since they received the treatment from Clay and the WHO, many of the Rathadi seemed to be showing signs of improvement—especially Dharr.

"What?" he called back over his shoulder.

"Nothing!" Alyssa panted.

They reached the top. She dropped to her hands and knees

then rolled to her back. Her lungs were on fire. She swallowed air in big gulps, willing herself not to throw up. Dharr stood next to her, his breathing even, facing over the slope.

Alyssa rolled to her stomach and lifted her head. She gasped. An impossible sight confronted her. A huge, pristine underground lake stretched as far as she could see. Pinpricks of light from sinkholes high above fell on the lake like spotlights hitting a stage.

She gazed up to Dharr, her exhaustion forgotten. "This... this is beautiful."

"Beautiful and functional," he replied.

"Is this why you chose this location?"

Dharr nodded. "The lake gives us practically unlimited fresh water, and the geothermal energy in this cave system provides us with the power we need."

"Geothermal energy? You mean I didn't have to feel guilty about taking long showers?" She stepped up to the lake. The water lapped at the black pebbles on its shore. She dipped her hand in.

"It's warm!" she called out.

"Several of the hot springs in this cave system flow into the lake."

The warm, pristine water was irresistible. She swung around to Dharr. "Can I... I mean, would it be okay if I...?"

Dharr gave her a smile. "You've earned it," he said. "And it will help you clear your mind."

Alyssa whooped. She stripped down to her underwear and raced into the lake, splashing around like a little girl. When the water reached her stomach, she dived in and kicked hard. She came up to the surface, but stayed facedown and opened her eyes under the water. It was crystal clear, and she could see the bottom beneath her despite the dim light. She flipped to her back, inhaling the damp air. She closed her eyes and moved her limbs slowly, just enough to stay afloat. A sea of tranquility washed over her, and for a few fleeting moments there was nothing but her and the water, lapping softly against her body.

She took one last deep breath and flipped back to her stomach, reluctantly. She swam to the shore and stepped out. Dharr had slipped off his backpack and stood next to it, waiting.

"Thank you," she said when she reached him. "For bringing me here."

Dharr opened his pack and threw a towel at her.

Alyssa eyed him. "You came prepared."

Dharr studied her. "How do you feel?"

"Better than I have in a long time."

"Good," he said. "Put your clothes back on." He turned and faced the lake.

Alyssa blushed at the thought, but she stripped off her wet underwear and finished toweling off quickly. Dharr stood with his back to her as she slipped into the stretchy black jumpsuit. She wrung out her wet underwear and wrapped them in the towel and placed it all on Dharr's backpack.

"I'm ready," she said.

Dharr turned and lifted his scaly, bald head. "Are you?" he asked, a dangerous gleam in his eyes.

Without warning he lunged at her, lighting fast. Before Alyssa realized what had happened, she flipped backward, avoiding his attack. She landed lightly on her feet. He followed up with a roundhouse kick to her head. Her arm blocked it instinctively. His next assault was upon her before she could blink. He moved his hands and legs in a flurry of rapid strikes. She knocked down a kick to her thigh, then a strike to her ribs, ignoring the pain the blocks sent through her forearms.

His onslaught continued, relentless and vicious. She kicked out her left foot, extending her heel, aiming for his gut. He sidestepped and countered with a palm strike to her head. Alyssa blocked and moved in with a straight right, anticipating the opening in his guard. She almost missed the small tilt of his lips as he pulled his strike short and seized her arm then pulled her hard, using her forward momentum against her. She struggled to regain her balance, but he crouched and spun his leg in a complete circle, sweeping her feet from under her.

Alyssa crashed to the ground, groaning as her back struck the hard stone. She stared at Dharr, her body frozen in terror and confusion.

Dharr stalked toward her—then an impish smile curled his scaly lips. He nodded approvingly. "Not too bad for a half-breed."

Alyssa's mind whirled as comprehension dawned. She exhaled a huge breath as her terror transformed into anger. "You've planned this all along!" she yelled.

"I told you we would try a different approach today," he replied calmly.

"You—!"

"Ah…" Dharr lifted his palm to stop her. "You should be respectful to your teacher," he said, but couldn't hide the grin that had spread across his rough face.

I'll show you respect… Alyssa huffed, but kept her mouth shut.

Dharr held out his arm. Alyssa hesitated a moment then grasped it, and he pulled her to her feet effortlessly.

Alyssa bent over, palms on her knees, taking deep breaths as her heart slowly made its way from her throat back down to her chest. She glared at Dharr, no longer angry, but hoping to seem ferocious. "I was terrified... I didn't know what was happening."

"You didn't have time to think about what was happening, and you reacted on instinct," Dharr said. He stepped to his backpack and reached inside.

"The fighting," Alyssa said. "I didn't know I could do—"

Dharr threw something at her feet, startling her. She blinked at the pair of daggers on the ground. She glanced up and her breath caught in her throat.

Dharr held a matching set in his hands. Alyssa gulped. Suddenly, the MMA-style butt kicking she was just handed didn't seem all that bad. "Uh... perhaps we should stick with the hand-to-hand combat for a while?"

"Trust your instincts," Dharr said. "Empty your mind."

She eyed the blades again. "Shouldn't we at least put on some kind of protection?"

Dharr patted the thick scales of his reptilian skin. "I did."

"I was more worried about myself!" Alyssa cried out.

"Think of it as an incentive to not get hit." He ran a scaly finger along the edge of one of the daggers. "These are supposed to be training blades and not very sharp, but I highly recommend you don't try to test just how dull they truly are."

"You're serious," Alyssa said, taking a step back subconsciously. "Shouldn't you first teach me some basics... or something?"

Dharr lifted up the blades. "The dual daggers have been Horus's weapon of choice for millennia. You have lifetimes of training and combat with them sealed within your mind. My charge is not to teach you. It is to unlock what is already inside you."

He flipped one of the daggers into the air and caught it, holding one of them blade-up, the other blade-down. He lifted his arms and lowered his stance, shifting the balance to his rear foot.

He regarded her, unblinking. "Pick up the blades."

Alyssa swallowed. She lifted the daggers from the stone floor.

A wave of familiarity rippled through her, stirring the small hairs on her arms. Without thinking, she flipped the dagger in her right hand into a reverse grip, blade out, and assumed the same stance as Dharr.

"Perfect form," Dharr said, appraising her smugly. "You see?" He stalked closer. "The less you think the easier it—"

He lunged at her, daggers whirling in the air.

————

THE STACCATO CLASH of steel against steel rang through the cavern. A tight pair of eyes scrutinized the combatants and their blades, shimmering in the dim light, striking and parrying, moving fluidly together as one, as if they were partners in a dance.

Heru-pa turned, his lips pressed into a tight line, and paced back to the camp.

"HE'S COMING!" Tasha whispered. She sprang to her feet, dashed to the metal door, and pressed her back against it. She clenched her fingers together into a stirrup. Paul mounted Tasha's grip, barefooted, and reached for the pipe that ran along the ceiling of their cell. The cold metal dug into his fingers as Tasha pushed him up. He swung his legs up and over the pipe.

Tasha rushed back to the far wall of the cell and dropped to the floor next to Paul's blanket just before the small window in the door slid open.

The guard scanned the room. Paul held his breath.

They had used Tasha's blanket and the empty plastic bottles to prop up his blanket, making it look like he was lying under it. Tasha put a concerned hand on the bundle where Paul's head would be. On the other side, the tips of his shoes peeked out.

The guard barked the usual order to Tasha, "Stay where you are."

Paul squeezed his legs around the pipe and gripped his shoelaces between his palms into a garrote. The back of his throat filled with acid as he considered what he was about to do. He swallowed it down.

It's either them or us.

He ignored the burning that began to set into his arms and legs as the guard unlocked the door and glanced inside.

"How is he?" the guard asked gruffly.

"Not well," Tasha said, her voice thin. "He's been asleep most of the time."

The guard took a step into the cell. Paul released the pipe and plunged down. He crashed onto the guard's back and flipped the shoelaces over the man's head and around his throat. Paul crossed his hands and pulled with all his strength. Tasha leaped up and tackled the guard's legs.

The Purean toppled back and hit the floor. Paul grunted as the weight of the guard came on top of him, but he continued to squeeze the shoelaces as he fought to wrap his legs around the guard's body. Tasha flung herself on top, pinning them both down.

The guard snarled and thrashed, trapped between them. Tasha grappled with the Purean's arms, doing her best to prevent him from raking at Paul's face. Paul's grunt turned into a feral growl, his muscles pushed to the breaking point.

After what seemed like an eternity, the Purean's movements slowed. A few seconds later he shuddered, then his body went limp.

Paul and Tasha lay motionless, panting, their limbs tangled with the Purean's lifeless body. Paul's pulse hammered in his temples as Tasha lay next to him, her rapid breaths grazing his neck. Without warning, his stomach churned, and he dry heaved.

Tasha rolled off and helped Paul get out from underneath the Purean. He couldn't bring himself to look at the man he had just killed.

"Take deep breaths," Tasha said, "then get your shoes. No time to think if we want to make it out of here."

Paul nodded. He grabbed his shoes from beneath the blanket and slipped them on as Tasha picked up the guard's automatic rifle. She flipped open his holster and pulled out the pistol. She handed it to Paul.

They peeked out into the corridor. Gray walls stretched in

both directions, dimly lit by fluorescent lights. Haphazardly suspended cables hung from the ceiling.

Paul glanced up at the cables. "Let's hope you're right," he said, and set off to the right. Tasha closed the cell door behind them and followed him.

They moved through the corridor on the balls of their feet, Tasha following Paul, holding the rifle at the ready. Paul's heart thudded in his chest as he scanned the hallway ahead.

They reached a junction and stopped. Paul pressed his back against the wall and inched forward then stole a quick look into the other hallway. The cables converged behind a closed door, midway down the right corridor. He slipped into that passage and crept to the door, with Tasha trailing closely behind. He pressed his ear against the door.

"I don't hear anything," he whispered over his shoulder.

Tasha nodded and lifted her weapon.

He reached for the doorknob and slowly pulled. The door creaked.

Paul froze, but the room remained silent. He clenched his jaw and pulled again, opening it wide enough for them to slip inside.

Paul's breath hitched when he spotted an old communications station resting on a metal table. Chips of its olive-green paint lay scattered on the floor and the equally worn chair in front of it. Scores of switches and dials protruded from a black metal panel.

"You were right!" Paul said.

"This thing has got to be fifty years old," Tasha replied. "And it looks like it hasn't been used in twenty."

"Then let's hope they built it to last—just like the pipes," Paul said.

Tasha leaned over the console and studied the dust-covered switches. She flipped one of them. Nothing happened. She toggled it on and off, but the station remained lifeless.

"I guess the Soviets were better at building sturdy pipes than reliable electronics," Paul said.

"Maybe there is a circuit breaker somewhere?" Tasha offered.

Paul glanced around the room. He spotted a metal box on the wall and rushed to it. He flipped open the lid and stared mystified at the panel and the jumbled descriptions.

"Uh… It's in Russian," he said.

Tasha moved beside him. She ran her finger down the descriptions next to the switches then toggled one of them. The lights on the console flickered. A moment later, the lights turned on, and the old station sprang to life with a soft whirr.

She gave Paul a half-grin. "Not just pipes!"

They moved back to the station. Paul slipped the pistol into his waistband and picked up the headset. "So how do we use this thing?"

Tasha pointed at the rotary dial on the apparatus. "How about this?"

"A rotary phone?"

"Do you know Clay's number?" she asked.

"How do you even dial out?"

"Try dialing double zero then the country code and his phone number."

Paul looked at her, uncertain.

"You do know his phone number, right?" she asked.

"Yeah, yeah… just give me second. I have him on speed dial, but I think…"

Paul stretched his memory. He spun the numbers for Clay's mobile phone digit by digit. The dial circled back painfully slowly. When he finished dialing, a short double beep sounded from the headset.

"Bloody hell…" he muttered under his breath. "Try Renley."

Tasha set down the rifle on the table and bent over the station. She dialed the numbers. After several agonizing seconds, the same tone sounded from the headset.

"Wait…" Paul rubbed his chin. "This is analog technology. It may not be compatible with digital cell phones. Does Renley have a landline?"

"Good thinking," Tasha breathed. She dialed another number. A few seconds later, a slow and steady beep signaled the connection.

"Yes!" Paul held his breath and squeezed Tasha's arm.

Another long beep. Then another.

"Come on…" Tasha whispered, "pick up…"

A click. "Renley Manor, this is Jacques speaking."

"Jacques!" Tasha called out.

"Miss Tasha?" Jacque's voice rose an octave. "Where are you? Lord Renley and Mr. Obono have been—"

"Jacques, listen to me. Get George now. And Clay! Hurry!"

"Yes, yes, of course… Oh, dear," he mumbled as he rushed through the manor. "Lord Renley! It's Miss Tasha!"

A moment later George Renley's voice came through. "Tasha?"

"George!"

"Thank goodness," his voice rang with relief. "Are you all right? Where are you?"

"We're somewhere north. Far north. An old Soviet Arctic station, I think."

"What? How did you—?"

"I don't have time to explain. We're in danger. You have to come get us. We're going to—"

Tasha yelped as she was yanked back.

Paul whirled. A Purean guard held Tasha in a choke hold and pinned one of her arms behind her. She screamed out in pain.

"Tasha!" Renley's voice called out from the headset.

Paul's surprise lasted only an instant. He pulled the pistol from his waistband and pointed it at the guard. "Let her go!"

"And where are you planning on going after you shoot him?" a woman's voice cut through the room.

Paul whipped around. Nephthys and two more guards entered the cramped room. They lifted their rifles at him.

Nephthys appraised Paul and Tasha, an amused expression rippling through her face. "I admit, I'm impressed."

Paul pointed the weapon at Nephthys. "Tell him to let her go or you die."

Nephthys's mouth twitched. "Do not threaten me, boy," she whispered, her voice colder than the Arctic air outside. "You have no chance of getting out of here."

"If I had a quid for every time—" Paul started.

The woman's motion was a blur. One second she stood at the door, the next she was beside Paul, a blade in her hand, slicing down on his arm.

Paul stood stock-still as he watched his right hand, still clutching the pistol, fall to the floor.

His eyes grew, his brain unable to process the image.

The pain came as suddenly as the realization.

He screamed.

———

ALYSSA AND DHARR doubled back to the base at a light trot when a figure appeared at the end of the tunnel. Alyssa squinted. The figure's dim outline morphed into Tef's familiar features. She was rushing at them, waving.

"We have been looking for you!" she called out.

Alyssa and Dharr sped up.

"What's going on?" Alyssa asked when they reached her.

"George Renley has been trying to reach you," Tef replied. "He's on the comm… I think something bad happened."

Alyssa broke into a sprint for the base, Dharr and Tef right behind her. A minute later they burst into the communications suite. Nel and the twins, Jawad and Vol, gathered around a console, their expressions grim.

The Rathadi moved aside when she approached, and she glimpsed Renley's face on the screen. She reeled at the pale color and the harrowed look in his eyes.

She moved in front of the camera. "Lord Renley! What's wrong?"

"I just heard from Tasha and Paul," Renley said, his voice trembling. "I fear something terrible has happened."

Alyssa's throat went dry. She stared at the screen.

"They called on the landline," Renley continued. "They

barely got out a few words. Then… I heard screaming and then… nothing," he finished, working hard to stay composed.

"Were they able to give you their location?" Dharr asked, moving next to Alyssa.

Renley nodded. "They did, but," he hesitated, "it didn't make much sense. Tasha said they were in an old Soviet Arctic station."

"A Soviet Arctic station? Why would…?" She stopped. "Maybe it's a trick. Nephthys playing with our minds, trying to mislead us?"

"I wish it were so," Renley countered. "It was Tasha. And whatever was happening was real." He shuddered, as if recalling the memory. "I do not believe it was a trick," he added quietly, almost to himself.

"Is there any way to track where the call came from?" Dharr asked.

Clay leaned forward into the picture. "I'm working on it," he said. Alyssa could almost see the gears in his brain spinning in overdrive. "We're unlikely to get a precise location from the short call, but we should be able to identify the relay stations through which it was routed. We can cross-reference it with satellite images and records in the areas that correspond to the hits. I can't imagine there being too many stations, so if we narrow the search to a reasonably tight geographical region, we should be able to locate them—assuming that what Tasha said is actually true."

"We have to go after them!" Alyssa cried out.

Dharr placed his hand on her arm. "We've been through this before. The council's orders were clear. We are to—"

"You heard Lord Renley!" Alyssa pulled her hand away.

"Something terrible has happened. They may be running out of time. Besides, this may be our best opportunity to find them before Nephthys makes her move again."

"Alyssa does have a point, Dharr," Tef said, and Alyssa eyed her gratefully. "I wouldn't be here if it wasn't for Paul. And neither would two dozen other Rathadi."

"Are we really discussing acting against the council's orders?" Nel chimed in.

"What if we asked to speak with the council again?" Alyssa pleaded. "The disease has been stabilized. They may—"

"They'll never agree to it," Dharr said. "Not until we have a full cure, and even then... Our elders and the young ones still suffer from the disease, and they need to be protected in case she attacks. Besides, the council will not allow you to endanger yourself."

Alyssa gazed at Renley. Fear and worry etched the lines of his face. He looked a decade older than when she last saw him. She turned to Dharr, her jaw set. "If you want me to continue training with you, you will help me get Paul and Tasha."

Dharr's features hardened. "Are you blackmailing me, Alyssa?"

"I will go after them all by myself if I have to," she said in the most somber tone she could muster. "You'll have to tie me down and lock me up to keep me here. Is that really what you want to do to your Legacy?"

"You would not do anything that—" Dharr started.

Renley cleared his throat. Dharr's head snapped to the monitor, his lips tight.

"I would not put it past her," Renley said.

"I will do whatever it takes," Alyssa said quietly. "But I would much rather do it with your support… please."

Dharr groaned in exasperation. His gaze swept the room, looking to the other Rathadi for support. Tef's face was a mask. Nel looked from Dharr to Alyssa then just shrugged. The twins broke out into a pair of matching grins, but their eyes remained sharp.

"She's certainly got spunk," Vol said.

"I think she will make a fine Legacy," Jawad threw in.

Dharr lifted up his hands in resignation. "I can't believe you are all considering this…" He took a deep breath and exhaled. "All right," he said.

Alyssa lit up. She opened her mouth. Dharr held up his palm. "I want your promise that after we return—if we return—you will dedicate yourself unconditionally to the training. No more excuses or whining. I want one hundred percent commitment."

"You shall have it," Alyssa replied.

"We are going against the council's direct orders," Dharr continued. "You know that none of you have to—"

"Oh, stop it," Nel interrupted. "You know damn well that you and Alyssa need us to pull this off, and even if you didn't, we wouldn't let you go by yourselves."

Alyssa offered her a grateful smile.

"Thank you," Renley said, placing his right palm over his heart. "I am in your debt."

"Very well," Dharr said. "It will take several days to gather the necessary intel and prepare this mission."

"I will let you know as soon as I have anything on the location," Clay responded.

Tef stepped forward. "We'll need a good cover story to take out the bird."

"We could just tell the council we need the jet to make another run for more meds," Alyssa offered.

Dharr shook his head and glanced at the monitor. "Did you teach her all that?" he asked Renley.

Renley put his palms up. "She came that way when I met her."

"You'll get used to it—eventually," Clay added.

PART 2

SACRIFICE

Alyssa reeled in horror as Paul charged her. His eyes shone with a feral glint, and his mouth was twisted into a manic snarl. He barreled into her, knocking her against the wall.

The pain snapped her into action. She slipped from his grip and swiveled, trapping his arm behind his back. Dharr rushed to help, but she waved him off with a shake of her head.

"Paul, stop!" she pleaded.

Paul thrashed and escaped her grip. He twisted and swung at her again with his right arm. She sidestepped, easily dodging his clumsy attack. Paul stumbled and fell. She sank to the ground next to him and clutched his head in her palms. Dharr scrambled to the ground across from her and pinned Paul's shoulders.

Alyssa stared at the stump that was once Paul's right arm as he thrashed violently in their grips, growling, his eyes rolling in his head. A wave of dizziness swept through her. "My God, what have they done to you?" she moaned.

Dharr leaned over Paul's head. "Look at his pupils. He's

been drugged, probably to keep the pain down." He slipped his hand into a pocket and pulled out an autoinjector. "I'm going to try to stabilize him." He pressed the pen-sized cylinder against Paul's upper arm.

Paul roared and bucked, spittle flying from his lips.

"Stop! It's me!" Alyssa cried out. She held his head back and leaned over him. "Paul! It's Alyssa!"

Paul's expression shifted for an instant. A glimmer of recognition flickered through him.

Alyssa fought back tears. "Paul…" she whispered.

Paul slowly focused on her face. "Alyssa?"

Alyssa's throat was too thick to form words. She nodded.

"But… how…?"

"We traced your call. We came for you. Dharr and I, and the other Rathadi."

Paul's eyes moved to Dharr then back to Alyssa. They glistened. He lifted his stump. "Nephthys… she…" His voice choked. "I didn't think you'd come… that I'd ever see you again."

"Oh, Paul…" Alyssa's voice cracked. She wrapped her arms around him and clutched him tightly.

Dharr gently squeezed her shoulder. "We have to move."

Alyssa pulled back and nodded.

"Tasha?" Paul asked.

"Nel and Tef are looking for her," she said.

Paul leaned on her as Dharr helped lift him to his feet. Alyssa moved to the door and glanced out. Three figures dashed through the hallway. Relief swept through her when she recognized the two Rathadi girls and the lithe figure between them. She dashed out and threw her arms around Tasha.

"You came for us," Tasha said, her voice choked.

Paul stepped out of the room, leaning heavily on Dharr, and the three women drew in a sharp breath.

Tasha rushed forward, and he reeled back like a spooked deer. She stopped. Her eyes moved to his stump. "Paul... I'm so sorry—"

A shot rang out and a chunk of the wall rained down on them. Dharr shoved Paul to the floor as a bullet struck the wall behind them, sending off another chunk of plaster. Alyssa hit the deck and slid the helmet over her head as rounds ricocheted all around her.

A hammer hit the right side of her ribs. She screamed.

The liquid polymer armor had stopped the bullet, but the pain was enough to cloud her vision and send flashes of light exploding through her head.

Gunfire erupted from the other side of the long hallway. Tef pulled Tasha behind her, and the three Rathadi surrounded Paul and Tasha, protecting them with the body armor.

The Rathadi lifted their weapons and returned fire.

Dharr grazed the bracelet on his hand. An instant later two of the marble-sized drones whizzed past their heads and down the corridor, aiming for the muzzle flashes. Two explosions rocked the hallway.

The firing ceased as quickly as it had started.

"Move! Now!" Dharr yelled. He pulled Paul to his feet and raced along the passageway, dragging Paul behind him.

Alyssa followed Dharr and the transparent arrows in the head-up display in her helmet. They arrived at a door and rushed through it and into a stairwell.

"Vol," Dharr's voice came through her headset, "do you have our position?"

"Affirmative. Four plus two guests. All accounted for," Vol replied, his calm voice a welcome contrast to the chaos and rapid breathing in her headset. "Get to the roof."

They raced up one flight. The stairs ended at a metal door. Dharr shouldered it open. Bright light and freezing cold enveloped them, then the familiar sound of the jet emerged. Alyssa's visor darkened to reduce the glare as the floor hatch on the jet opened and several lines dropped down.

"Prepare to clip in," Dharr's command echoed through their headsets.

A brief flash of light from the ground was the only warning before the jet rocked with an explosion. Alyssa screamed as they toppled to the rooftop, debris crashing down all around them.

The jet veered sharply to the left, narrowly missing the satellite dishes and array of antennas spiking up from the roof. She heard Vol growl as he fought to regain control of the wounded aircraft.

Alyssa snapped her head to the source of the flash. A Purean soldier kneeled in a shooter's stance on the snow, a missile launcher on his shoulder. He aimed it at the jet again.

"Watch out!" she screamed just as Dharr lifted his weapon and fired at the soldier. The shots went wide, impacting the snow around him, but the Purean flinched when he fired the missile and it blew past the jet.

"Vol, get out of here!" Dharr boomed. "You're no good to us if the bird is toast. Meet at the rendezvous point!"

Alysa didn't hear Vol's response, but the plane's rear thrusters came to life an instant later and it roared away.

"What now?" Alyssa called out.

"The snowmobiles!" Dharr yelled back. He pushed Paul to her. "Take him!" He pointed to the far side of the roof, away from the soldier. "Go!"

Alyssa hesitated for the briefest of moments before she clutched Paul's arm and dragged him with her, racing to the edge of the roof.

"Wh-what are you doing?" Paul stammered, panic rising in his voice.

"Just follow me!" she called out then she launched herself off the roof, pulling Paul with her.

They fell twenty feet to the ground and sank into the snow-bank up to their thighs.

Alyssa held on to Paul's hand as they waded through the deep snow. A moment later Tasha landed behind them, followed by the three Rathadi. They high-stepped through the powder for the snowmobiles parked at the entrance. Alyssa reached the first one and hit the starter, and the engine purred to life.

"Climb on!" she yelled to Paul.

He stared at her, shivering, his lips turning blue.

She slipped off her parka and wrapped it around him. Instantly, the bitter cold cut through her body armor.

Nel and Tef jumped on the second snowmobile, and Dharr and Tasha mounted the third. Dharr pushed his weapon into Tasha's hands and started the snowmobile. Tasha held on to Dharr with one arm and cradled the rifle in the other. If the sub-zero temperature bothered her, she didn't show it. *A Siberian ice princess in her element.*

"Let's move!" Dharr called out.

They sped across the snow, the wind howling in Alyssa's ears through the helmet. She followed the arrows in her head-up display.

"Vol?" Dharr's voice sounded in the headset. "How is the bird?"

"She's hurting, but she'll get us home," Vol replied. "Jawad is patching up what he can."

"We're thirty seconds out," Dharr said.

The sound was something between a cannon blast and a thunderbolt. It lifted the snowmobile off the ground. Alyssa flew through the air and tumbled into the snow, lost in a powdery white haze. Her ears rang as she lay facedown, stunned. She shook her head and tried to push herself to her hands and knees.

A bullet pinged into the side of the snowmobile as gunfire peppered the snow around her. She pulled Paul next to her behind the snowmobile and peeked over it.

A heavy, truck-sized vehicle barged at them, its tracked wheels carving deep furrows into the snow. Three Pureans stood on a platform, shielded by a half moon shaped armor plate behind the enclosed cab, strafing them with gunfire.

Nel swung the second snowmobile around and skidded to a stop beside Alyssa and Paul. She and Tef dived into the snow and crouched behind their snowmobile. Behind them, Dharr and Tasha swerved to a stop and hunkered down behind their sled.

"Are you both okay?" Nel yelled.

Alyssa assessed Paul. He seemed stunned, but she didn't see any additional injuries on him. "I think so," she managed.

Alyssa peeked out at the massive vehicle careening for them then gasped when a second one, farther back, came into view— just as the jet screeched in and hovered above them.

"Vol, take out the snowcats!" Dharr's sharp command cut through the gunfire.

Alyssa held her breath, waiting for the gunfire from the jet, but the vehicle continued plowing through the snow at them.

"Vol!" Dharr yelled.

Vol let out a curse. "The weapons are jammed," he grunted.

Alyssa's blood pounded in her ears as she watched the first snowcat draw closer by the second. A Purean leaned out of the window, holding a rocket launcher.

"Vol, get out of here!" Dharr yelled.

"I'm not leaving you to get captured!" Vol shot back.

Tasha sprang to her feet and onto the snowmobile. She glanced at Alyssa. "I'm sorry I couldn't keep Paul safe," she said. She gunned the engine and whipped the sled around before taking off for the snowcat at full speed.

"Tasha!" Alyssa and Paul cried out in unison.

The snowmobile raced for the heavy vehicle, Tasha hunkered low over the handlebars, her auburn hair whipping in the wind. The Purean swiveled the rocket launcher from the jet to the snowmobile and fired.

Alyssa screamed.

Tasha banked the sled sharply, and the rocket impacted the snow, the explosion covering her in powder. She zig-zagged for the snowcat, her jagged course defying the Pureans' aim as she sped toward it. The driver tried to veer the heavy vehicle out of the way, but Tasha adjusted her line.

Alyssa held her breath as the two vehicles closed in on a

collision course. The Pureans on the platform leaped off an instant before Tasha dived off the snowmobile, and it slammed into the snowcat, exploding in a ball of fire. Tasha rolled to a stop in the snow as the heavy vehicle ground to a halt.

Dharr's distraction lasted only a moment. "Vol, drop the lines, now!" he yelled.

A moment later the lines hit the snow. Alyssa couldn't tear her eyes away from the scene before her. Tasha staggered up as more Pureans swarmed out of the burning snowcat. One of them raced for the rocket launcher in the snow. Tasha moved to intercept him.

"Alyssa, clip in, now!" Dharr yelled as Tef and Nel fastened a harness around Paul and clipped him to a line.

"We have to go back for Tasha!" Alyssa cried.

Dharr assessed the second snowcat closing in.

"There is no time," he said. "I'm sorry." He clipped her in.

Alyssa stood frozen as the Purean bent down for the rocket launcher.

Tasha barreled into him, driving him to the snow. She surged up as a second Purean soldier charged her then she danced aside, making him miss.

Alyssa didn't feel the jerk of the harness as it lifted her up, or the sting of the cold biting through her armor as she was reeled into the jet.

Another pair of soldiers reached Tasha. She fended them off, keeping them away from the rocket launcher, but her movements began to slow.

"Close the hatch and get out of here," Dharr ordered.

"No! We have to go back for her!" Alyssa pleaded.

Dharr pointed at the second snowcat, his scaly lips twisted into a grim line. "If we don't leave now, we'll never get out."

Alyssa's heart faltered. She screamed and slammed her fist into the hatch retract button.

"Vol, get us out of here, now!" Dharr called out.

The jet banked sharply and accelerated away. Alyssa's vision blurred as she stared helplessly through the small window in the hatch. The shapes on the ground grew smaller as a dozen shadows converged on a lone figure in the snow beside the burning snowcat. The shapes grew smaller still, slowly turning into nothing more than black dots on a pale canvas before completely blending into the white and disappearing from her view.

ALYSSA LIFTED her head when the door to the operating suite opened. The Rathadi surgeon stepped out and pulled down his mask. His face was long and skinny with a deeply etched forehead and wedged ears that tilted toward his black, penetrating eyes.

He approached the bench where she and Tef had been perched for the last four hours since their arrival, and since Paul had been rushed into surgery.

Alyssa stood. "How is he?" she asked.

The Rathadi pulled his lips back, reminding her of a neighing horse. "The amputation was clean, almost surgical, but his wound has been neglected for several days," he replied. "Fortunately, I was able to remove most of the necrotic tissue. He will need additional surgery, but he is strong and will recover well."

"And his infection... is it...?"

"There appears to be no trace of the pathogen in his blood."

Alyssa exhaled, emotions welling up inside, clenching her throat.

"You may go in and see him now, if you wish."

"Thank you," Alyssa said. "For everything you've done."

She entered the room and headed for the narrow bed. Tef followed her and stepped across to the other side. Her features mirrored Alyssa's concern as they approached Paul.

He rested, wrapped in a white blanket. An oxygen mask covered his face, and an IV line ran from his arm to a bag suspended on a metal pole at the head of the bed. Alyssa forced herself to look at the freshly bandaged stump that lay atop the white blanket across his stomach. Anger and fury sparked within her, twin flames searing through her body. She didn't quell the blaze, but let it pass through her, drawing strength from it.

You're going to pay for what you did to him. For what you've done to everybody you've hurt.

She bent over Paul, reaching for his face when the door slammed open. She whirled.

Heru-pa stormed inside, glaring at her. "Do you have any idea what you risked with this stunt of yours?" he spat.

Tef stepped in front of Alyssa before he had a chance to get closer. "Not now, Heru-pa," she warned.

"Not now?" He grimaced. "Does she realize that if anything had happened to her, the Legacy she carries inside her right now—*our Legacy*—would be lost forever?" He pointed his finger at Alyssa, but faced Tef. "Is this the person you want to lead the Rathadi? Reckless and stupid?"

Tef grasped the front of Heru-pa's shirt and shoved him against the wall. "How about loyal and decisive?" she fired back. "I will always choose somebody who shows loyalty and commands it through their actions over a cowering rabbit who hides behind tradition because he is too afraid to face the truth."

Heru-pa's jaw clenched. He curled his fingers into tight fists.

"Tef!" Bes's voice carried into the room from the doorway. "Release him!"

Tef flinched at Bes's tone. She relaxed her grip and stepped back. The old Rathadi approached, his ancient gray eyes burning through them from beneath a furrowed, scaly brow.

"Your behavior is shameful. We are struggling to survive, and the two of you quibble like Rathlings?"

"You cannot condone their behavior!" Heru-pa challenged. "What they did—"

"You will not tell me what I can or cannot do," Bes said, his voice cold as flint, matching the tone in his reptilian eyes. "We shall deal with everything, but this is neither the time nor the place."

Heru-pa opened his mouth to speak then closed it with a snap. He swiveled about and stormed out of the room.

Bes regarded Tef and Alyssa and took a long, pained breath through the two vertical slits that made up his nose.

"What you did was in direct violation of an order from the Council of Elders."

"It was all my fault," Alyssa started. "I—"

"You will all be held accountable for your actions," Bes continued, his voice tight. "Dharr is pleading your cause with the council as we speak, but I doubt even his impressive skills of persuasion will suffice to talk his way out of... out of—"

Bes coughed and red splotches of blood covered his palm.

"Bes!" Tef cried out and rushed to him. "Are you—?"

Bes held up a gnarled hand. "Do not concern yourself with me," he said. "You have much greater worries."

"What will happen now?" Alyssa asked.

"The council will decide your fate," Bes replied. "You will report to the council chamber in one hour." He straightened his back and headed for the door.

"Bes," Alyssa called after him.

Bes stopped and turned.

"May I contact my friends to tell them Paul is safe?" she asked. "And to inform Lord Renley that Tasha…"

He nodded.

"Thank you," Alyssa whispered.

"Thank Ra you are home safely," Bes said, then he left the room.

Alyssa smoothed Paul's hair. She looked to Tef. "Will you stay with him while I contact Clay and Renley?"

"Of course," Tef replied.

Alyssa slipped out of the operating suite and paced to the communications room. The bitter taste in her mouth grew with every step she took. She sank into the chair and initiated the connection. A moment later Clay's image filled the screen.

"Thank God you're back," he said. "Did you get them?"

The bitterness ripened into an ache that filled the back of her throat. "Where is Lord Renley?" she asked.

Clay's lips twitched. "I will get him."

Five minutes later, Alyssa forced herself to keep Renley's gaze as he and Clay digested her words. Renley's skin had paled to a dull gray.

"I promise you I will do everything in my power to get Tasha back," Alyssa said.

Renley slumped back into the chair and covered his head with his palms.

Clay stood beside him, his forehead wrinkled. He lifted his hand and reached out to Renley, hesitated, then put it on the older man's shoulder and squeezed. Renley reached up and patted Clay's hand.

"How is everybody else faring?" Clay asked after several moments.

"I'm not sure," Alyssa said. "Something is happening. I think the infection may be getting worse. Bes, one of the elders... he coughed and spit up blood."

Clay's expression pinched even more. "We've hit a wall developing further treatment," he said, his voice ringing with frustration. "I ran simulations based on the initial analysis and sent the specifications to Kamal. It should work, but for some reason they are unable to reproduce the results in their lab. They haven't been able to fully isolate the antibodies from the blood samples to narrow down on the—"

"Our best chance to find the cure is to access Horus's memories," Alyssa cut in. "And Dharr said it's the only way to defeat Nephthys—and get Tasha back."

"Are you making progress?" Clay asked.

"Some," Alyssa replied, "but I'm afraid it's not fast enough."

Renley lifted his head. "Do you truly believe that accessing Horus's memories will help us save Tasha?"

"Nephthys is holding her," Alyssa said. "And we cannot hope to defeat Nephthys without Horus's memories."

Renley leaned forward as if getting ready to say something, then he appeared to change his mind.

"Lord Renley?" Alyssa asked. "What is it?"

"I may be able to offer a potential solution," Renley said.

"With Horus's memories?" she asked, surprised.

"An... old friend... has developed technology for deep brain stimulation and neuromodulation for the purpose of memory extraction."

"What?" Alyssa asked.

Clay's brows drew closer. "I haven't heard about this research."

"Think about the potential applications of scientific knowledge that will permit accessing and manipulating memories," Renley replied. "This is not the kind of technology that is publicized and patented to be sold on the open market."

Clay scratched the stubble on his chin. "Fair point."

"Furthermore, since the work is highly experimental, there have been... regrettable mishaps with some of the test subjects."

"How do you know about this? And who is this old friend?" Alyssa asked.

Renley hesitated. "Suffice it to say that he owes me a favor."

"So, how do we get a hold of him?" Alyssa pressed.

Renley took a deep breath. "Unfortunately, his common sense is not at par with his scientific prowess, and he made some very powerful enemies. His whereabouts are not easily—"

"Can you reach him or not?" Alyssa interrupted.

"Stop right there, the both of you," Clay broke in, giving

Renley a sidelong glance before turning to Alyssa. "What part of the side effects section of the label did you not hear? You're talking about stimulating the hippocampus and mucking about with the memory cortex. I shudder to think about all the thousands of things that could go wrong that could fry your brain and turn your gray matter into porridge."

The door opened and Dharr stepped in.

Renley's expression darkened at Clay's words, but he nodded slowly. "I'm afraid Mr. Obono's assessment of the situation is correct," he conceded. "My grief for Tasha clouded my judgment. I should not have suggested it."

"Suggested what?" Dharr asked, approaching the comm station.

"Lord Renley may be able to help us access the memories," Alyssa said. "Clay thinks it's too dangerous, but what if it worked?"

Dharr pointed to the door. "The council is waiting," he said. "We can discuss it on our way."

"Don't forget to mention the porridge part," Clay urged.

Alyssa shot him a look then said her goodbyes and ended the call.

They paced along the corridor while Alyssa filled Dharr in on Renley's suggestion. They stopped in front of the door to the council chamber.

"Are you out of your mind?" Dharr asked. "We are making good progress. Horus's last living memory will reveal itself to you, and the rest will follow. We just need more time and more training."

"More time and more training?" Alyssa snapped. "You said yourself it may take years. Years we don't have." She sneered.

"Paul is crippled. God knows what hell Tasha is in after we abandoned her. And the Rathadi may all be dead by the time we uncover these memories!"

Dharr put his palms on her shoulders. "You must continue your training."

"I don't want to train anymore!" Alyssa yelled and shrugged off his palms. "We've been at it for weeks and have barely scratched the surface." She glared at him. "Ever thought that you might just suck as a teacher?"

Dharr's jaw twitched. "You gave me your word you would continue your training if we went after them." His voice was colder than the Arctic air that had bitten into her skin, but the hollow look in his eyes was worse.

"We were supposed to bring them both back," Alyssa said, her voice cracking. "I don't want to do this anymore. I just don't have the strength."

Dharr appraised her silently for several moments. "We will discuss this after the meeting," he said, and he opened the door.

They entered the council chamber, and all heads turned to them. They moved in front of the long table, joining the rest of Dharr's team. Nel and Tef slid to the right and the twins to the left, their usual easy-going smiles replaced by matching solemn expressions. Alyssa and Dharr took their places alongside the other Rathadi as they all faced the table of the Council of Elders. As before, Bes occupied a tall chair between the two other elders, and Heru-pa was perched on a smaller chair at their side.

"How nice of you to join us," Heru-pa sneered.

Bes shot him a look, but remained silent. The rough skin of his face was taut with a pained expression.

He looks really ill… or dreading what he has to do…

The ancient Rathadi steadied himself before he spoke, his voice weaker than usual, but still filled with the ring of command. "Commander Dharr, son of Kherr and Hu, you have violated a direct order from the Council of Elders." The young Rathadi faced Bes unblinking as the elder scrutinized all of them. "You and your team have not only risked your own lives, but worse, you have jeopardized the most valuable asset to our people. Do you have anything to say in defense of your actions?"

Dharr stepped forward. "I understand and take full responsibility for our actions," he said. "I stand ready to accept any punishment the council sees fit, and I only ask leniency for my team."

"His actions put us all at risk," Heru-pa said. "There is only one punishment that befits the seriousness of the crime. Dharr must be banished."

Dharr tensed but kept silent.

"No," Alyssa jumped in. "He was trying to convince me not to go. If anybody should be punished for this, it should be me!"

"We will get to each one of you!" Heru-pa snapped.

Bes lifted his hand, silencing him. "Heru-pa's argument is valid."

"You are considering banishing your best warrior at a time of war?" Alyssa challenged. "How wise a decision is that?"

"You will show the council the respect it deserves!" Heru-pa warned.

"Or what?" Alyssa shot back. "You're going to imprison me? Keep me locked up until Horus's memories reveal themselves to me?"

Elder Xin flapped his thin arm at her. "Do not test our resolve," he warbled, his high-pitched voice bringing a chill to her skin.

Tef stepped forward. "If Dharr goes, we all follow him." A moment later Nel and the twins joined her at Dharr's side.

"This is outrageous!" Heru-pa spat.

"We stand together," Tef said.

Elder Sia stood, her gray feline fur bristling. "You are Rathadi soldiers and you will do as commanded!"

Alyssa moved forward and joined the rest of the team. "Esteemed Elder Council," she pleaded. "May I—?"

"You have no voice here!" Heru-pa scoffed aloud.

"She stands accused with the others," Elder Bes said. "She has the right to be heard."

Alyssa nodded gratefully. "Esteemed Elder Council," she said, trying to keep the tremor out of her voice, "I know you understand the importance of Horus's memories revealing themselves to me. I can never accomplish this without Dharr. He and I have been training tirelessly and have made good progress."

"We shall find another Rathadi to continue your training," Heru-pa said.

"Dharr was the first Rathadi I saw after Horus transferred his consciousness to me. I believe this allowed Dharr and me to form a unique connection that I will be unable to replicate with any other Rathadi." Alyssa placed a palm on Dharr's arm. "I need Dharr to continue my training. He is the finest teacher I— or anybody—could ask for."

Dharr shot her a sidelong glance that she pointedly ignored.

"Don't you see what she's doing?" Heru-pa fumed. "She is

trying to manipulate all of you. You can't be foolish enough to—"

"Silence!" Bes commanded. He started to cough, but clamped his jaw and fought it back down. He took a steadying breath. "Alyssa, daughter of Horus and Anja, we will take your words under consideration." He exchanged glances with the elders flanking him. "Elder Sia, what is your judgment?" he asked.

The feline Rathadi scrutinized the group before her. Finally, she spoke. "They must be punished for their actions. Dharr shall be banished, and the other offenders shall be stripped of their ranks."

Heru-pa's lips turned up into the barest of smiles.

Bes turned to the Rathadi on his left. "Elder Xin, what is your judgment?"

The avian elder puffed out his chest as he weighed the options. Alyssa pleaded with him through her silent gaze. "Banishment during these trying times does not appear to be the wisest course of action," he said. "I judge in favor of a more moderate punishment."

Bes placed his scaly palms on the table. "Your judgments have been heard. Given the extraordinary circumstances, I too judge against banishment."

Alyssa breathed a sigh of relief.

"However, you shall all be stripped of your military ranks and privileges, and shall resume civilian duties." He addressed Dharr. "Your main duty shall be to continue as Alyssa's instructor. You shall surrender your command band."

Dharr's face was expressionless. "I accept the council's

wisdom and judgment," he said. He removed the wide bracelet from his left forearm and placed it on the table in front of Bes.

"You are letting them off this easily?" Heru-pa ranted. "This is an outrage. After what they have done and risked? This amounts to nothing more than a slap on their—"

Bes pushed off his chair and slammed a heavy fist on the table. "Enough! You will respect the judgment of the council!" He coughed again and leaned forward, his breathing labored. "You w-will..." He coughed again and bright splotches of blood sprayed out of his mouth, splattering the table and Dharr's bracelet. He gasped, his body tensing. He lifted his hands as if reaching for something invisible before him then collapsed to the floor.

Dharr cried out and leaped to his side, dropping to his knees beside the old Rathadi. He grasped Bes's head between his hands.

"He's not breathing," Dharr called out, his voice faltering. "Get a healer!"

ALYSSA STOPPED when she reached the door. She faced about for the one hundredth time and doubled back five paces to the narrow cot in her room. She sighed.

Patience...

Almost an hour had passed since the healer arrived in the council chamber and Bes had been whisked away. Dharr had refused to leave his mentor's side, so after a brief standoff he and Tef were allowed to accompany the old Rathadi to the infirmary. Alyssa was ushered back to her room and told not to leave. She huffed at being confined, but decided not to press her luck any further.

At least they haven't started locking my door.

Yet.

A knock interrupted her thoughts. She rushed to the door and swung it open.

Tef's usual shimmering scales had faded to a dull gray. Dharr stood next to her, his face hollow.

"Bes is dead," Tef said.

No…

"Why? How?" She reached out to Dharr. "I'm so sorry…"

"His immune system failed, and the infection overwhelmed him," Tef continued as she stepped inside. Dharr followed her, his shoulders slumped.

"I thought the infection was stabilized?"

Tef shook her head. "The older Rathadi and the children are growing sicker. It seems that the treatment fails to protect those that are most vulnerable. It's just a question of time until Bes's fate befalls all of them."

Dharr slumped onto the side of the bed. He scrubbed his hands across his scaly face and bald head. "We may have an even more immediate problem."

Alyssa and Tef turned to him.

He took a moment to collect himself, but the pain carried through his voice as he spoke. "With Bes gone, I fear it's only a question of time before Heru-pa sways Elder Xin to vote with Elder Sia against us."

Alyssa's stomach clenched. "You mean they'll vote to banish you?"

Dharr nodded. "If I'm not here to protect you, Heru-pa may try to convince the others that he is the rightful heir to Horus's consciousness."

Alyssa felt the blood drain from her face as she took in the full meaning of Dharr's words. "But you said they wouldn't force me to—"

"Without Bes on the council and with the excursion we just pulled…" Dharr pressed his gray, rough lips together, leaving the implication hanging.

"What do we do?" Alyssa asked.

"We need to get you out of here," Dharr said.

"And then what?"

"Then we'll figure out the rest. But first and foremost, we must ensure your safety. We cannot allow anything to jeopardize your training."

"So what do you propose? Even if we could somehow slip out of here, there's no way we could carry enough supplies with us to make it far, let alone anywhere our friends could reach us quickly."

Tef eased down onto the bed next to Dharr and patted his thigh. "I don't think slipping away quietly into the jungle is what Dharr had in mind."

Dharr gave her a small nod. "The jet will have the supplies we need."

Alyssa's breath caught in her throat. "You want to steal the jet?"

"Dharr has a point," Tef said. "That's our best chance to make it anywhere. And it beats walking through the jungle." She shuddered. "Have you seen the size of the centipedes around here?"

"The jet will need to be fueled," Dharr said. "And the security around it has been tightened. This will not be easy."

"We're going to need Nel and the twins," Tef said.

"There is also the small issue of retrieving my command band," Dharr said.

Tef stood. "Leave that to me."

Dharr fixed Alyssa with a steady gaze. "Get Paul. Bring only what you need. One backpack each. Meet me in the tunnel outside the hangar in twenty minutes."

Twenty minutes later, Alyssa faced a young Rathadi stationed outside the heavy metal door that led to the hangar cavern. His rigid spine was the embodiment of poise, but the white-knuckled grip on his weapon betrayed him as he shifted his weight from one foot to the other.

"What do you mean, my access has been revoked?" Dharr asked, the tone of his voice chipping away at the guard's confidence.

"I'm sorry, Commander… uh… I mean… Dharr," he stammered. "No civilians are allowed inside the hangar at this time." His face pinched painfully at his own words. "Heru-pa emphasized that you are not to go near the jet."

"Since when does Heru-pa give orders to our soldiers?"

The guard swallowed. "He said he spoke for the council."

Dharr tensed.

Alyssa stepped forward and said, "And you also know that the highest priority for the council, and all Rathadi, is for me to recover Horus's memories. The jet is where he transferred his Legacy to me. I need to immerse myself in that environment for the purpose of our training." She paused. "Unless, of course, you want to explain to the Council of Elders why you are keeping me from this most important task."

The guard pressed his lips together in a grimace. His eyes dashed from Alyssa to Dharr. "I need to clear this with the council first," he said, his voice trembling. "I'm certain you understand."

Alyssa gave an exasperated sigh. "We don't have time for—"

Dharr placed a calming hand on her arm. "Of course," he said, a hard smile building on his face. "Go right ahead, we'll wait." He took a step back and turned aside.

The guard lifted the radio to his mouth. The moment his eyes left them, Dharr closed the distance and pressed his hand against the guard's neck. The young Rathadi convulsed violently then slumped. Dharr caught him before he fell and eased him to the ground. He stepped back and holstered the small stun gun he had palmed in his hand.

"I wish that hadn't been necessary," he said. He whistled, and Nel and Paul slipped out from behind the bend in the corridor. Paul moved gingerly, leaning on the Rathadi as they approached.

Dharr eyed him. "You up for this?"

Paul stood straighter and nodded, his jaw tight.

"Good," Dharr said. "Take his weapon." He pointed to the guard then opened the heavy metal door into the cavern.

The lights inside the hangar were dimmed, but Alyssa could easily make out the contours of the jet, parked against one of the cavern walls.

Dharr and Nel pulled the guard inside the hangar and moved him behind a metal crate.

"Will he be all right?" Alyssa asked.

"He'll come around in a few minutes," Dharr said. "I want to be long gone before then." He pointed across the hangar to the pumping station.

"Start fueling the jet," he said.

Nel and Alyssa dashed to the station. Nel picked up the fuel hose and ducked under the right wing. She attached the end of the hose to the fuel tank and signaled Alyssa, who turned on the pump.

The pump whined softly and seconds later the smell of kerosene filled the cavern. Paul sniffed the air. "The jet runs on regular airplane fuel?" he asked, a hint of disappointment in his voice.

Nel nodded. "Mostly. Why?"

"I guess I was hoping for something more advanced... you know, like a flux capacitor, or at least some kind of fusion device. A bit of a letdown that this bird uses the same fuel as a commercial airliner."

"A flux capacitor?" Nel said, pinching her lips. "I'm not sure I'm familiar with that propulsion technology."

"Just ask Clay about it," Alyssa said, trying not to crack a smile. "He'll explain it to you in extensive detail."

Nel cocked her head.

"Enough chatter," Dharr said. "Three minutes until Vol and Jawad open the main gate." He threw an anxious glance at the door. "Where is Tef with the command band?"

"She'll be here," Nel said.

"Once they realize the jet has been fired up without proper authorization, they'll activate emergency protocol and lock this place down," Dharr said. "If we're not past the gate at that point, we'll be stuck in here."

"Let's make sure that doesn't happen," Nel said. "I have no desire to ever see the inside of the council chamber again."

The door to the hangar opened. Dharr's eyes lit up, then they narrowed when he recognized the figure standing in the door.

"I knew you could not be trusted!" Heru-pa's voice carried

across the hangar. "You are nothing but traitors and thieves."
He pulled out a pistol. "Move away from the jet!"

Alyssa stood, frozen. Dharr lifted his hands. "Heru-pa, think
about what you're doing," he said.

Heru-pa aimed the weapon at Dharr and approached him
wearily. "I will not allow you to leave."

Alyssa spotted another figure creeping into the hangar
behind Heru-pa and stalking him, hiding in the shadows.

Tef!

Dharr tensed.

He must have noticed her, too.

Dharr spread out his arms and moved slowly toward Heru-
pa. "We're all on the same side. We are not the enemy. Nephthys is. The infection is. If we do nothing, we will all perish!"

"We have to trust in our elders and our ways," Heru-pa shot
back. He pointed at Alyssa. "She poisoned you," he hissed,
eyes shifting from Dharr to Nel. "She poisoned all of your
bodies and your minds." He leveled the weapon at Nel. "Disconnect the fuel hose."

Nel stood motionless.

"Do it!" Heru-pa yelled.

Dharr glanced over his shoulder and nodded to Nel. She
disconnected the hose and closed the fuel latch. Dharr moved in
front of Heru-pa, his arms open at his sides. "I understand how
you feel, and what this looks like, but please, you have to
trust us."

"Trust you?" Heru-pa snorted. "After everything you've
done?"

Dharr gave a shallow sigh. "We were brothers once."

Heru-pa's face tightened.

"Will you truly shoot your own when we are trying to save our kind?" Dharr asked.

Heru-pa's arm wavered, and he began to lower his weapon.

Alyssa kept her focus firmly on Heru-pa as Tef crept up to him from behind, holding a metal wrench in her hand.

The sound of the heavy gate opening at the far side of the hangar rang through the cavern. Heru-pa glanced to the gate. Dharr charged him.

A shot rang out.

Dharr screamed and lurched back, clutching his shoulder.

Heru-pa's eyes grew wide. "Dharr! I—"

The next word was cut off when Tef clobbered him with the metal wrench. Heru-pa's eyes glazed over, and he slumped to his knees then collapsed to the ground.

"Dharr!" Tef yelled as Alyssa rushed to him.

"I'm fine," Dharr replied through clenched teeth, hand pressed to his left shoulder. "The command band!"

Tef threw the wide bracelet to Dharr. He snatched it out of the air with his right hand and pushed it onto his left wrist, wincing. He tapped a button, and an instant later the jet's engines roared to life and the aft ramp lowered.

"Get inside!" he commanded.

Paul and Nel raced up the ramp. Alyssa and Tef helped Dharr to his feet and followed them inside. A moment later the plane set out for the open gate at the entrance of the cave.

"Strap in!" Tef called out as she darted to the forward cabin and into the cockpit. "It may get bumpy!"

Alyssa eased Dharr into a jump seat, then threw a glance over her shoulder. Heru-pa staggered to his feet and shook his head, as if trying to clear it. He stared at the jet rolling for the gate then broke out into a dead sprint after it.

"Heru-pa is coming after us!" Alyssa yelled.

A red light flared up and sirens blared through the hangar.

"They're locking us down!" Nel called out.

"The gate is closing!" Tef's voice rang from the cockpit an instant before the engines powered down.

Alyssa glanced back. Her breath caught in her throat as Heru-pa closed on them. She rushed to the aft ramp and jabbed the button to raise it.

"He's gaining on us!" Alyssa warned as the jet continued to slow down.

"They're trying to override the AI remotely!" Tef yelled.

"Go to manual!" Nel urged, her voice tense.

Two seconds later, the engines spun up again, and the jet swung around to the cave exit. Alyssa's eyes darted between the closing gate in front of them and Heru-pa behind them, sprinting for the rising ramp.

The jet rolled through the gate and onto the rocky overhang that served as the landing and takeoff pad.

"Hang on!" Tef called out.

The engines roared. The jet lifted and cleared the overhang. Alyssa glanced back.

Time seemed to slow as Heru-pa launched himself from the cliff side at the jet's closing ramp. For an instant, he appeared to plunge to the darkness below, but his arm stretched and his fingers locked around the edge of the ramp. He swung himself into the jet a moment before the ramp sealed shut, and rolled to the floor.

Before Heru-pa had a chance to gain his feet, Dharr leaped

from the jump seat and surged into him, driving them both to the floor. Dharr screamed as he fell on his wounded shoulder, but he held on tight.

Paul roared, pounding across the cabin, and barreled into Heru-pa, slamming his elbow into the Rathadi's ribs. Heru-pa gasped, contorting with pain. Alyssa dived into the jumble of bodies, grappling with Heru-pa's arms. He snarled, twisting and writhing. Alyssa groaned as she felt Heru-pa's arms slipping out of her grasp, then his body went limp.

Nel pulled a spent autoinjector from Heru-pa's thigh and rose up, wiping her brow.

"What's going on back there?" Tef's voice rang from the cockpit through the open door.

Dharr stood slowly, wincing, keeping his left arm tight against his body. He gave Nel a pat on the shoulder with his right. "It's all good," he replied, breathing heavily.

Alyssa and Paul untangled themselves from Heru-pa's limp body and scrambled off the floor. She gaped at the blood seeping through Dharr's shirt. "Your arm…"

"The bullet just grazed me," he said. "I screamed like a Rathling."

"You screamed like a Rathadi soldier who got shot point blank," Nel said. She moved closer to him. "Let me take a look at it."

Dharr pushed her away. "Later," he said. "After we figure out how to deal with our extra passenger. What did you hit him with, anyway?"

"A high enough dose of tranq to knock out a horse," Nel said. She pushed Dharr back down with an expression that brooked no argument. "There's more where that came from if that's what it'll take to let me treat you." Dharr resigned and stopped resisting as she unbuttoned his shirt.

Tef stepped into the cabin. "I blocked their signal. AI has the plane," she said. She stared at Heru-pa lying motionlessly on the floor. "Looks like I missed something."

"We just added kidnapping to our rap sheet," Dharr said. "What the hell are we supposed to do with him?"

Nel took off Dharr's top. Tef grimaced at the ugly gash that ran across his right shoulder, coating his arm in blood. "Is lowering the ramp and giving him a boot out the plane an option?" she asked.

Nel gave her a look.

"I was joking," Tef said. "Sort of," she added under her breath.

Tef made eye contact with Alyssa as Nel attended to Dharr's wound. She nodded to the ramp release button and made a kicking motion at Heru-pa. Despite everything that had happened, Alyssa's lips curved into a brittle smile.

———

THE HUM of the jet filled the silence as Renley and Clay took in Alyssa's words.

"Was Bes the only one?" Clay asked.

"Bes is the only one we know of," Dharr replied.

Clay remained silent, a vacant expression pasted onto his young face.

"Clay," Alyssa said. "You and the others at the WHO did everything you could. Because of you, hundreds of Rathadi still have a chance to be cured."

"I don't understand it," Clay said, his shoulders sagging. "The second generation of the treatment should provide additional protection, but Kamal hasn't been able to confirm it in the lab yet."

"We must find a cure before more Rathadi die," Alyssa said. She tapped a finger against her head. "Our best chance of achieving that is locked in here, and we can't afford to waste any more time." Her voice was tight when she spoke. "Lord Renley, I want to go through with the procedure you mentioned."

"Alyssa—" Clay started.

"Clay, this is my decision."

Renley cleared his throat. "You are willing to go through this even though you're aware of the risk?"

"Yes," Alyssa said, trying to sound braver than she felt.

"And what is your opinion on this matter, Commander?" Renley asked Dharr. "The Rathadi have much to lose, should the procedure go awry."

"Alyssa is right," Dharr said with a grim twist to his mouth. "We are out of time. Our children and elders are becoming sicker by the day."

Clay stirred. "The initial treatment was never intended to be a full cure. It was meant to help keep the disease in check. Those with the weakest immune systems are affected most severely, and—"

"Please forgive me if I sounded ungrateful," Dharr said. "We are all in your debt for what you have been able to accomplish."

Clay leaned back. "I'm sorry, I didn't mean to…" He rubbed his forehead. "It's just so bloody frustrating."

Renley put a calming hand on Clay's arm. "At least the disease is not infectious anymore."

Clay nodded. "The tests confirmed it. Its virulence has been greatly reduced with the treatment."

"So, hypothetically speaking," Renley continued, "if the Rathadi were to meet with somebody, there would be no danger to that person?"

"That's correct," Clay replied.

Renley placed a palm to the temple, as if massaging a headache. "Very well," he finally said. "Continue due west. I shall contact Xander and will send you the exact coordinates after I confer with him. If things go as planned, we shall meet you there." He pushed the chair back and stood.

"Thank you," Alyssa said.

"How is Paul?" Clay asked as Renley stepped away.

"Better, I think," she replied. "He's been sleeping since we took off."

Clay gave a small smile. "It will be good to see you."

"And you," Alyssa said and hung up. She leaned back. Two vertical grooves furrowed Dharr's forehead. "What's bothering you?" she asked. "Other than the obvious."

Dharr tugged at the scales of his chin. "I can't get the image out of my mind."

"What image?"

"Heru-pa," he said. "After he shot me. I've never seen him so terrified."

"I don't understand," Alyssa said.

"I don't either, that's the problem. I get why Heru-pa confronted us in the hangar. I even understand him trying to scare me and pull a weapon on me. But why did he risk his life to get on board? He knew he wouldn't be able to take us all on."

"It was the heat of the moment," Alyssa said. "He seemed pretty determined to stop us at all costs."

"Perhaps," Dharr said, sounding unconvinced. "But in all the years I've known Heru-pa, I can count on two fingers the times he did something in the heat of the moment." He gave a small chuckle. "Both of them involved girls."

"Was one of them Nel?" Alyssa asked.

Dharr's scaly lips curved up as Nel stepped out of the med bay. "Speak of the..."

Nel tilted her head. "Yes?"

"Nothing," Dharr replied, the smug look pasted on his scaly face for another second before turning serious. "How is he?"

"He's okay, for now. I hit him with a heavy dose, so I'll need to monitor his vitals," she replied, looking almost guilty. "He'll be out for a while. How's the shoulder?"

"Almost like new," Dharr said, moving his left arm up and down gingerly. "I almost forgot what a fine field medic you were." He stood. "Speaking of wounds, I should check on the bird again. I'm not the only one nursing a broken wing."

"Is the jet going to be okay?" Alyssa asked.

"She took a wallop, but Jawad and Vol were able to patch up the critical systems. She'll get us where we need to go," he said then stepped to the cockpit.

Nel eased into the chair across from Alyssa. An uncomfortable silence stretched between them.

"I'm sorry," Alyssa said. "I know this can't be easy for you."

Really?

Nel peered at her from beneath her blond curls. "Oh?"

A flush crept across Alyssa's cheeks. She pointed to the med bay. "You know… since you guys have… uh… history?" *Did I just end a statement with a question?* She felt the heat invade the capillaries of her face and spread over her body.

"We were just a couple of kids," Nel replied, saving her from further humiliation. "It's been over for decades."

"Wait, what?" Alyssa froze. "Decades? How old are you?"

"Thirty-nine," Nel replied.

"I thought you were my age!" Alyssa's mind spun at the revelation. "What about Dharr and the others?"

"Dharr is forty-eight. A year away from adulthood. Tef and the twins are thirty-five."

Alyssa shook her head, absorbing Nel's words.

A shadow of a smile ghosted the Rathadi's full lips as she curled a strand of her hair around her finger. "We used to spend all of our time together. Not just Heru-pa and me, but all of us. Dharr, Tef, the twins."

"You were all friends with Heru-pa?"

"Heru-pa was a different person back then." Nel glanced wistfully out the little window. "As he got older, he became consumed by his training, with his role as Horus's heir, his Legacy. Before long, he was not the Heru-pa we once knew."

"Sounds like the only Heru-pa I know."

"Being Legacy is not a role to be taken lightly," Nel said, her tone growing harder. "When we broke up, he completely closed himself off. He wouldn't even acknowledge any of us."

Another silence stretched between them. The intercom buzzed with Dharr's voice. "Alyssa, can you come up to the cockpit?"

Alyssa bounced up, glad for the diversion. "Sorry... I should..."

"Go ahead," Nel replied. "I need to check on Heru-pa again. And I'll keep an eye on Paul."

Alyssa gave her a grateful smile and paced to the cockpit. Tef was strapped into the pilot's seat, and Dharr occupied the seat to her right. He glanced over his shoulder as Alyssa entered. "We received the coordinates," he said. "Looks like we're going to Nigeria."

"Nigeria?" Alyssa furrowed her brow. "Do we have enough fuel to get us there?"

Dharr looked to the gauges. "Barely, assuming these coordinates are even correct."

"What do you mean?" she asked.

He motioned to a monitor and brought up a satellite image. "The coordinates point to a location in the middle of the jungle. Doesn't seem like there are too many places to set the bird down."

Alyssa leaned closer to the screen. A sea of green covered the entire image. "Can you zoom in?"

Dharr touched a button, and the image enlarged. Alyssa could make out the individual trees in the dense forest, but nothing else.

"I hope this heading is taking us somewhere we want to be," Tef said.

It has to. "I'm sure the coordinates are right," Alyssa said out loud.

"Well, eight hours from now we'll know for sure," Dharr said. "I do hope you're right."

Alyssa swallowed. *So do I.*

ALYSSA SQUINTED at the dense canopy through the cockpit window. The forest seemed to stretch for hundreds of miles in each direction. Tef glanced over her shoulder from the left seat, keeping one hand on the flight yoke. "We're getting close."

"ETA at coordinates in five minutes," Dharr said. He took a look at the fuel gauge. "And less than twenty before we start to glide."

"The jet glides?" Alyssa asked.

"Yeah," Tef chuckled. "Like a brick."

Alyssa scanned the treetops below them with renewed fervor, willing a clearing to appear through the thick canopy.

A minute later, the radio crackled, and a man's voice rang through the speaker. "Aircraft on heading two-seven-zero, identify yourself." Alyssa flinched at the voice and possibly the thickest Texas drawl she'd ever heard.

Tef activated her microphone. "This is Romeo Alpha niner-five-four. We are... uh... with Alyssa," she said.

A moment of silence followed. "What is the last step before

serving dessert? And what type of car does this Alyssa like to drive—and bugger up?"

Tef glanced back quizzically. Alyssa gave her a little smile. "Crumbing the table, of course. Porsche 911, preferably black. And I'm really sorry about that."

"Crumbing the table," Tef repeated. "A black 911. And she's really sorry about that."

A few seconds of silence followed again.

"You are cleared for approach, Romeo Alpha niner-five-four. Reduce airspeed to two-zero-zero knots and follow your current flight vector for eight miles."

Tef repeated the message in acknowledgment and complied with the instructions.

"Romeo Alpha niner-five-four. Reduce airspeed to three-five knots," the voice instructed a few moments later.

"There!" Dharr said and pointed ahead of them.

Alyssa leaned forward and did a double take. A large section of the tree canopy ahead of them appeared to slide open, revealing an empty space below. Alyssa gasped, realizing she was looking at a retractable roof that had been covered with tree branches to make it blend in seamlessly with the forest around it.

"Romeo Alpha niner-five-four. You're clear to land."

"Curiouser and curiouser…" Tef muttered as she guided the plane to the landing zone.

Dharr hit the intercom button. "Nel and Paul, saddle up," he said. "And make sure our passenger is strapped in."

"Transitioning to vertical flight," Tef reported as Alyssa buckled into the jump seat in the back of the cockpit. Tef flipped several switches, and the jet gradually slowed. "Somebody doesn't want to be found," she said as they came to a stop and hovered above the open canopy.

Tef maneuvered the plane into the space below and set it down next to three long-range helicopters. She shut down the engines and exhaled deeply, glancing at the fuel gauge. "Look at that, twelve minutes of flight time to spare."

Alyssa unbuckled from the seat as the canopy began to close above them. She moved to the back of the plane, joining Nel and Paul at the ramp. A moment later, Dharr and Tef came up behind her.

Dharr glanced to Nel and Tef. "You two stay on board for now. Keep an eye on Heru-pa—and be ready in case we need backup."

Tef gave a brief nod. "My thoughts exactly."

"I'll be right behind you and Paul," Dharr said to Alyssa.

Alyssa squeezed Paul's arm and activated the ramp. Her heart skipped a beat as the ramp lowered, revealing Clay and Renley standing next to a burly, middle-aged man. She dashed out and hopped down the ramp before it had touched the ground. She pulled Clay into a tight hug. "It's good to see you again," she said.

Clay held her close for several seconds, then broke the embrace. His face caved when he spotted the bandage around Paul's right arm. He grabbed him in a bearhug, wordlessly.

Alyssa shook Renley's hand. "It's good to see you, Lord Renley," she said, but her voice sounded hollow. *I'm so sorry about Tasha.*

Renley regarded her as if reading her thoughts. He swallowed and nodded to her and Paul. "Miss Morgan, Mr. Matthews, may I present an old friend, Mr. Xander Hart."

Alyssa eyed the man. If there was a polar opposite to George Renley and his bespoke suits, this man must surely have been it. Fleshy lips and a craggy nose stuck out in his sunburnt face, and a bushy beard and a set of ruddy, unkempt hair protruded from beneath a huge cowboy hat. A massive revolver hung lazily under his sizable belly, and a fat unlit cigar dangled from the corner of his mouth. He removed the cigar and hat with his left hand and offered Alyssa his right.

"Your reputation precedes you, Miss Morgan," Xander Hart said with definitely the thickest Texas drawl Alyssa had ever heard. "But your entrance is even more spectacular than I could have imagined." Despite everything, she found it easy to return his smile. She accepted his hand and shook it.

He eyed the plane with a spark. "If you do not mind my queryin', just what kind of an aircraft is—" He stopped midsentence, his mouth gaping open. He stared over Alyssa's shoulder as Dharr came down the ramp. All color drained from his face.

Alyssa stepped aside as the Rathadi approached.

"Gentlemen, please meet Commander Dharr," she said.

Dharr shook Renley's and Clay's hands. "It is a pleasure to meet you both in person," he said. "On behalf of the Rathadi, thank you for all your assistance." He held out his hand to Xander. "And thank you for your hospitality, Mr. Hart."

Xander's eyes ping-ponged between Alyssa and Dharr in rhythm with his mouth, opening and closing soundlessly. Finally, his voice returned. "Are you…? Are you…?" he stammered.

"Tired?" Dharr replied. "Yes, quite a bit. And hungry, too. It's been a long flight, and we forgot to pack provisions."

Xander ogled him wordlessly for three heartbeats before he bellowed out in laughter so loud it sent the birds scurrying from the nearby trees. He grabbed Dharr's hand and shook it enthusiastically.

"I have hosted more generals, ministers, and world leaders in this humble compound than I care to remember—or admit, but you are by far and away the most fantastic guest these eyes have ever seen. Please forgive my rudeness and lack of manners." He stepped aside and pointed behind him. "Welcome to Hart Ranch. I have dinner prepared for you, and you may freshen up—"

"Mr. Hart—" Alyssa interjected.

"Xander," he said. "You must call me Xander."

She took a breath. "Xander," she said, "we truly appreciate your hospitality, but we don't have much time. And we've encountered some... complications on our trip. If you don't mind, we would like to discuss the reason for our visit."

Xander's brow furrowed a fraction of an inch beneath his straggly hair, but it relaxed almost as quickly as it had tensed. "Yes, of course," he said. "I completely understand. Please follow me." He put on his hat. "Is that all of you?" he asked.

Dharr started to nod, but Alyssa jumped in. "We left several of our friends on the plane," she said. "For maintenance and repairs."

Dharr gave her a sidelong glance.

Xander nodded. "Very well," he said and turned to the entrance.

The compound was surprisingly large, a sprawling two story structure that sat back in the middle of a thick stand of trees behind a tall wall that circled the entire building. Dense vines curled around the trees above and hung in long, thick ropes onto the roof and walls. It was nearly impossible to see through the branches intertwined around the house. Alyssa marveled at the way the compound appeared to be a part of the jungle, blending in perfectly with the surrounding forest, when Dharr pulled her back gently.

"It may not have been wise to tell him about the others," he whispered in her ear.

"We're planning to put my life in this man's hands," Alyssa whispered back. "I don't want to start our relationship with a lie. Doesn't seem like we have much of a choice."

"One always has a choice, Miss Morgan," Xander said over his shoulder as they passed through a gate in the wall. Alyssa's skin tingled under his gaze. She hadn't expected him to hear their exchange. "But having dealt with deception and lies most of my life, your honesty is a breath of fresh air—and much appreciated," he added.

She glanced at Dharr. He kept his mouth pressed into a tight line.

As they approached the entrance, the door slid open. Alyssa gasped. As much as the outside blended into the forest, the inside looked like she had stepped into a modern art museum. The entire space was open, covered in gray polished marble and decorated in white furniture with simple, clean lines. Arrangements of paintings and modern art sculptures lingered about, tastefully illuminated by soft overhead spotlights. A single winding staircase, an elongated helix of oak with raw bark at the edges, dominated the house and led up to the second story. A faint smell of burned tobacco permeated the space.

That's unexpected, she thought, eying Xander again. *Never judge a book…*

Xander led them to a metal door and took his cigar out of his mouth. He pressed his right palm on a scanner and blew into a tube. Xander caught Alyssa's quizzical look.

"The palm print and breath sample are used as biometric keys," he said as the door opened, revealing an elevator. "You can cut a hand off a corpse, but it's harder to make it breathe," he chuckled and put the cigar back between his teeth.

Dharr leaned over to Clay as the others entered the cabin. "Are we sure this is the right man? He strikes me as a bit… odd."

"Xander Hart may be the smartest man on the planet you've never heard of," Clay whispered back.

"I appreciate the sentiment, Mr. Obono," Xander said, turning in the elevator. "I shall strive to live up to the reputation." He motioned them inside. "Shall we?"

A flush crept across Clay's cheeks. He snapped his mouth shut and shuffled into the cabin, eyes glued to the floor.

The elevator descended and opened into a large space. The lights turned on as Xander stepped out and motioned them to follow. The hall was filled with tables packed with electronic instruments and gadgetry. Clay perked up, his earlier embarrassment washed away. He fidgeted and squirmed, his eyes bouncing from one contraption to another as they followed Xander to the center of the room. *A puppy in a dog park,* Alyssa mused.

They stopped in front of a wide table. Alyssa followed the neatly crimped cables that ran between the instruments and computers on top of the table and a desk-sized metallic gray box on the floor.

Alyssa's smile wilted. "This is it." It was more a statement than a question.

Xander nodded. "This is why you're here."

Alyssa studied the equipment skeptically. "So what exactly does it do?" she asked.

"It uncovers memories," Xander replied.

"When you say uncover, you mean…"

He pointed at the screen on the desk. "It displays your thoughts."

Alyssa froze. "It *displays* them?" she asked, unable to hide the anxiety that spread through her and crept into her voice. "I thought it was only going to help me trigger memories."

Xander took off his hat and set it on the table. "There are organizations whose entire existence is based on uncovering what others are thinking, not simply making them remember things. Let's just say that it was quite important for these organizations to see what was in other individuals' heads after they were able to… get their hands on them."

"You built it to interrogate people?" Alyssa asked, her shame giving her voice a sharper edge than she had intended.

Xander gave a heavy sigh, misreading the true reason for her tone. "You may judge me with good reason, Miss Morgan, as many others have before. I assure you, I am not proud of many of the things I have done. But some may argue that this is more humane than torturing information out of people."

"How is that even possible?" Paul jumped in. "The technology to do this…" he trailed off, shaking his head.

Xander pointed to the instrument on the floor. "This is a

high field strength functional MRI that uses deep brain stimulation and neuromodulation."

Alyssa blinked, glad for the distraction. "MRI as in…"

"Magnetic resonance imaging," Xander said. "Same tech they use in a hospital to take pictures of your brain. Except this machine does it at a much, much higher resolution."

"High enough resolution to see memories?" Paul's voice rose a fraction.

Xander gave a booming laugh. "No, Mr. Matthews. That would be like using a magnifying glass to look for pictures on a hard drive. The process is a bit more sophisticated and complex."

"Come on," Clay said, rubbing his hands. "I've been waiting to hear all about this since we got here." He glanced at Alyssa. "Xander refused to give me details until you arrived."

"Sorry… we got here as fast as we could," Alyssa said, dryly.

Xander lifted up a plastic skull cap from the table. It was studded with electrodes, and wires ran from it to the other devices on the table. "In a nutshell, the equipment first uses a neural network algorithm to map out brain activity in response to specific images. Once that's accomplished, this algorithm is then used to interpret unknown brain impulses— memories—and convert them to images then display these images."

"That's bloody brilliant…" Clay whispered.

"Well, thank you kindly, Mr. Obono," Xander said with a small bow.

"How about you try again," Paul said to Xander. "For those of us who have not grown up making computers out of toasters

—or however you chose to spend your childhood, mate," he threw in, flipping a glance at Clay.

"Out of microwave ovens, not toasters," Clay said. "Toasters don't have the necessary logic boards to—"

"Clay," Alyssa said, "not now."

Clay closed his mouth and put his hands in his pockets.

Xander nudged Clay. "Fascinating. We have to compare notes on that sometime." He turned back to Alyssa and the others. "But back to the task at hand. There are two parts to the process. Think of the first part as learning the brain's own language—"

"The language of the neural impulses that correspond to the various visual clues," Clay butted in, unable to contain himself.

"Precisely," Xander said, not seeming to mind the interruption. "Once that language has been deciphered, we can extract information from it and display the impulses as images."

"Doesn't the brain already have a language?" Paul asked. "Isn't it called talking?"

Xander chuckled. "That's the language we developed for communicating among ourselves. The brain's own language consists of electrical impulses through the vast network of neurons and synapses. Every image we form in our mind, every word we utter and every thought we have is represented by these impulses. Impulses that are unique to each brain."

"So, wait… you can map these impulses at the level of individual neurons?" Paul asked.

Xander shook his head. "Your brain consists of roughly a hundred billion neurons. Each neuron has an average of ten thousand synapses. So that's a hundred billion times ten thousand, or one quadrillion synapses."

"That's a one followed by fifteen zeros," Clay offered.

"Thanks, mate," Paul replied. "'Stonking big' would have sufficed."

"There is no technology advanced enough to allow for that," Xander said, "so we concentrate on the part of the brain and the impulses that deal with images."

Clay leaned over the equipment, staring unabashed. He ruffled his thick black curls. "I've heard of research that teaches computers to interpret brain patterns that correspond to speech and then translates brain impulses into voice. Effectively reading thoughts. But this… This is so much more complex!"

Xander gave Clay a pat on his shoulder. "Extending technology beyond its current limits is simply a question of money, time, and elbow grease. By focusing our technology on the regions of the brain that deal with forming visual memories, we learn the brain's own language of how the images are stored and are then able to recreate a crude representation of the images or snapshots of memories by stimulating the brain accordingly."

He picked up the goggles. "These are used to present the subject with a rapid series of visual cues, developed specifically to map the areas of your brain that responds to this visual stimulation, especially areas in the hippocampus."

"The hippo-what?" Paul asked.

"The hippocampus," Clay chimed in again. "A small organ located within the brain's temporal lobe that is associated with memory, in particular long-term memory."

"Ah…" Paul said. "So you train your computer what the brain impulses look like based on specific images."

"Images, thoughts that are evoked by the images, even feelings," Xander continued. "Then we stimulate the hippocampus with images that are related to the suppressed memories, in hopes of inciting subsequent memories that are then decoded and displayed.

"Impressive," Dharr said.

"Told you he's smart," Clay grinned.

"How long does all that take?" Alyssa asked.

"The first part, to train the algorithm—learn the language of the brain—takes the most time… a couple of weeks, possibly a month."

A heaviness roosted in Alyssa's chest at his words. "A month?"

"It's a complex and computationally challenging endeavor," Xander replied. "Our servers aren't half-bad, but unless you brought a supercomputer in that fancy plane of yours."

Alyssa hung her head. *The Rathadi don't have a month.* Her mind raced, then—

She sat up. "Well, we don't have one in the plane, but we do know where one can be found."

Paul stared at her with a blank look. He shook his head as comprehension dawned. "Oh, bloody hell, no," he said. "No way. You're crazy."

Clay shook his head in unison. "As much as I would like to play with the Society's quantum rig," he said, "let me just concur with my mate here that you're bonkers for even thinking about it. Besides, we have no idea whether they even got it up and running again after you left it a proper shambles."

"You said it yourself, Clay," Alyssa said as Xander followed the exchange, teeth nibbling on his fat cigar, "it's one of the fastest computers on the planet. And Nephthys killed two dozen of their people. If we can help them defeat her—"

"I blew up their ship!" Paul burst out, throwing his arms in the air. "I probably maimed or even killed some of them in the process! Do you really think they'd want to help us?"

Alyssa's lips tightened. "Lord Renley?" she looked to him, pleading.

Renley rubbed his brow. "I am quite certain I have burned my bridges with the Society during our last interaction, and undoubtedly they are not thrilled with what you two have done to them. Still, your intent was not malicious. Nephthys, on the other hand, conspired to kill and masterminded the execution of more than twenty of their own. They are not likely to forget that. And they may be able to forgive your digressions in light of Nephthys's deplorable actions."

"The enemy of my enemy is my friend?" Paul's voice was strained. "Really? That's our best angle now?" He kneaded the back of his neck. "We don't even know if the memories will truly be able to tell us how to defeat Nephthys."

"The alternative is to wait for either the infection or Nephthys to overwhelm the Rathadi," Alyssa offered.

Paul opened his mouth, but closed it again, swallowing.

Renley's hand moved to straighten the already perfect knot of his tie. "I cannot quite convince myself to endorse this idea," he said, "but Mr. Matthews, despite his intentions, may have correctly assessed our situation. Approaching the enemy of our enemy may indeed be our best opportunity at an alliance—and success."

Dharr stepped forward. "We have been observing the Society for decades," he said. "Despite their... eccentricities...

their actions have largely been governed by rational behavior—"

Alyssa cleared her throat noisily.

"With notable exceptions," Dharr added. "Still, I do believe there is a chance that they will at least listen to the proposition."

Paul crossed his arms. "Sure," he said. "Let's have tea with the Society. What's the worst that can happen?"

"Would you like me to contact them?" Renley asked Alyssa.

She shook her head. "I will do it," she said. "There was an Italian woman. A scientist."

"Dr. Claudia Tibaldi?" Renley offered.

"That's her! Do you think you can help me reach her?"

Renley nodded as Paul grumbled his irritation, his jaw set tight.

"Brilliant," Xander said, his eyes sparkling. "It sounds like we have consensus, and a plan." He leaned forward. "Now that we're all in agreement, would you mind letting me know who this Society is that you've been discussing so passionately?"

Paul sighed, resigned. "A bunch of zealous crackpots who are dead set on ruling the world. Filthy rich, ruthless, and mad as a hundred hatters."

Xander chewed on his cigar vigorously, digesting the words. He removed it from his mouth and flashed a tobacco-stained grin. "Sounds like my kind of folk. Can't wait to meet 'em!"

———

CLAUDIA TIBALDI BROKE the surface of the azure water and grasped the diving ladder of her forty-foot catamaran. She squinted in the rays of the Caribbean sun, its reflection bouncing with the waves when a distorted shape approached the diving platform of the cat and stood above her.

She slipped off her foggy mask and looked up. Her lips curved into a smile when she took in the shirtless body of her private steward.

"Did you enjoy your dive, Dr. Tibaldi?" Rafael asked, offering her his hand.

She lifted her arm to him, and he grasped it in a strong grip, pulling her out of the water with one hand and handing her a towel with the other.

"Thank you, Rafael, I did," she replied, brushing her long dark hair from her eyes.

She toweled off and moved to the bow, easing herself into the trampoline that stretched between the two hulls. She slipped on her sunglasses and took a sip of the freshly made margarita and a deep breath, letting the lemon tang mix with the salt in the air. The well-deserved vacation had been a welcome break from the pace of the last few weeks on board of the *Valediction.*

The Society was still in an uproar about what the Hybrid woman had done to them. After weeks of investigating and spending more money than she cared to admit, they were no closer to finding out what had really transpired on the night when more than twenty of their own had lost their lives. To make matters worse, Yuri Korzo's trail was growing colder by the day. There were rumors that he'd turned up dead in Hong Kong, but they hadn't been able to substantiate them. On top of it all, the mess the Morgan girl made still gave Claudia heartburn every time she thought about it. At least they've been able to repair the damage to the ship and the server.

Enough, she admonished herself. *This is supposed to be a vacation. A break from it all.*

She forced herself to take in another deep breath and exhale, and focused again on the warmth of the sun caressing her body and the smell of the salty moisture of the sea air. The warm Caribbean breeze washed over her bikini-clad body as she listened to the waves lap lazily at the twin hulls. Her breathing slowed and her eyelids grew heavy, and she began to drift off into a contended catnap.

"Dr. Tibaldi," Rafael's voice stirred her. She opened her eyes, annoyed at the intrusion. Her irritation melted away when Rafael appeared on the deck.

"What is it?" she asked, glad for her sunglasses as she took in his flawless body.

"You have a call on your private phone," he said, his Colombian accent drawing out the rounded sound of vowels and stunted *V*s. "A young woman, sounds American."

"Did she say who she was?" Claudia asked and took another sip of her margarita.

"She said her name was Alyssa Morgan."

The sip stuck in her throat and she coughed, almost dropping the drink.

"Dr. Tibaldi," Rafael said, "are you—?"

She waved him off. "Give it to me," she rasped between coughs.

Rafael blinked, but handed her the phone.

She lifted it to her ear, her lips pressed into a white slash. "Yes?" she managed.

"Dr. Tibaldi?" the voice on the other end of the line greeted her. "This is Alyssa Morgan."

Claudia Tibaldi took off her sunglasses and squinted in the glare.

"Of all the people…" she replied, struggling to contain herself. "I suppose I have George Renley to thank for divulging my number."

"Yes."

"Do you know how much trouble you have caused us? Not to mention the amount of money?"

"Did anybody die in the explosion?" Alyssa asked.

Claudia blinked at the question. "Several crewmen were injured, but they all recovered."

Alyssa exhaled. "Thank God."

"I'm touched by your care," Claudia said, not trying to hide the sarcasm in her voice, "but I doubt you called just to check in on the welfare of our crew." She fought the urge to disconnect the call, or better yet, chuck it into the clear waters.

I wish the girl were here herself…

She sighed softly at the mental image of throwing Alyssa overboard along with the phone.

"I can help you find and defeat the Hybrid woman who killed your people," Alyssa said.

Claudia's sigh caught in her throat. She snapped back from her therapeutic fantasy. "You have my attention."

"Her name is Nephthys. She is extremely powerful and dangerous."

Nephthys? Claudia clenched her jaw. The Society spent six weeks and a small fortune investigating leads all over the world, and the Morgan girl just gave her information they haven't been able to obtain. She managed to keep her voice calm. "Go on."

"To find and defeat her, I need something from you and the Society."

"I'm shocked," Claudia said.

"I need access to your computer."

"The quantum computer you almost destroyed?" Claudia asked, exasperated. "There has got to be a joke hidden in there somewhere. Do you know how much it cost to repair the damages to it?"

"I am truly sorry for the damages I have—"

"You're sorry for the damages..." Claudia barked a laugh. "That's supposed to make up for it?"

"Do we have a deal or not?"

Claudia scowled. "I am unable to give you an answer without discussing this with my associates."

"There is no time," Alyssa said. "I know you have leverage within the Society. I want to deal with you, nobody else."

"Let me get this straight," Claudia said, struggling to keep her voice calm. "You call me up out of the blue, interrupt my vacation, and want me to convince my associates to let you back on board the ship you and your boyfriend blew up, and use the computer that you all but destroyed because you think you know how to find the woman that killed our people."

"I can help you defeat her," Alyssa said.

Claudia remained silent for several moments. After a while, she chuckled softly. "You know, if you weren't such a pain in the ass, you and I may have gotten along quite well."

"Does that mean we have a deal?"

"I'll see what I can do."

"I need more than that," Alyssa pressed.

Claudia's lips tightened. "I believe I can convince my associates to agree to your terms."

"And I need a guarantee that we will have safe passage to and from the ship."

"You shall have it," Claudia said.

"Thank you, Dr. Tibaldi." Alyssa ended the connection.

————

ALYSSA SHOT Paul a small victory grin. He stared at her with his mouth open, then looked to Renley and Dharr.

"You're really planning on going through with this, aren't you?" he asked.

Alyssa nodded.

"And what prevents them from shooting us the second we set foot on their ship?" he pressed.

"She gave me her guarantee that we'll be safe."

"Are you even listening to yourself? A guarantee from the Society? You're going to risk our skin on a guarantee from the same nutters who had you shot and kidnapped?" He ran his hands through his hair. "Oh, and they did the same to me, too!" he added.

"That was Drake," Alyssa replied. "The people I saw on the *Valediction* condemned his actions. Believe me, I do not trust them and wish we had another option, but I know they want Nephthys more than they want us."

"We *think* they want Nephthys more than us. And what if they decide they can have their Nephthys and eat us, too?"

"We will not be helpless. We will have the Rathadi with us and we'll have something to offer them."

"Don't you have a say in this?" Paul asked Dharr. "It does concern the Rathadi."

Dharr returned Paul's gaze calmly. "Alyssa's memories may hold the only key to helping my people."

Paul blew out a frustrated sigh. He looked to Renley. "Lord Renley, perhaps you can infuse a dose of sanity into this madness?"

"We cannot discount the inherent risks involved in the proposed course of action," Renley said. At this Paul brightened. "However," Renley continued, "Dr. Tibaldi is a highly regarded member of the Society, and recovering the memories in Miss Morgan's mind appears to be our best opportunity to reach Nephthys—and to saving Tasha. Given what we learned today, we will not be able accomplish either in time without utilizing the server on board of the *Valediction*."

Paul's shoulders slumped. "I have a really bad feeling about this," he muttered.

Xander stood up from the chair and took the cigar out of his mouth. He patted Paul on his back. "Well, it may not be unanimous," he said, "but I've done things that were far more thickheaded." He stretched his back. "I'm on board"—he shot Dharr a glance—"as long as I get to fly in that fancy bird of yours."

THE FLASH of lightning set fire to the sky, and Paul's stomach lurched into his throat when the jet hit another air pocket and bounced in the turbulence. The clouds appeared as thick as milk, and the rain drops left horizontal streaks on the oval window panel. He moved his hand to tighten the seatbelt, but his fingers missed the buckle.

He looked down and froze at the sight of the bandaged stump of his right arm.

The images flashed through his mind like a set of exploding lightbulbs.

The blade slices through his arm...

His hand falls to the ground, fingers locked around the pistol...

His ears rang and his vision closed in. The sinking feeling in the pit of his stomach threated to overwhelm him again. He forced himself to breathe.

I am alive.

Things *were* getting better. At least he didn't feel like he was going to be violently ill every time the memory flashed into this mind.

I am alive, here with Alyssa and the others, he reminded himself again. *Tasha needs us.*

He pressed a button, and the small window dimmed again. Renley slouched in the seat across from him with his head drooped onto his chest. His jacket lay folded in the seat beside him, and he had loosened his tie. His cheeks puffed out when he exhaled, accompanied by a distinctly unaristocratic sound.

Well, what do you know? His Lordship nose-whistles just like the rest of us, he snickered.

At least he's able to sleep.

He had tried taking a nap himself earlier, but a million things kept rushing through his mind. His time with Alyssa has been woefully short. She'd been holed up in the forward cabin with Dharr, continuing her training for almost the entire flight. Paul's chest tightened. He wasn't sure whether it was at missing Alyssa next to him or the idea of returning to the *Valediction.*

His mind wandered to the last time he set foot on the Society's ship. At over six hundred feet, the *Valediction* was the world's largest megayacht. It had been constructed in secrecy with one main purpose, to hide the members of the ultra-secretive and ultra-rich Society from prying eyes—and to keep them out of reach of governments and international law enforcement, if necessary.

Another air pocket rocked the jet. Renley snorted and opened his eyes. He sat up in his seat and straightened his tie. He studied Paul in silence for several moments.

"You look quite bothered," he said.

"Truly?" Paul replied. "The last time I set foot aboard that bloody ship almost turned me to fish chum, and Alyssa was only able to escape because we blew out a chunk of its hull."

"I do remember," Renley said. "Distinctly."

"My point exactly," Paul replied. "And the Society isn't likely to forget that, either, regardless of what kind of a deal Alyssa thinks she made with that Italian woman."

"Dr. Tibaldi is a brilliant scientist and well-respected around the world. She will keep her word. And Xander's device will work."

"I do hope you're right," Paul said.

He threw a glance over his shoulder into the cargo area where Xander and Clay huddled over the equipment, their heads almost touching, talking in hushed voices. Xander seemed to be explaining something to Clay, who nodded enthusiastically. He looked up at Paul and shot him a grin. At first glance, the two men could not have seemed more different. Xander's huge frame, ruddy complexion, and unlit cigar hanging from his mouth, adorned by a huge cowboy hat and massive belt buckle stood in stark contrast to Clay's slender build, dark skin, curly hair and stubbled chin, all packaged into a black T-shirt and ripped jeans. Despite appearances, the pair had connected immediately, both in their element, oblivious to everything else around them.

Birds of a feather.

"I have no other choice than to believe I am right," Renley said, interrupting Paul's thoughts, deep furrows lining his sharp features. "That's the only thing keeping me sane now, knowing that… that woman has my Tasha."

"We will get her back," Paul said.

Renley gave a slow nod, a far-off look in his eyes.

Paul cocked his head. "What is it?"

Renley drummed the armrest with his fingers. "Just an odd feeling," he said. "Like I may not be coming back."

Paul opened his mouth, but Renley continued. "My life has been filled with wondrous experiences and adventures of which most people can only dream. Yet I would trade all of it and all of my possessions without the slightest hesitation to ensure Tasha's safety." Renley leaned forward, his eyes glowing with fierce intensity. "Mr. Matthews, over the past few months, I have come to respect you—and trust you—a great deal."

"Thank you, Lord Renley," Paul managed.

"I would like to request something from you that is of utmost importance to me."

Paul swallowed. "Of course."

"Should something happen to me, please promise me that you will look after her," Renley said.

A bubble of laughter caught in Paul's throat, stopped short by Renley's expression. "We're talking about the same Tasha, right? Of all the people I know, she seems most capable of looking after herself."

"I am the only family she has," Renley said. "And she is more vulnerable than she lets on."

Paul contemplated Renley's words before replying. "You have my promise, Lord Renley."

Renley leaned back in his seat again. "Thank you, Mr. Matthews. You have my abiding gratitude."

"Everything is going to be fine. Remember, we've got Alyssa and the Rathadi with us. If the Society keeps their word and Xander's machine works, our divine girl will do her part."

Renley gave a slight smile. "Speaking of 'our divine girl,'

there are some items that I should discuss with Miss Morgan prior to our arrival at the *Valediction*."

Paul sighed. "She's training with Dharr."

"Oh," Renley said. "I should not interrupt."

"They've been at it for hours," Paul snapped. "She could probably use a break." He unfastened his seatbelt a tad too eagerly. "I'll go fetch her."

Renley's lips quirked. "If you think so, Mr. Matthews."

Paul stood and moved into the forward compartment. He stopped in front of the cabin next to the medical bay and knocked. No response. He knocked again, harder.

"Who is it?" Dharr's voice rang from inside.

"It's Paul. I have to talk to Alyssa."

A moment later Dharr opened the door. Paul peeked into the small cabin. The light was dimmed, and Alyssa kneeled on the floor, eyes closed, her face drawn in.

"How is she doing?" Paul asked quietly.

"We are making some progress," Dharr replied, but the tight tone of his voice betrayed his frustration.

"We are getting close and Renley needs to talk to her before we land."

"Now?" Dharr asked.

Paul nodded.

"We aren't quite finished."

Alyssa opened her eyes. "I could use a break."

"We don't have time for breaks," Dharr said over his shoulder.

"I'm not getting anywhere," Alyssa shot back. "I don't know where you see progress."

"You should be meditating, not listening to this conversation," Dharr griped.

Alyssa stood. "I need a break," she repeated and walked past him and Paul. "I'll be with Renley."

"Alyssa," Dharr called after her. He moved through the door to follow, but Paul lifted his arm and wedged it against the frame. The Rathadi tensed and snapped his head, yellow eyes flaring. The men sized each other up through the uncomfortable silence, the constant hum of the jet the only sound surrounding them.

Finally, Paul said, "I think you're pushing her too hard."

"What?" Dharr asked.

"She is exhausted. She will break before she ever has a chance to face Nephthys again."

Dharr took a deep breath, and his body relaxed. "I never thanked you for what you did."

Paul blinked.

"Saving Tef and the other Rathadi," Dharr said. "What you did earned you much respect. Defeating a Purean warrior is not an easy task."

"Thank you," Paul said, awkwardly. "I did owe you, after all."

"The Purean you fought. He was a formidable opponent, was he not?"

Paul nodded.

"You were lucky," Dharr said. "Resourceful, no doubt, but very lucky." He curled his upper lip. "Next to Nephthys the person you fought is a mere foot soldier. She could best him without breaking a sweat." Dharr moved closer to Paul, their faces separated only by a handbreadth. "Nephthys is the most dangerous being on Earth. She was cunning enough and powerful enough to defeat the most powerful Rathadi who has ever lived, someone your people worship as a god." He let his words sink in. "And sooner or later, Alyssa will face her."

Paul stared at him, unable to swallow the lump that had grown in his throat.

"Alyssa is no longer the girl you met. If she is not successful in unlocking Horus's memories, Nephthys will over-power her, and then she will either kill her, or worse, force Alyssa into becoming her vessel. The Rathadi will die of the illness that is still ravaging them, or Nephthys will find another way to annihilate us, and your world may follow the same fate. Right now, Alyssa is the only chance we have to prevent this from happening." He paused to take a breath. "So now, please tell me again, Paul. Tell me that I am pushing Alyssa too hard."

Paul continued to stare at Dharr, unblinking, searching his brain for a response, but remained silent.

Dharr put his hand on Paul's arm and moved it out of his way. "We should prepare for landing," he said then stepped out and into the cockpit.

THE JET TOUCHED down on the helipad of the *Valediction* with the slightest of jolts amid the torrential rain. Alyssa curled her fingers into tight fists to keep her hands from trembling as the engines spun down and the helipad lowered into the glass-covered hangar. The anxiety of landing in the storm was nothing compared to the tightness in her chest at seeing the inside of the hangar once again.

I can't believe I'm coming back here. Willingly.

She took deep breaths, trying to focus on the task at hand. After her initial phone call with Claudia Tibaldi, they had communicated only once more to discuss the details of their engagement and to obtain the current location of the *Valediction*. Even though Dr. Tibaldi had managed to convince the other decision makers of the Society to let Alyssa and her team come on board, it wasn't likely to be a friendly reception.

She did keep an ace up her sleeve. She and Renley had decided not to tell the Society about the Rathadi until their arrival. She recalled Renley's words: *An image is worth a thousand words, especially when it's a living and breathing image.*

The helipad reached the floor of the hangar, and Alyssa unbuckled from her seat and stepped next to Renley as the ramp opened into the ship.

Alyssa studied the line of people standing at the far end of the hangar, away from the rain that pelted the jet through the open ceiling. She made out Claudia Tibaldi, front and center, wearing a tight-fitting white dress. Despite the five inch stiletto heels, she was still a head shorter than the boulder of a man to her right. Sergeant Torin was dressed in his usual military fatigues, Claudia Tibaldi's slim form making him appear even larger and more intimidating. The pair was flanked by more than a dozen guards armed with automatic rifles.

Quite an honor guard, Alyssa thought.

The ramp touched down on the metal deck with a clang. Moments later the canopy slid back in its place, covering the roof above them and reducing the gush of rain to a soft ringing against the glass ceiling. Torin sized up the plane suspiciously, then turned to her. She tensed.

Maybe Paul was right. I am crazy for coming back here.

Renley leaned in to her. "Keep your head up and don't let them intimidate you," he said quietly. "You are the Daughter of Horus. They fear you more than you realize."

Alyssa straightened her spine, taking strength from Renley's words. "Let's do this," she whispered and set off down the ramp with as confident a gait as she could muster. She stopped in front of Tibaldi and Torin.

"Welcome aboard," Claudia Tibaldi said, her voice tight despite her expressive Italian accent. She did not extend her hand. "I must admit, I did not think I would ever see you again, much less under these circumstances."

"I'm certain you understand that I prefer these circumstances to being forced to do your bidding at gunpoint," Alyssa replied.

Claudia Tibaldi's lips twitched, the subtle scowl somehow managing to emphasize her high cheekbones and elegant lines. She pointed to the man next to her. "You remember Sergeant Torin," she said.

Alyssa craned her head. Now that she was closer, she noticed the fading red gash that ran down the right side of his face, from his temple to the jaw line.

"Vividly," she replied. She appraised the men with the rifles, held at the ready. "Is all of this for me?"

"You have a lot of gall coming here after what you pulled last time," Torin said. "Give me one good reason why I shouldn't have my men detain you and tear whatever information we need from you piece by piece."

"We have assurances from Dr. Tibaldi!" Renley scoffed. "You would not—"

Alyssa stepped forward and looked up at the huge man, her golden eyes hard as flint.

"I will give you three good reasons, Sergeant Torin," she said. She lifted her hand and signaled to the jet. An instant later a panel opened beneath each wing, and a pair of massive guns slid down and rotated toward them.

The guards lifted their rifles, alarmed, but Torin held up his hand.

"Reasons number one and two," Alyssa said, pointing at the pair of guns. "I'm sure you realize these will shred your men to pieces faster than they can say Edgar Cayce." She paused. "And reason number three—because I know that even more than making me pay for the damage I caused to your ship and the quantum rig, you want to hold accountable the woman who murdered two dozen of your own."

Torin's face twitched, but he remained silent.

"So, Sergeant," Alyssa continued, unblinking, "why don't we stop comparing the sizes of our guns and get to the real reason we're here."

Torin held her gaze for several moments, then the corners of his lips tilted into the barest hint of a smile.

"Very well, Miss Morgan." Torin signaled his men, and they shouldered their rifles.

A moment later the jet's guns retracted back into the wings.

"Right," Alyssa said. She composed her face stoically, but her stomach churned and flipped. "Now that we have that out of the way." She addressed Claudia Tibaldi. "You told me you would grant us access to your server. May I assume that your offer still stands?"

"You promised me information about how to find and defeat this woman… Nephthys, you called her," Dr. Tibaldi replied.

"That is correct," Alyssa said.

"When can we expect to receive this information?"

"After we have accessed your server."

"Perhaps a piece of the information prior to that could serve as a sign of good faith in our arrangement?" Dr. Tibaldi pressed.

"I'm afraid that's not possible," Alyssa replied.

The woman's voice firmed. "You're unwilling to show a sign of good faith?"

"That's not it. The information is inside my head, but I can't remember it."

"You can't remember it?" Torin spoke up. "Are you holding us for fools?"

"No," Alyssa said. "We brought a device with us that will help me access these memories."

Dr. Tibaldi raised a perfectly manicured eyebrow. "You are playing a dangerous game, Miss Morgan," she said. "I had to convince senior members of the Society that we should—"

Renley stepped forward, interrupting her. "Nephthys is holding Tasha." His voice strained under the weight of his words. "I don't even know if she is still alive."

Dr. Tibaldi's face darkened, and her eyes softened. "I am truly sorry to hear that, George," she said.

Renley gave a slight nod, acknowledging her words. "I personally guarantee that Miss Morgan is planning on fully cooperating and honoring the terms of the agreement." He moved closer. "Time is of the greatest essence, Claudia," he said, pitching his voice low. "Everything you and I have achieved up to this day pales in comparison to the challenge we are facing."

Dr. Tibaldi processed his words. "There must be more to this. What are you not telling us?"

Alyssa glanced at the armed guards. "The fewer people who know about it, the better."

Dr. Tibaldi stood quietly for several moments then turned to Torin. "Sergeant, please tell your men to leave."

Torin hesitated. "Are you certain?"

Claudia Tibaldi nodded.

"Fall out," Torin addressed his men. "Station outside the hangar door and standby."

Alyssa waited for them to leave. She moved closer to Dr. Tibaldi. "What if I told you that there is not just this one Hybrid woman, but an entire race of Hybrids? True Hybrids. Hundreds of them."

Dr. Tibaldi's shot a fleeting glance at Renley. "Hundreds?"

"And that they've been at war with this woman for millennia," Alyssa continued. "I'm sure you heard what happened in Hong Kong a month ago. That was Nephthys's doing. She attacked the Hybrid's home. They got away, but she infected them with a deadly disease. The infection has been contained and slowed down, but it continues to kill them even now. My memory holds the key to curing the infection. And to defeating Nephthys."

Claudia Tibaldi regarded Alyssa. "That sounds dubious at best and insane at worst," she said after she found her voice. "How can you expect me to believe anything you're saying?"

Alyssa turned and waved to the plane. A moment later Dharr and Nel appeared on the ramp. Dharr's slitted yellow eyes and Nel's feline irises locked on Torin's and Tibaldi's forms as they approached them.

Torin reached for his sidearm, but Dr. Tibaldi placed a palm on his arm. She stared at Renley as Dharr and Nel approached.

"George, is this for real?" she asked, her voice quaking, forgetting to blink.

Renley nodded to her wordlessly. He stepped aside as the pair fell in between him and Alyssa.

"Dr. Tibaldi and Sergeant Torin, meet Dharr and Nel of the Rathadi," Renley said. "Descendants of the Island Kingdom of Atlantis."

———

AN HOUR LATER, Alyssa stood in the expansive medical bay of the *Valediction* among six state-of-the-art hospital beds and stacks of medical equipment.

Most hospitals don't even have these machines, she thought. *Then again, why should I be surprised?*

Xander Hart hunched over the instruments they had brought down from the jet. It had taken them several trips since they insisted on handling everything themselves, while Sergeant Torin and his men ensured they didn't have any accidental encounters with the crew. Xander glanced up as if sensing her eyes on him.

"Just making some final adjustments and running through the calibration protocols," he said. "The interface to the Society quantum computer is almost in place."

Paul and Clay had gone to the server room to set up the link from that end. Renley had been snagged by Claudia Tibaldi who insisted that he share with her everything he knew, and Nel had returned to the plane to stay with Tef to watch over Heru-pa —and as a backup in case things turned sour. They had gone over their bug-out plan several times. The jet could be off the ship in a matter of seconds if it came down to that. Everything seemed to be going smoothly—at least for the moment, but Alyssa couldn't shake the sinking feeling in her stomach. She had not expected Xander's procedure to lay bare her memories for others to see.

What if they uncover what really happened that night?

She had wanted to tell them the truth, of course, but... At least it sounded like it would take a while before they got to that part.

They have to know before—

Clay and Paul entered the room and she pushed the thought aside. Paul's face was as glum as it had been when they first decided to go through with this plan. In contrast, Clay seemed to bounce across the room to Xander's equipment. Alyssa didn't know whether it was the anxiety of what they were about to do or the buzz because he got to play with the Society's quantum computer. She suspected the latter. Clay shot her a boyish grin and approached Xander.

"I gave the techies the specs we discussed during the flight," he reported. "You should be all set to hook up your contraption to their quantum rig."

Xander tapped on the keyboard. "I see the interface."

"So everything's going well?" Alyssa asked.

"Smoother than expected, actually." Xander shot an approving glance in Clay's direction. "Thanks in no small part to this young man. I've never seen anybody figure things out this quickly. We need to run some final calibrations, but we should be set and ready to go shortly."

Paul stepped over to Clay and patted him on the back. "He may not look it, but he's a pretty bright bulb," he quipped.

Clay feigned a hurt look before hunching back over the instruments.

"It's true," Alyssa said. "If it wasn't for Clay, we would never have been able to figure out what was on the crystal." She watched Clay as he hunkered over the device. For an instant, she was back in the cheap hotel room, watching Clay hunched over the VR setup.

It seems like a lifetime ago.

She moved closer to the equipment. "You mentioned there are two parts to this procedure, right?" she asked Xander. "This first part is where you're learning my brain's language before you actually try to find out what it's trying to tell you."

"Precisely," Xander said.

"So what exactly will happen during the first part?"

"You will be exposed to various visual stimuli for about six hours," Xander said, "and this device will record your brain's responses to them."

"What kind of visual stimuli?"

"An extensive and diverse collection of pictures selected as the most suitable building blocks of the alphabet and language of the memory centers of your brain," Xander responded. "Once your brain's responses to the images are mapped, the computer will process the data to train the neural network."

"To decipher this visual language of my brain," Alyssa said.

"Sounds like you're getting the hang of it," Xander replied.

"And that's the part that takes a long time," Paul said.

"Well, long is relative," Clay jumped in. "Based on the preliminary benchmarks I ran, rather than two weeks to a month, the quantum rig will crunch through the data in a couple of hours, max."

Alyssa cringed. *That soon?*

"You okay?" Paul asked.

"Yeah…" Alyssa replied, "I'm fine… just… a bit spooked about this whole thing." She forced herself to focus on the task ahead. "What do I have to do?"

"Just watch the images and try to relax," Xander said. "The more you can clear your mind and have it respond naturally to the images, the more precise the alphabet will be."

"Sounds easy enough," Alyssa said and sank into the chair next to the equipment.

Xander picked up a cap with electrodes attached to them. He approached Alyssa and lifted it to her head.

Paul moved closer to her. "Is this dangerous?" he asked.

"Not at all," Xander replied. "This part is completely harmless. It's just like watching a movie and taking pictures of your brain as the images are flying by."

He slipped the cap and a pair of goggles over her head then pulled a large device closer and around the back of Alyssa's head.

"These will record a variety of signals from your brain. It is a combination of a functional magnetic resonance scan, computer tomography and EEG to measure the electrical impulses."

Clay whistled, impressed. "That's a lot of tech in a portable package."

Xander adjusted the equipment around Alyssa. "Are you ready to start, Miss Morgan?" he asked.

"Let's do this," she replied.

Xander tapped on the keyboard. A moment later, images began to flash in front of her eyes. The pictures changed slowly enough not to blur, but too fast to allow her to focus on what they were. Some lingered longer in her conscious mind, but most just went in and out.

Xander glanced to the controls. "How are you doing, Miss Morgan?"

"Just swell," she replied. "I feel like I'm flipping through somebody's photo album at a ridiculously high pace. Can't really recall anything I've looked at so far."

"She's right," Paul said, glancing at the monitor that displayed the same images. "That's going awfully fast. How can you learn anything from it?"

"The frequency of the images has been exactly predetermined," Xander replied. "We want to ensure that the brain's response is genuine and unspoiled. We want her mind's subconscious reaction to each image before she realizes what she's looking at." He touched Alyssa's shoulder. "Get comfortable, try to empty your mind and focus on the pictures." He pulled a cigar from his breast pocket and stuck it between his teeth. "This is the boring part. Let me know if you need a break."

"Let's just get this over with," Alyssa said and settled more comfortably into the chair.

SIX HOURS and two bathroom breaks later, Alyssa rested on one of the medical beds, the pressure behind her closed eyes finally ebbing to a dull ache. A hand gently moved a strand of hair from her face and tucked it behind her ear. She gave a weak smile before opening her eyes.

"How are you doing?" Paul asked quietly, perched on a metal chair next to the bed.

"Better now," she said, massaging her temples. "It was like watching a triple-feature of a French impressionist movie."

"That bad, huh?"

She chuckled then winced at the noise.

"Your eyes…" Paul said. "Your pupils are still moving, jittering."

"I feel like I'm still flipping through images. Kind of like returning to land after being out to sea—you still feel like you're rolling from side to side." She sat up and glanced around the medical bay. "Where'd everybody go?"

"Renley and Dharr are talking with Dr. Tibaldi, and Clay

and Xander are monitoring the data crunching in the server room. Xander said it should be done in less than an hour."

Alyssa scowled.

"What's up?" Paul asked.

She shrugged. "Nothing."

"Come on, I know that face by now." Paul nudged her with his finger. "Spill it."

Alyssa's teeth tugged at her bottom lip. "It's about Horus... the way he died," she said. "I'm afraid you may find out something about that night in Hong Kong... something that will make you think differently about me."

Paul reached out and lifted her chin to him. "Nothing could make me feel differently about you."

Alyssa pulled back slightly and whispered, "I need to talk to Heru-pa."

Paul cocked an eyebrow. "Isn't he sedated? Probably a good idea to keep him that way, if you ask me."

"I just think... If I just have a chance to talk to him, one-on-one, maybe I can get through to him." *And tell him the truth about his father.*

"Don't count on it."

"Still... he deserves to know."

Paul looked at her quizzically.

"I mean he should be here when we try to access Horus's memories," Alyssa said.

"You sure about that?"

No... "He is Horus's son," she said. "I took so much away from him. Perhaps this can make up for it in some way."

"Are you doing this for him or for yourself?" Paul asked.

Alyssa held still, unable to answer.

Paul took her hand. "Okay, let's go talk to him."

Alyssa shook her head. "I've got to do this by myself." She squeezed his hand before letting go and jumping down from the bed. Paul drew his eyebrows together, but he remained silent as Alyssa left the room.

She arrived at the hangar and stepped inside the jet. She opened the door to the medical bay. Heru-pa lay in the narrow cot, eyes closed. His arms and legs were secured to the metal bars on the gurney. Nel and Tef glanced up.

"How is he?" Alyssa asked.

Tef pointed at the IV line hooked into Heru-pa's arm. "Nel's cocktail is keeping him well sedated," she said.

"Can I talk to him?"

Nel tilted her head. "Are you sure that's a wise idea?"

"I have to try."

Nel glanced to Tef who gave a small nod. "Very well," she said and reached to the IV controls, dialing back the sedative.

"May I have some time with him alone?" Alyssa asked.

"Now I'm quite certain *that's* not a good idea," Nel replied.

"He's restrained and still sedated," Alyssa said. "And both of you can be right outside the door."

The Rathadi stared at Alyssa wordlessly.

"Please," Alyssa pressed. "This is really important to me, and may be to him, too."

Nel wrinkled her nose. "Okay, but he stays restrained."

"Understood," Alyssa said.

"And we'll be right outside," Tef added before she and Nel stepped to the door. Tef glanced at Alyssa over her shoulder. "Just yell if—"

"I will," Alyssa said. "Thank you both." She waited for the door to close before she approached the cot.

"Heru-pa," she said softly.

Heru-pa's face twitched and his eyes fluttered. He groaned.

"Heru-pa," she repeated. "Can you hear me?"

His eyes opened slowly, and his pupils darted back and forth as his mind seemed to struggle to catch up with his surroundings. He focused on Alyssa and recollection rippled through his face. "How is Dharr?" he asked.

"Dharr is fine," Alyssa said. "The bullet just grazed him."

A wave of relief seemed to wash over him before his eyes hardened again. "What do you want?"

Alyssa thought over the words she had prepared. All of them seemed woefully inadequate now.

"The Rathadi need us united," she finally said.

Heru-pa sneered. "A mere month ago, you did not know of the Rathadi's existence, and now you presume to tell me what the Rathadi need. What could you possibly know of our needs?"

Alyssa looked down and remained silent, unable to form a reply.

"The Rathadi need a leader who is one of their own," Heru-pa said.

Alyssa nodded. "You are right," she said, still facing the floor. "I was not born a Rathadi and was not raised into your way of life. You are the one who has been trained since birth to be Legacy. You are Horus's son. Of that, there is no doubt." She lifted her chin. "But, whether you approve or not, I am his daughter. And we cannot change what happened." She moved closer to the cot. "You know that if I hadn't been there, if Horus hadn't transferred the consciousness to me, it would have perished that night with him. Tell me, is that really what you wanted to happen?"

Silence stretched, their gazes locked. "No," Heru-pa finally said. He grimaced. "For as long as I can remember I have been training for this role, preparing for the moment when I become Legacy, when I will lead the Rathadi. Then, in one day, everything I've worked for, everything I was and would ever be... all vanished."

"I'm sorry," Alyssa said. "I understand how you must—"

"Do you? Really?" Heru-pa barked a laugh.

"Then help me," Alyssa pleaded. "Help me understand, and help me become who I need to be. For the Rathadi. For your father."

Heru-pa seemed to consider his next words carefully. "A true leader must be willing to sacrifice themselves for the Rathadi, to die for them. Even when others do not understand the sacrifice." He paused, and a strange expression flickered through his face. "Are you prepared to sacrifice everything?" he asked, his eyes burning into her.

"Yes," Alyssa said, "if it gives us a chance to unite the Rathadi and find the cure. If it can help us defeat Nephthys. Even if I must pay for it with my life—or my mind."

Heru-pa appraised her with a piercing gaze. "Nephthys is the one who will pay," he said, his lips twitching. "For killing my father."

Alyssa steeled herself. "Heru-pa," she said, "there is something you have to know. About the night in Hong Kong. The night when Horus died." She moved closer to him and reached out.

He jerked his hand back. "Do not lay your hands on me," he hissed. His eyes were clearing up, resolve surging within.

"I-I'm sorry..." Alyssa stammered. "I just wanted to tell you..."

Heru-pa stared at her with fervor that woke chills beneath her skin. "I have heard enough from you today."

"But—" Alyssa started.

"You should leave," Heru-pa said. He laid back down and closed his eyes.

A line of curses crackled through Alyssa's mind. She fought down a surge of temper and an urge to put a fist through Heru-pa's smug face.

The door opened, and Tef peeked in. She stared at them for a moment, noting the tension. "Uh... Clay said the algorithm is finished," she said. "They're ready for you."

Alyssa forced down her anger. *He deserves to know...*

"You talked about sacrifice," she said to Heru-pa. "We found a means that may help awaken Horus's memories in my mind. It carries a great deal of risk, and if it doesn't work..."

Heru-pa opened his eyes.

"I would like you to be there," she said.

He regarded her. "Shackled and sedated like a wild animal?"

Alyssa stared at the shackles, her chest tightening. "No," she said quietly.

"Alyssa—" Tef started.

"Please..." Alyssa said.

Nel stepped in. "Give Alyssa your word that you will not attempt to harm her or interfere."

Heru-pa straightened his spine. "As Horus's son, you have my word."

Alyssa's skin tingled when she reached for Heru-pa's restraints and unfastened them.

THE DOOR to the medical bay opened. Paul forced his lips into a smile when he saw Alyssa despite his somber mood at what they were about to do. He spotted Heru-pa behind her, and the hair on the back of his neck bristled. *I guess she convinced him.*

Dharr leaped up when he noticed Heru-pa, but Alyssa gave him a slight shake of her head. He stared at her, vexed, but he remained still. Nel and Tef followed Alyssa and Heru-pa into the room.

Xander glanced up from the terminal, cigar between his teeth. He raised his eyebrows when he spotted the new face.

"This is Heru-pa," Alyssa said before Xander could ask. "I asked him to join us. I hope that is okay?"

Xander narrowed his eyes for a fleeting moment before his expression relaxed again. "Of course," he said and leaned back over the equipment.

Alyssa approached Paul and Dharr as Heru-pa settled against the wall, flanked by Nel and Tef who seemed determined not to leave his side. Dharr motioned to Heru-pa with his head, his scaly lips curling down. "Why is he here?"

"Horus was his father," Alyssa said. "He has a right to witness this. He gave me his word that he would not cause any trouble."

"You should have discussed this with me first."

"Would you have allowed it?"

"Of course not," Dharr replied. "This is a terrible idea on top of an already terrible idea."

"Right…" Alyssa said. She turned to Xander. "So this is the scary part, huh?" Her easy-going words were at odds with her tight shoulders and the tremor in her voice.

Xander nodded solemnly.

"Well, are we going to do this before I change my mind, or what?" she asked.

Xander took the cigar out of his mouth. He looked at it wistfully for a moment then chucked it into the trash can. "I know we've been through this, but in light of the risks, I am compelled to once again emphasize the seriousness of the potential consequences."

Paul's heart thudded dully in his chest. *Please come to your senses, girl.*

"If everything works as expected," Xander continued, "we will uncover the hidden memories. However, if things do not go as well as we all hope—"

"I may lose parts or all of my memories forever," Alyssa finished the thought. "I understand."

"There is also a risk of introducing false memories that could feel one hundred percent real to you," Xander said. "Are you willing to go through with this, despite the risks?"

Alyssa swallowed hard. "Yes."

Paul gave a long sigh as Xander nodded. "Very well," he said. "I will initialize the sequence."

Xander's fingers tapped the keyboard, then he glanced at Clay who stood on the other side of the equipment. Clay gave him a thumbs-up.

"We're all set on our side." Xander motioned Alyssa to the chair. "Whenever you are ready."

Clay moved next to Paul. His expression was as dour as Paul's mood. Alyssa shot them both a forced grin. "Hey, what's with the glum mugs? We've been through a lot worse."

The lump in Paul's throat robbed him of speech. He simply wrapped his arms around her and held her close. *Just tell her to stop.*

His mouth opened, about to spew out a thousand reasons not to go through with this, but he closed it and remained silent.

She hugged him tightly, the pasted-on smile at odds with the trembling body she pressed against him. Paul worked to find his voice. "Don't you fret," he managed to whisper in her ear. "Clay and I will have your back."

She broke the embrace and stepped back, holding on to his arms. "I know," she replied, unable to hide the tremor in her voice. Clay gave her a silent hug and pat on her back before she slipped into the chair. Renley and the Rathadi stood by, the anxiety in their faces mirroring Paul's own worries.

"Are you ready?" Xander asked.

Alyssa nodded.

He strapped the skull cap on Alyssa's head and arranged the panel of instruments around her. "The equipment will stimulate parts of your brain and elicit specific memories." He pointed at the large monitor on the wall. "They will be displayed on the screen and recorded for analysis. We will start with a field strength of one Tesla and go up from there."

"Okay," Alyssa said, her voice sounding weak.

"Here we go." Xander tapped the keyboard.

The equipment hummed to life and digital noise appeared

on the monitor.

"How are you feeling?" Xander asked.

"So far, so good," Alyssa replied.

Xander scrutinized the monitor and the instruments, frowning. "The memories seem to be buried deeper inside your hippocampus than anticipated," he said. "Increasing the field strength to two Tesla."

The display flickered briefly then went back to the digital noise.

"Three Tesla," Xander said.

Paul's throat tightened. "Is that safe?" he asked.

Xander shot him a look. "She is aware of the risks." He tapped the keyboard again.

Alyssa's body contorted with a spasm.

"Alyssa!" Paul cried out. He stared at Xander, alarmed.

Xander put a calming hand on his shoulder. "This is a normal response," he said. "We have successfully activated the memory center."

Alyssa's body relaxed, and the screen flickered to life.

"We are now going to stimulate the visual cortex with the last known images of Horus before his passing," Xander said.

"The inside of the jet," Paul said.

Xander nodded. "This should trigger the target memories within her and prompt the memory sequence."

The digital noise on the screen slowly transformed into the inside of the jet.

Paul moved closer to the display. "Are these really…?"

"Yes," Xander said. "We are seeing her memories."

Alyssa's face appeared on the monitor, twisted with anguish.

"No," Heru-pa said. "Not *her* memories. These are *his* memories. We are watching my father's memories before he died."

Paul inhaled sharply at Heru-pa's words. He stood still as shivers crept down his spine, freezing his feet to the floor. He stared at the monitor, unable to blink.

The screen continued to show Horus's point of view as he reached out to Alyssa, his palms joined in the sacred Rathadi blessing. He placed his palms on her head.

"The sacred Bond of Legacy..." Tef whispered.

The image of Alyssa's face slowly flickered in and out.

"He is dying..." Nel said, her voice breaking under the weight of her own words.

The image disappeared, replaced by darkness. Slowly, pinpricks of light broke through the dark, like stars shimmering in a night sky. Gradually, one of the lights grew brighter, larger. Paul gasped as features emerged from the light, transitioning into an image of a young woman wearing a white dress with a high collar. Her strikingly beautiful face was marred by dirt and blood, and fear shone from her feline eyes.

"Who...?" Paul started.

"Amah," Alyssa whispered, her voice sounding strange and ethereal.

"Horus's mother," Heru-pa said softly. "This is his last thought, his last memory before he died. The face of his mother."

Complete silence stretched through the room, nobody willing to break the spell of the moment. Their eyes were glued to the monitor, mesmerized.

The fear in the woman's face was replaced by resolve. She

glanced behind her into a dark alley then looked out with a piercing stare before leaping away.

"No, *Amah*…" Alyssa whispered. "Don't leave…"

The image flickered. Slowly Alyssa's face filled the screen. Nephthys stood in the background.

"This was in Hong Kong!" Paul cried out. "On the night of the attack—when Alyssa and Horus fought Nephthys."

Paul's mind reeled as Alyssa lifted her arm and pointed a pistol directly at the screen. He recoiled when the gun flashed three times, accompanied by collective gasps in the room. The image on the screen shook and blurred, then tilted down. Paul recognized Horus's golden armband as he pressed his palms to cover the red-stained spots on his shirt.

Paul's chest blazed with searing pain, as if his ribs had punched a hole right through his lungs. For a second nobody spoke or moved, then Heru-pa broke the stunned silence.

"She murdered Horus!" he screamed.

Dharr stepped between Heru-pa and Alyssa. His frozen expression reflected Paul's own dread.

Alyssa's eyes snapped open, and she ripped the cap off her head. The images on the screen vanished. "What…?" she stammered, confused.

"You murdered my father!" Heru-pa cried out.

"No! You… you don't understand!" Alyssa cried. "I wanted to tell you! It was Nephthys, she controlled my mind—"

"You're a murderer and a liar!" Heru-pa spat. "Unworthy of his Legacy!" His gaze swept the room, burning into the other Rathadi. "What more proof do you need?"

He rushed Alyssa.

"Heru-pa!" Dharr cried out, holding him back. "You shall

honor your vow."

Heru-pa stopped, and his face turned expressionless. "I shall not blemish my honor because of *her*," he seethed. "By the ancient Rathadi custom, I invoke the Rite of Retribution."

Dharr froze, and his face caved.

Paul blinked at the change in Dharr's demeanor. The challenge in the Rathadi's eyes vanished. "Uh... retribution?" Paul asked.

"Heru-pa, consider your words," Tef said.

"The Rite of Retribution has not been called upon in millennia," Dharr said.

Heru-pa glowered at Alyssa. "It is my right as his son."

"What is he talking about?" Paul asked.

Heru-pa shot Alyssa one final scathing glare then stormed out of the room.

"Heru-pa, wait!" Tef shouted then rushed after him.

Dharr stared at Nel. "This is madness."

"It may be madness," Nel said, eying Alyssa, "but it is Heru-pa's right." She followed Tef out.

"What are you talking about?" Alyssa's voice wavered, her gaze bouncing from Dharr to the others. "What is this retribution?"

Dharr's voice was grim when he spoke. "When one Rathadi commits a grave offense against another, the victim may forego the judgment by the Council of Elders and instead demand the Rite of Retribution by challenging the transgressor to a duel."

Paul felt the blood drain from his face. "A duel? Heru-pa just challenged Alyssa to a duel?"

Renley stepped forward. "To the death?"

"It may as well be," Dharr said. "If Heru-pa wins, Alyssa

must relinquish her claim to Legacy."

"So what does that mean?" Paul said.

"I will have to transfer the consciousness to him," Alyssa said.

"And would that be so bad?" Paul asked. "You didn't ask for this. Giving it up may be the best thing that's happened to you. It has brought you nothing but pain. You could—"

"Transferring the consciousness would kill me," Alyssa said.

Paul's breath caught in his throat. His vision narrowed as the words sank in. "This can't be happening…" he muttered.

The door opened again and Tef barged in. She slammed the door behind her.

"He is such a—" she kicked the chair closest to her, crashing it into the wall. Xander drew back and adjusted his hat.

"He refuses to change his mind," Dharr said. It was a statement rather than a question.

"And Nel!" Tef yelled. "I thought she would help me talk him out of it, but… but… she's taking his side!"

"Surely there must be—" Renley started.

"This is insane!" Paul burst out, finally finding his voice. "You can't honestly expect Alyssa to fight him! She said Nephthys controlled her mind! An hour ago, Heru-pa was your captive. Now you're letting him challenge Alyssa?"

"Heru-pa is within his rights to do so, given the circumstances," Dharr said. "We must honor our laws."

"Well… what if… what if…" Paul's mind raced, the throbbing in his chest growing stronger by the second. "What if she refuses to fight? He can't make her fight!"

Dharr looked at him aghast. "She cannot. Refusing would

forfeit her right to Legacy. She would have to transfer the consciousness to Heru-pa."

"The only way to avoid the duel was for Heru-pa to recall the challenge," Tef said. "I thought Nel would help to convince him, but…"

"There's got to be another way!" Paul cried out. "I'm not going to stand by and watch you fight to the death."

"You heard Dharr," Alyssa said quietly. "If I don't accept his challenge, I will forfeit the Legacy."

"And if he defeats you, it'll be the same outcome!"

"Then I will make sure he doesn't," she said.

Dharr nodded. "We must do everything to ensure that he does not."

"Where is this… duel supposed to happen?" Alyssa asked.

"By tradition, the challenge is to be fought at the tallest elevation," Dharr said.

"So highest deck?" Alyssa asked.

"It must be under open air," Dharr said.

"The helipad?" Tef offered. "When it is raised, it's the tallest deck on the ship."

Paul slammed his fist on the table, rattling the equipment. "Stop talking about it like this is going to happen!"

"Paul—" Alyssa said.

"You don't have to do this. We could run away—" he started.

"I'm afraid that is not an option," Dharr cut in. "By law, she must accept the challenge after it has been issued."

"These are your laws!" Paul shot back. He grasped Alyssa's hand, pleading. "You don't have to abide by them."

Dharr faced Paul, a dangerous gleam in his yellow eyes.

"Alyssa is the daughter of Horus and his Legacy," he said, his voice quiet, but icy. "Our rules are her rules now." He turned to Alyssa. "We don't have much time. We have to prepare," he said and stepped out of the room.

Paul held on tight to Alyssa's arm. "Ally, please…" he said.

Alyssa gently moved Paul's hand from her arm. "I'm sorry, Paul." She followed Dharr out of the room.

Paul stared after her, a gnawing numbness settling into his limbs.

———

ALYSSA KNEELED on the soft carpet, focusing on her breathing. *In… Hold… Out…* She listened inward, sensing her hammering heartbeat. She erased all thoughts from her mind, gradually taming the swirl in her head. *In… Hold… Out…* Her heartbeat slowed.

She sensed Dharr's presence more than she heard it as he approached her. She opened her eyes. He kneeled down before her, holding a bundle in his hands. He set it on the carpet between them and unfurled it. A glint of metal flashed through the cloth.

"Heru-pa is the challenger, so by rite you have the choice of the weapon," Dharr said, lifting a pair of dual daggers to Alyssa. "Horus has wielded dual dagger in many battles. Your body will remember, and your mind will catch up."

Alyssa took the blades from him. She studied them, acutely aware of their weight in her palms and their texture against her skin.

"Heru-pa is a formidable opponent," Dharr continued, "but

he does have weaknesses. He is brash and arrogant. You can exploit these traits to your advantage."

Without thinking, Alyssa spun the blades in her hand. A sense of calmness washed over her. Images hovered at the edge of her awareness… the familiar sense of electricity before a battle. Her senses heightened.

A knocking sound drew her back. Alyssa blinked, focusing on her surroundings again.

The door opened, and Renley and Paul stepped inside.

"Dr. Tibaldi and the Society have agreed to our request," Renley said.

"That was easier than expected," Alyssa mused.

Renley offered a pensive smile. "The Society has spent decades and millions of dollars looking for any clues that may lead them to the Rathadi. Today, we brought them to the *Valediction*'s proverbial doorstep. It's not surprising that the Society does not want to stand in the way of an ancient rite that involves the Rathadi, after they welcomed them as guests." He paused. "Dr. Tibaldi and Sergeant Torin did have one condition."

Dharr looked at him expectantly.

"They wish to witness the duel."

Dharr clicked his mouth, irritated.

"It is their ship," Renley said. "The demand is not unreasonable."

"What about video surveillance?" Dharr asked.

"If we allow the two witnesses, they agreed to turn off surveillance of those areas," Renley said.

Dharr mulled this over. "Very well," he said. "Please inform Dr. Tibaldi and Sergeant Torin that their terms are acceptable."

He turned back to Alyssa as Renley stepped out of the room. "Are you ready?"

"As ready as I'll ever be," she replied, suddenly aware of the weight of her limbs. She shot a fleeting glance at Paul who stood at the door with his arms folded across his chest. He caught her glance and moved closer. A sad smile ghosted his lips.

"You're really going to do this, aren't you?" he asked.

Alyssa took his hand. "I need you by my side for this."

He pulled her up and put his arms around her, drawing her close. "I have never left it," he said.

Alyssa's vision blurred as she squeezed her body against him.

———

THE HANGAR WAS heavy with damp air and the pungent smell of ozone, serving as a reminder of the storm that had passed over the *Valediction* earlier in the day. Alyssa kneeled on the helipad with her eyes closed, taking in the sound of the wind and ocean as they rushed into the hangar through the open ceiling.

The anticipation of the fight tingled through her body, her senses on edge, sharper, but also disconnected, as if she were in someone else's dream. The weight of the blades on her belt, foreign at first, now seemed as much a part of her as her own limbs. She moved her palms to the hilts and a familiar energy stirred within her.

She opened her eyes. Heru-pa kneeled across from her on the opposite side of the circular platform. Clay and Paul stood with Renley and Xander along one side of the perimeter of the helipad. Dharr, Nel, and Tef lined up along the opposite side. Claudia Tibaldi and Sergeant Torin completed the circle around Alyssa and Heru-pa, their eyes filled with awe and anticipation.

Dharr stepped forward. "Heru-pa, son of Horus and Ma'at," his voice rang out, "has challenged Alyssa, daughter of Horus and Anja, to the ancient Rite of Retribution. The winner of this duel will be proclaimed Legacy." He swiveled to Alyssa. "Do you accept this challenge?"

"I accept," Alyssa said.

The helipad raised skyward. "When the platform reaches the apex, you may begin," Dharr called out. His gaze flickered to Alyssa, and his voice pitched lower. "Be decisive and quick. Trust your instincts," he whispered, his voice tense. "Horus's strength lives within you. Let it guide you."

He stepped back, joining the circle the others formed around Alyssa and Heru-pa. The platform rose, emerging over the arrow-shaped glass structure that enclosed the ship above its hull. The setting sun painted the sky a blood red. Alyssa squinted.

The helipad stopped.

Heru-pa leaped to his feet and drew two silver daggers from the sheaths in a single motion. He rushed Alyssa. She barely managed to roll aside and draw her own weapons.

He charged after her, the blades a perfect extension of his limbs, knives relentlessly slicing in tandem.

Alyssa backed away, somehow managing to evade his strikes, more on instinct than intent.

As fast as the attack started, it stopped. Alyssa panted as Heru-pa appraised her, his chest barely moving, his breathing slow and steady.

He's toying with you.

He lunged at her again in another flurry of strikes, even faster than before. The left dagger slashed for her temple in a blur, the right aimed for her flank. She managed to just block the strikes with her own blades, but it left her exposed. His follow-up opened a gash in her right arm.

The bite of the blade was like a burning leash. Alyssa screamed, and the dagger fell to the helipad with a clang. Heru-pa pressed on with a savage roundhouse kick to her left side, his shin connecting viciously with her ribs. The pain shot through the rest of Alyssa's body, robbing her breath. Her left knee buckled, sending her to the ground.

"Alyssa!" Paul's scream cut through the air.

Alyssa gasped for breath, doubled over in pain, as Heru-pa stalked toward her. The blades in his hands loomed menacingly.

"Do you yield?" he asked.

Alyssa met his gaze unblinking. "No," she breathed.

Heru-pa moved to the dagger on the ground and kicked it to her.

"Pick it up," he spat.

Alyssa hissed in a breath as she moved her right arm. Pain seared through her biceps, an angry red line of blood seeping from her upper arm to her wrist. She wrapped her palm around the hilt and gained her feet.

They took stock of each other, the edges of their blades reflecting the crimson color of the sky.

I have no chance against him here...

Alyssa threw a sideways glance over the glass structure that extended the entire length of the vessel. Midship, an antenna tower rose high above the glass.

Heru-pa lunged forward.

Alyssa turned and leaped from the helipad onto the glass, twenty feet below her. The gasps of the others faded above her as she landed and rolled out of the fall. Her wounded arm sent stabs of pain to her shoulder as she pushed off the glass to her feet. She was in a full sprint to the tower when she heard Heru-pa land behind her and give pursuit.

She tucked away her daggers. As she drew nearer, the enormous scale of the antenna array became clear. Metal rungs led up the five foot wide mast that rose sixty feet in the air. Midway up the structure, a pair of horizontal beams cut across the mast, jutting out like four arms. Each of the arms was lined with countless antennas rising up to the sky like swords and held one of the four radar domes at its end.

She leaped up and caught a rung in mid-stride and swung herself up. She climbed the tower, hand over hand, adrenaline dulling the spikes lancing through her right arm with every pull.

Heru-pa reached the tower below her.

"Is this how you expect to lead the Rathadi?" he mocked her. "By running away like a scared rabbit?"

Alyssa kept climbing the mast until she arrived at the first crossbar. She stopped and looked down, her heart beating wildly against her chest. Heru-pa sheathed his blades and reached for a rung. He pulled himself up with ease and followed her up.

Alyssa took a tentative step out onto the metal arm, holding on to the parallel beam above her. She weaved between the antennas, forcing herself not to think about the thirty foot drop to the glass, or the shimmering water a hundred feet beneath it.

Heru-pa reached the horizontal beam. He pulled out one of

his daggers and used his other hand to steady himself on the crossbar above.

Alyssa made it to the end of the beam. She pressed her back against the radar dome as Heru-pa stalked toward her.

"You have nowhere to go, little rabbit," he taunted.

Alyssa gathered all her strength and wrapped both arms around the crossbar above. She swung herself onto the upper beam and carefully gained her feet, balancing against one of the antennas rising from the metal arm.

Heru-pa growled below her. "You can't run forever," he spat.

I'm not planning to...

Alyssa grabbed hold of one of the thick antennas and swung down in an arc, kicking her legs out at Heru-pa.

He snarled, surprised, and almost lost his balance, but managed to avoid her legs. Alyssa landed on the lower beam and followed up with a snap kick to his head. Heru-pa blocked it and slashed at her with the blade. Alyssa dodged behind one of the antennas, and he grunted as the blade connected with the metal.

Alyssa pulled free one of her daggers and struck out. He evaded it easily and advanced. Alyssa parried and dodged, backing away. Her feeble attempts at counter strikes succumbed to his blade before they could inflict any damage. Heru-pa had gained initiative once again, and he bore down relentlessly, his strikes precise, driving her back against the radar dome.

Alyssa panted, her lungs burning. Heru-pa drove his blade forward with new intensity, his face fierce and alive with concentration. She raised her dagger just in time and parried the blow, but the force of the impact jolted her wrist. She gasped when the dagger slipped from her grasp and fell to the glass below.

Viper-quick, Heru-pa's dagger lanced out. She let her body respond and leaped back, pivoting. The blade missed, but her move knocked her off balance. She teetered on the edge of the beam, reaching for the antenna. Panic surged as her fingers grasped air and she fell backward.

Desperate, she twisted her body and stretched for the beam. Her fingers found metal and locked around it. She swung in the air, clutching desperately to the lower crossbar.

Heru-pa glowered from above, eyes shining brightly. Terror bled through her as the throbbing in her right arm grew into a stinging bite that sent waves of agony through her muscle.

"Do you yield?" Heru-pa asked again.

Alyssa's arms shook with invisible tremors as exhaustion came over her in a wave, starting in her muscles and sinking into her bones. She looked down to the glass then to the water all around her. She closed her eyes. Slowly, the panicky daze cleared. Pain and exhaustion yielded to a sense of peace.

Alyssa let go. Time seemed to slow as the glass rushed at her. Then she smashed into it, her feet and legs absorbing the brunt of the force, but the impact jarred her bones and rattled her teeth. She crashed to the glass, spreading cracks through the pane beneath her like giant spiderwebs.

She stared into the empty space below. The inner courtyard stretched on the main level of the ship, twelve decks beneath her. She moaned and rolled to her back, peering up at Heru-pa.

He stood on the antenna array, his arms spread wide like a wraith, his open shirt blowing in the wind. "It is time to end this," he called out. "On this day, the Legacy returns to the rightful heir." Fire filled his eyes and he leaped down, his dagger gleaming brightly in the fading sunlight.

Alyssa groaned. With a final effort she rolled aside and onto the neighboring pane of glass. Her palm grazed the hilt of the dagger and locked around it, then she drove the blade into the cracked glass pane. More spiderwebs shot out, spreading across the glass to the metal frame just as Heru-pa landed. He stood still in time for an instant before the cracked glass splintered into hundreds of pieces under his weight, and he fell into thin air. He twisted and reached for the other pane, but his hands came up short.

Alyssa's palm shot out and snatched his wrist in mid-air. She screamed with the pain and effort as he jerked to a stop, suspended from her injured arm, twelve floors above the deck. She locked her other hand around his arm.

Heru-pa looked up at her. For an instant, the ghost of a smile edged his lips before his face darkened, and his eyes hardened again.

She willed her arms to keep their grip. Every nerve fiber of her injured arm screamed at her as she pulled up and dragged him onto the glass pane beside her. She collapsed on the glass next to him, panting.

Alyssa pushed herself to her knees, grunting with the effort. "I don't want to be your enemy," she said to Heru-pa, finally able to catch her breath.

Heru-pa glared at her in a silent reply.

She pushed to her feet and spotted the others rushing to them across the glass. Dharr reached them first. He put his hand on her shoulder, gleaming with relief and pride. He turned to

Heru-pa and leaned over him as Paul approached Alyssa, his eyes bright.

Paul's expression turned to terror.

"Watch out!" he screamed an instant before Heru-pa's dagger whipped past her, missing her neck by the width of a hand.

She whirled.

Heru-pa glowered at her, growling in frustration. He stood over Dharr, clutching a command bracelet as Dharr lay on the glass, cradling his face. Heru-pa slipped on Dharr's armband and tapped it. An instant later the jet crashed through the glass ceiling of the hangar, the aft ramp lowering as it hovered above the ship.

Heru-pa sprinted for it and leaped to the ramp.

Torin slid out his sidearm and fired a rapid series of shots as Heru-pa swung inside the jet before it banked sharply and away from the ship. Torin continued firing until his slide locked.

Everybody stood still, as if frozen in place, watching the plane disappear in the distance.

Paul reached Alyssa and held her against him. "Are you okay?" he asked.

She managed to give a small nod and turned to Dharr.

Tef leaned over him. A cut over his right eyebrow trickled blood into his face. He brushed off Tef's hand and stood. "I was not prepared for that," he said, grimacing.

Sergeant Torin reloaded his weapon and approached Alyssa, eyeing her with respect. "You fought well," he said. His gaze moved to the huge gash in the glass roof, and he scowled. "But I am growing weary of your destroying my ship every time you set foot on it."

Alyssa sucked in air and dug her left hand into the thin mattress as Nel injected the anesthetic around the wound in her right arm. A cool hand slipped into her fingers and squeezed gently. She glanced up at Paul and eyed him gratefully.

"Try to hold still," Nel said. She reached up to the handle on the surgical light and readjusted it.

"We have more important things to do than to worry about a scratch on my arm," Alyssa offered through clenched teeth.

"Unless you want that *scratch* to get infected, you'll sit quietly and let me take care of it," Nel replied.

Alyssa held still as Nel put in a suture and tied it off. She worked adeptly until she covered the length of the cut with tidy stiches that held the skin together. She tied off the last knot and cut the suture.

"All done," Nel said. "See how much easier it is when you let me do this without squirming around?"

Alyssa inspected the work, impressed. She flexed her arm a couple of times. "Thank you," she said.

Nel nodded and taped a dressing over the cut. An awkward silence stretched. Nel swallowed. "I owe you an apology," she said.

Alyssa remained silent. She felt Paul squeeze her hand again in support.

"It was wrong of me to doubt you," Nel continued. "I—"

"It's okay," Alyssa said. "The last few weeks have been difficult on all of us." She reached out and touched Nel's arm. "With all that's happened and the past you and Heru-pa share... it couldn't have been easy on you."

"I didn't realize how much he had changed. I did not think he was capable of—"

Nel stopped when the door whipped open and Dharr stormed into the medical bay, frowning. Tef trailed after him, her lips pinched tight.

Alyssa's stomach sank. "What now?"

"We were able to reach the elders," he said.

"Isn't that a good thing?" she asked.

"They didn't believe me. They think we're making it all up to cover for stealing the plane."

"What?" Alyssa called out. "That's ridiculous!"

Dharr grumbled. He paced the large room. "We are running out of time... Without the amulet, the elders will continue to sit on their hands, doing nothing!"

"Any luck trying to reach Heru-pa?" Nel asked.

Dharr shook his head. "Not surprisingly, he has not responded, but..."

"But what?" Alyssa asked.

"We were able to track the plane," he replied. "It appears that he's heading north. Way north."

Alyssa's mind reeled at the implication. "He's going to—"

"Nephthys," Dharr confirmed.

"Why would he do that?" Paul asked.

"The enemy of my enemy…" Alyssa whispered. She shook her head. "I didn't know he hated me that much."

"What could he possibly hope to accomplish?" Paul asked.

Dharr let out a forceful breath. "I have a suspicion, but I loathe to think about it."

Before Alyssa could press him, the door opened again and Clay came in, a victorious smile lighting up his face.

"I could use some good news," Alyssa said.

"I was finally able to get through to Kamal," Clay replied. "And, better yet, Kamal said he should be able to route a call to Kade."

Alyssa hopped off the cot. Her knees buckled, but she managed to catch herself before Paul could reach for her. She waved him off when he gave her a concerned look. "When can I talk to him?"

"I'm keeping the line open and routed the call to your guest cabin," he said. "I figured you'd appreciate the privacy. Kamal is waiting for you on the line."

Alyssa rushed to the door. "Thank you," she breathed. She stopped and turned around. "Umm… where exactly is my guest cabin?"

"I'll take you there," Clay offered.

Alyssa followed Clay to the glass elevator. They entered, and he pressed the button for the suites.

"I think you'll be happy with your digs," Clay said, giving her a wide grin. They exited and paced along the hallway. He pointed at a double door. "Here it is."

"Thank you," Alyssa said and gave him a quick hug then opened the door. Her head buzzed with excitement at talking with Kade, and she barely noticed the spacious cabin appointed in leathers and exotic woods as she dashed to the phone on the wide desk. She picked up the handset.

"Hello?" she said.

"Alyssa!" Kamal's voice sounded from the other end of the line. "Thank goodness you're all right. We have been so worried!"

Alyssa slumped into the plushy chair. "Kamal... How is Kade? Is he still... in jail?"

"Yes, the police department isn't budging on this matter, but the minister has been surprisingly helpful and ensured preferential treatment."

Alyssa exhaled. *At least he's safe.* "Thank you, Kamal, I know you're doing what you can." She paused. "When can I speak with him?"

"In just a moment," Kamal said. "I was able to pull some strings to arrange a private conversation. He should be dialing in any time."

Alyssa waited for a few moments, then she heard a click.

"Alyssa?" Kade's voice rang through the handset. Alyssa tried to answer, but her voice failed. Tears welled up behind her eyelids.

"Alyssa?" Kade repeated. "Are you there?"

"Kade... Dad..." Alyssa whispered.

"Ally..." Kade's voice faltered.

"How are you?" she asked. "Are they treating you well?"

"Don't you worry about me, Ally, I've got the best cell in all of Cairo," he chuckled. "Running water, a bed, and three decent meals a day. They even let me read, so I can catch up on my reading list." Alyssa smiled at Kade's words despite everything. "But enough about me. How are you?" he asked.

"I…" Alyssa started. Without warning her head swam as a wave of emotions welled up inside, and the events from the past several days threatened to overwhelm her. "I'm okay," she managed.

"Where are you?" Kade asked.

"You would not believe me…"

"Are you safe?"

"I… I think so, for now."

"You think so?" Kade's voice grew tight.

Alyssa took a deep breath.

"What's going on, kiddo?"

"There's so much that's happened," she said. "I don't even know where to start."

"Tell me, Ally."

Alyssa took another deep breath, then the words spilled out of her.

————

THIRTY MINUTES LATER, Alyssa luxuriated on her plush king-sized bed, processing her conversation with Kade. She hadn't planned on telling him as much as she did, but once she started talking, she couldn't stop. She needed to share with him, get things off her chest. Somehow knowing that he knew made it more bearable.

The knock on the door pulled her back. The door opened, and Paul's head peeked into the room.

"Are you finished with your call?" he asked.

She nodded and pushed up slowly. Every muscle in her body seemed to be screaming at her. She bit back a moan.

He stepped inside. "How are you feeling?"

"Like I could really use a hot shower." Alyssa eyed her torn and bloody clothes. "And a new outfit."

Paul stepped up to the closet and opened it. He whistled at the ensemble of clothes. "Nice..." He picked up one of the dresses. "Brand new," he said, impressed.

Alyssa forced herself to stand and moved next to him. She lifted one of the outfits and looked at the brand then at the rest of the clothes. "My dad's yearly salary is hanging in this closet."

She cut across the cabin to the bathroom and opened the door, taking in the gleaming granite countertops and marble floors. She wistfully sized up the jacuzzi tub that stood in front of the panoramic window. *Perhaps tomorrow...* She turned to the huge walk-in shower on her left and shook her head. "The shower is as big as the entire cabin they gave me last time."

Paul stepped beside her and peeked in.

"Nice," he quipped. "A toilet fit for the Legacy."

Alyssa smiled, but it was sad and distracted.

Paul eyed her. "I'll let you clean up and get some sleep," he said.

"Please don't leave," Alyssa said. "I don't want to be alone now."

He blinked, tilting his head. "Of course," he said. "I'll wait."

She closed the door and stripped off her clothes then stepped inside the glass enclosure. The shower turned on at the touch of a button, the temperature perfect. She looked at the controls and switched on the full body jets.

She let the water soothe her tortured muscles for a few minutes, then washed her hair and bathed her skin before turning off the water reluctantly. She dried off and wrapped a small towel around her hair. Her gaze fell to the body lotion on the granite sink, and she took a sniff. *Coconut and watermelon?* She rubbed it into her skin, taking care not to press on the cuts and bruises that scattered her body, then slipped into the plush robe that hung at the door and tied the belt around her waist. She opened the door.

Paul rested on the side of the king-size bed. He looked up.

"Feeling better?" he asked.

Alyssa nodded and moved to the bed. She eased down next to him and put her hand on his right arm. She could feel him tense as she moved her hand down to the stump. He yanked away as if her touch hurt him.

"Don't," he said.

"Paul," Alyssa whispered, and she reached for his arm again.

"Why?" he asked her, his lips twisted into a grim line.

"I'm sorry," she said, suddenly aware of the growing tightness in the pit of her stomach. "I never got to tell you. I'm so sorry…"

"I don't want your pity."

The bitterness in his voice felt like a slap. She felt burning behind her eyelids and turned away so he wouldn't see the tears. She blinked to hold them back.

"I'm not offering you pity," she said. "I… I know we haven't been able to spend time—"

"I don't even know who you are anymore," Paul said and his voice cracked. He coughed to cover it up.

"I don't even know myself," she whispered.

"Do you know how hard it is to put your socks on with only your left hand? Not to mention to cut an apple?" He gave a bark of laughter that sounded like a cry. His lips quivered.

Alyssa wrapped her arms around him and held him tight. He tensed, but then relaxed, and they sat on the bed for a long time, soaking in each other's presence. After some time Paul pushed back gently.

"I'm sorry," he whispered. "I'm an idiot. I shouldn't have—"

"I've caused you so much pain," Alyssa said.

"It's not your fault. You must not blame yourself." He touched her arm.

She shivered at the touch of his fingers. His fingertips were warm and soft, and her skin remembered the trace of his touch after he lowered his hand.

"Even after everything. That day in the Internet café," he said. "I would do it all over again."

Alyssa's throat tightened. She felt tears well up again, but this time she didn't try to hold them back.

"I should go," Paul said and stood.

Before she realized what she was doing, Alyssa grabbed his arm and held him back.

He looked at her, a confused expression in his eyes.

She pulled him back next to her. "I would have been lost without you."

Alyssa leaned over and kissed him on his cheek. She looked into his eyes, and the fluttering that took hold in her stomach spread through her whole body. Paul's pupils were large. His breathing came in ragged breaths.

Alyssa stood slowly and faced Paul. With unhurried movements, she unfastened the towel that she had wrapped around her head and shook out her dark, long hair. Paul stared at her, unblinking. Her breathing quickened as her hands shifted to the belt around her waist. Paul's eyes widened as she untied it and let the bathrobe slide off her body and onto the floor. His eyes stayed glued to her face for several quickening heartbeats, then followed the curves of her breasts and hips, down to her legs, then back up to her face. He swallowed.

"Are you—?" he stammered, his voice hoarse.

"Don't you fret," she whispered and leaned forward. "What's coming up doesn't require both hands."

————

NEPHTHYS SAT in the plush chair when the phone rang. She looked at the number and answered the call.

"Yes?"

"The girl just made contact with Kade Morgan," the man on the other end of the line said.

"What have you learned?" she asked.

"There has been a development. Unforeseen, but it may play into your hands."

Nephthys remained silent.

"Horus's son invoked an ancient rite and challenged the girl for his right to the Legacy."

Nephthys's mouth twitched. "The Rite of Retribution? I

would not have thought the cowards on the council would allow the risk."

"They are operating without the council's approval. They are renegades. Apparently, they went to the Society and are aboard their ship."

"The Society? What could they possibly want from those zealots?"

"I'm unsure, but I will find out," he said.

"What about Kade Morgan?" Nephthys asked.

"I have ensured that he remains in jail for the foreseeable future. He will not be allowed to interfere, and the girl will not be able to reach him again."

The words tugged one corner of Nephthys's mouth into a shrewd smile as she leaned back into the chair. "You have been valuable, Kamal, and you shall be rewarded."

HERU-PA KEPT his eyes trained on the compound ahead of him as he hovered over the compacted snow that served as the makeshift runway. The jet blasts kicked up billowing clouds of snow around him while he maneuvered through the final descent. The wheels touched down and sank until the wings almost reached the snow before finally stopping. He exhaled and powered down the engines. As the white clouds around him settled, a dozen white-clad Purean soldiers appeared, their weapons pointing at the plane.

His stomach churned. They had not acknowledged his attempts at communications, but he took solace in the fact that they had not shot him out of the sky on sight.

I must not fail.

He left the cockpit. His jaw clenched when he stepped into the aft compartment, past the spot where Alyssa kneeled in the sacred Bond of Legacy with his father, when he realized his life would forever be changed. The memory of holding his father's lifeless body threatened to overwhelm him once again. Rage seethed through him. Clean, perfect, focusing rage.

Soon she will pay the price for what she did. For what she stole from me. For what she stole from all the Rathadi.

He stepped through the cabin and activated the ramp. He raised his hands and waited at the edge of the platform as it lowered to the snow. Before it touched down, the Purean soldiers rushed him. A pair of hands shoved him to his knees while another dozen held their rifles pointed at him.

"I am Horus's heir. I have a proposition for Nephthys," he said, repeating the words of his radio transmission.

One of the Purean soldiers struck his back with the butt of a rifle, and Heru-pa fell forward into the snow. He grunted with pain, but didn't move as the soldiers pinned his arms behind his back and searched his body.

He clenched his jaw when one of them pulled his father's dagger out of the sheath at his hip and held the onyx-black blade to his face.

"Do you come seeking an audience with Nephthys armed?"

A pair of hands yanked him to his feet then shoved him forward, to the entrance of the compound.

———

THE DARKNESS ENVELOPS me as I'm falling.

A distant gleam of light hovers in the distance. I rush down to it. A ship. Countless panes of glass reflect the moonlight, gleaming like facets of a diamond above the jet-black water. I draw nearer. A tower rises from the glass. White domes and

metal shafts line up like spears. I continue rushing at it, faster.
There... a glint of gold. I race for it. Closer. I reach out—

Alyssa woke shuddering. She blinked, trying to recall
the dream.

The *Valediction*. The antenna tower where she fought Heru-
pa. *Was it just a dream, or...?*

She rolled over, and her body touched another. She froze.

Paul!

Memories rushed back. For a moment her dream was
forgotten as she reveled in her memories. She took a deep
breath and exhaled, drawing herself back to the present, then
glanced at the clock. *4:15 am.*

She turned over carefully, trying not to stir the mattress.
Paul lay next to her, his chest bare, a white blanket covering his
lower body. His breathing was calm and even. She studied his
face in the darkness, her new vision bathing it in a red glow,
surrounding his features like a halo. She recalled the first time
she saw him this way, in complete darkness. It was on this ship,
only four weeks ago. On the night when she thought she had
lost him forever.

She touched his cheek gently and slipped out of bed then
crossed the cabin to the closet and opened the door. A soft light
illuminated the clothes. She flipped past the cocktail dresses
and pantsuits before stopping at a pair of black yoga pants and a
matching long sleeve top.

She dressed quietly then tiptoed to the cabin door and
pulled it open. The door creaked softly as the light from the
corridor filled the room. Paul stirred. Alyssa held still and
glanced back. Paul roused, squinting.

"Where are you going?" he asked sleepily.

Darn it... She closed the door, and the room darkened again.

"I'm sorry, I didn't mean to wake you," Alyssa whispered.

Paul rubbed his eyes and sat up. "Were you trying to sneak out? So we wouldn't have to talk?" he asked.

"No... I mean... yes," Alyssa stammered, "but—"

The warm glow of Paul's face dulled to a reddish gray. "Do you regret... what happened?"

Alyssa moved next to the bed and kneeled beside Paul. She took his hand between her palms. "Paul, I've been imagining last night for almost as long as I've known you," she whispered, her eyes glued to his. "For months, I've been hoping, looking forward to this. My only regret is that we can't stay in this room forever."

His color brightened. "Then why were you leaving?"

She hesitated. "After Hong Kong... I've been having these dreams... visions."

"Like last time? After the crystal?"

"Yes, except..."

"Except what?"

"They've always been the same. I'm falling, out of control... Every time I tried to remember Horus's memories... it was the same."

Paul squeezed her hand. "Did you tell Dharr?"

"No."

"Why not?"

"Because..." She avoided his eyes even though she knew he couldn't see her in the darkness. "They were about me..." she hesitated. "About me shooting Horus."

Paul inhaled sharply.

"That's why I could never get any closer to Horus's memories. Like… there was some kind of a block that prevented me from it." A warmth washed over her body at her own words. Sharing this with Paul felt like some huge weight had just been lifted off her shoulders.

"And you just had one of those dreams?" Paul asked.

"Yes. But this one was different. I was falling at first, but then it was almost like—like I was soaring. And I saw the *Valediction*, and where Heru-pa and I fought, and there was… something. I… I can't explain it…" Alyssa struggled for words. "I just felt drawn to it."

"So you were just going to go up there by yourself and check out what it was you were drawn to?"

"Yes," Alyssa said. "I know it sounds silly."

"No. Checking it out isn't silly. Doing it by yourself is." He grabbed his clothes and shuffled to the bathroom. "Give me two minutes," he said over his shoulder. "Don't go anywhere." He closed the door.

"Paul, you don't have to—"

"Two minutes," he called from the bathroom.

He was out in ninety seconds, fumbling with the buttons of his shirt. Alyssa moved to help him, but he waved her off. They left the room and headed for the hangar elevator. They stepped inside the cabin, and Alyssa pressed the button for the top floor.

"I seem to remember seeing a hatch in the ceiling of the hangar," she said. "It looked like it could be opened from inside."

The elevator stopped, and they entered the hangar. The gaping hole in the ceiling had been covered by a massive tarp that was tied to the metal support beams, and the floor beneath it had been swept clear of the glass shards. Alyssa pointed to the ladder in the far corner. "There it is."

They crossed the hangar, and Alyssa reached for a rung, then turned and looked at Paul's arm. "Can you climb with one hand?"

"I *will* climb with one hand," he replied, grim confidence in his voice.

She nodded and stepped on the ladder. She scaled it at a slow pace and glanced down after a few steps. Paul hooked the crook of his right arm around each rung before reaching up to the next. He labored up the ladder slowly, but he was making good progress.

"Brings back memories, huh?" she said.

"And I thought it was arduous with two hands," he grumbled between heavy breaths.

Alyssa reached the top of the ladder and pushed open the hatch. The fresh breeze of the ocean air filled her nostrils. She climbed out and helped Paul onto the glass structure. A waning moon glared down at them like a white and watchful eye.

She took a moment to take in the view and inhale the salt-tinged air before they moved midship, to the communications array. They gave the tarp a wide berth. It appeared sturdy, but she wasn't about to find out. She had suffered enough falls to last a week.

When they reached the tower, Alyssa turned to Paul and said, "Wait here."

She climbed up swiftly to the first beam then stepped out on it and sneaked between the antennas.

There. Near the white radar dome. A metallic glint…

She moved closer. As she neared the object, her muscles weakened. Suspended from one of the clasps of the radar dome hung a golden chain with a large amulet, a triangular hole embedded in its center. The amulet's brilliant polish reflected the moonlight streaming between the clouds.

"Do you see anything?" Paul called out from below.

She reached for it, brushing it with her fingers. Memories flooded her mind.

The smell of metopion oil. My mother reaches out to me, holding the golden medallion. I bow my head, and she slips the chain around my neck.

Alyssa jerked back her hand and staggered. She fell to her knees.

"Alyssa!" Paul cried from below.

She gripped the beam and took slow breaths. "I… I'm fine," she yelled down after she found her voice.

She unwrapped the golden chain and lifted it off the clasp. She hooked it around her elbow and moved back to the ladder.

———

NEPHTHYS WATCHED her guards drag the Rathadi into the room and shove him to his knees before her. He lifted his head.

Her lips curled down. Heru-pa's likeness to his father was unmistakable. Even on his knees, surrounded by her guards, his chin was held high, the lines of his face sharp and proud. He glared at her defiantly.

One of the guards stepped forward and bowed. "He was armed only with this," he said and presented a dagger to her.

Nephthys took the weapon and studied it. It was perfectly balanced, its blade black as onyx and sharp as a scalpel. She placed the dagger on the wooden armrest of her chair and turned to Heru-pa.

"A magnificent weapon," she said. "Worthy of Horus's heir."

Heru-pa looked at her, his lips a tight line.

"I hear you have a sister," Nephthys continued. "I suppose congratulations are in order," she said, not trying to hide the sarcasm from her voice.

"She may be my father's offspring, but she will never be a true Rathadi," Heru-pa spat.

"Not a *true* Rathadi," Nephthys mused. "Is that why you challenged her to retribution?"

Heru-pa returned her gaze, the tightening of his jaw barely recognizable. Nephthys's lips curved into a smile at his surprise.

"I challenged her because she killed my father," he said. "Because the Rathadi deserve a true leader."

"And does a true leader of the Rathadi attempt to kill the victor of a challenge?"

This time his face twisted. Nephthys's smile broadened.

"I can deliver her to you," Heru-pa said.

"And why would I want her?"

"I know she is important to you."

Nephthys remained silent.

"I know you wish to make her into your vessel."

Nephthys sized him up for several moments, letting the silence stretch.

"Leave us," she said to the guards.

The six Purean soldiers bowed and moved to the door, following her command without hesitation. She waited for them to leave the room then motioned for Heru-pa to stand. He gained his feet. Nephthys rose from the chair and approached him.

"Why would you turn against your own?" she asked, her golden irises burning into him.

"Turn against my own?" Heru-pa bristled, matching her steady gaze. "I am protecting my own. She killed my father. She and her band of traitors want to usurp the Legacy."

"And what is it that *you* want?" she asked. She slowly circled him, keeping her gaze on him. She could sense him tensing as she moved behind him, and she savored his unease.

"Only what is rightfully mine."

"And what do you need from me?" she asked.

Heru-pa turned. "The cure for the illness."

At that Nephthys smiled. "Perhaps I don't have it," she teased. "Perhaps you placed yourself in this delicate position for nothing."

"I know you have it. You cured Paul Matthews."

Nephthys smiled a cold smile. "What makes you so sure?"

Heru-pa's cheek twitched, but he remained silent.

"Let us assume that I do have the cure for the illness that is plaguing your people," Nephthys continued. "How do you imagine this… trade?"

"Once she returns to the Rathadi, I can convince the elders to give her up in exchange for the cure."

Nephthys scoffed. "They would never agree to it."

"Saving the Rathadi is paramount to them," Heru-pa said,

his eyes burning bright. "You underestimate their desire to survive."

———

PAUL WATCHED Alyssa descend from the antenna tower. He stared at the amulet in her hand. "Is that what I think it is?"

Alyssa nodded.

"But… that doesn't make any sense," he stammered. "Why challenge you, if he was going to give it up, anyway?"

Alyssa shook her head.

"Perhaps it came off by accident," Paul offered.

"No, it was hung there for somebody to find it." She paced quickly to the hatch. "Even if I hadn't found it, sooner or later they would have picked up an issue with the radar and checked." She stared at him. "This was no accident."

Paul's mind raced as he struggled to keep up with Alyssa. "If he's really going to Nephthys, perhaps he left it because he didn't want it to fall into her hands?" Paul suggested as they stopped at the hatch. He went in first, then Alyssa, who closed the hatch above them. He kept his lips sealed through the litany of curses that bounced in his head at his glacial pace as he made his way down the ladder. He jumped down the last five rungs. Alyssa joined him a moment later.

They paced through the hangar and stepped inside the elevator. Paul pressed the button for their floor, and the doors closed. Alyssa stared at the floor display as the numbers flashed, nibbling on her lower lip.

"What is it?" Paul asked.

"When I talked to Heru-pa," Alyssa said. "There's something he said." She pinched her lip as she tried to recall. "He said that a true leader must be willing to sacrifice himself, even if others don't understand the sacrifice."

"That does sound like something he'd come up with," Paul said.

The elevator doors opened. Paul moved to step out when he realized somebody was in his way. He looked up and stared into the face of a lanky young man. The man took a step back and gave a small yelp. His mouth opened and closed like a fish, and his bushy eyebrows danced on his forehead like a couple of sparring caterpillars before he was able to utter a sound.

"J-James?" he finally blurted out.

Before Paul could react, he was wrapped tight into a bearhug. "It is you!" the young man yelled.

Paul's mind leaped. "Dan? Dan Malone!"

"In the flesh!" The lanky Aussie squeezed him again and patted him on the back affectionately before releasing him.

He shifted to Alyssa.

"Jane?" He pointed to her hair. "But... your hair... not blonde... and no glasses... and... the eyes... color... wow..." He took a breath.

He turned back to Paul as if looking for answers when he spotted the stump of his right arm. His jaw went slack, and he pointed at it.

"Oh..." he stammered. "Oh, mate... Whatever happened to you? I'm so sorry."

"Later, Dan," Alyssa jumped in, sparing Paul the explanation. She gave Dan a hug, trying to distract both men.

Paul eyed her gratefully.

Consoling others about his own loss hasn't gotten any easier for him, she thought. *Will it ever?*

"What in the world happened to youse both that night?" Dan asked when Alyssa broke the embrace. He faced Paul, his lips almost turning into a pout. "You go bush and completely ghost your roomy. With all that commotion and secrecy, I feared the worst. Oh, and you would not imagine the grilling I got from Sergeant *Thor* and his security team. They tore me a new one with all their questions. And—"

"I'm sorry, Dan," Alyssa broke in. "We didn't mean to get you in trouble."

"And you wouldn't believe all the furphy stuff going on now," he continued, leaning in. "They have me deliver a breakfast spread to the VIP conference room mad-early in the morning. I was told to drop it off and get out. The corridor is completely empty... spooky stuff, I tell you." He paused "And now you two are here again, just in time." He leaned even closer to them and whispered, "You should hear folks talking. They say we have alien technology on board. And maybe even aliens!" He spread out his arms for emphasis.

Alyssa put a calming hand on his arm. "Dan, this is really fascinating, but we really have to get—"

He looked down and spotted the amulet in her other hand.

"Crickey! That's one sick piece of bling!" he exclaimed.

"What?" Alyssa asked, taken off guard. "Yeah... uh... family heirloom," she said, clearing her throat.

Paul gave her a sidelong glance.

"Seriously?" Dan asked.

Paul stepped forward. "I'm really sorry, mate," he said. "We're kind of in a big rush."

"But we just—" Dan started.

Alyssa jumped in. "Dan, I promise we'll catch up, but we have to run right now."

Dan stepped back. "You're in on it, aren't you?" His eyes grew big. "I knew it!"

Alyssa shushed him then pitched her voice lower. "Keep it down."

Dan's expression shifted, and he nodded in understanding. "Good on ya," he whispered, looking around. "You never know who may be listening."

Alyssa nodded. Suddenly she froze, then perked up. "What did you say?"

"Ya know," Dan said. "There's always somebody listening to what you're saying and doing."

Alyssa's eyes brightened. "Of course!" she cried out. She grabbed Dan and pulled him into a hug. "You're a genius!"

"I am?" he muttered with a bewildered expression.

"Heru-pa!" she yelled. "That's what he was doing!"

"What?" Dan asked, perplexed. "Whose pa?"

Alyssa was already racing full speed down the corridor.

Paul threw a glance at Dan. "Sorry, mate… gotta run!"

"What? But we just—"

Paul rushed after Alyssa as she dashed to Dharr's room. She banged on his door.

"Who is it?" Dharr's sleepy voice came from the inside.

"It's Alyssa!"

Paul heard commotion inside as Dharr rushed to the door and ripped it open.

"Is everything—?"

Alyssa barged inside, dragging Paul behind her, and closed the door. "What Heru-pa did—it was all an act!" she cried.

Dharr blinked. "What?"

"He must have known that Nephthys had spies." Alyssa continued. "That she knew what was happening here. He needed to make sure this was convincing."

Paul put his hand on her arm. "Alyssa, slow down," he said.

Tef glanced up, perplexed. She rubbed her eyes and sat up in bed, pulling the sheet around her. Heat flushed in Paul's cheeks when their gazes met. "Sorry..." he muttered, staring down at his shoes.

Alyssa took a moment to collect her thoughts. "When I talked to Heru-pa on the jet, he told me that a true leader must be willing to sacrifice himself for the Rathadi. Even if nobody else would understand their sacrifice. That's what he meant. He's been planning this all along!"

She grabbed Dharr's arm. "That's why he risked his life to get on the jet. He knew he would ultimately have to challenge me. He must have known about Nephthys's mind command from the beginning. He had to make sure that the information about him challenging me and trying to kill me would get to Nephthys."

"Why would he do that?" Paul asked.

"To be able to get close to her. 'The enemy of my enemy.' You said it yourself. If I'm his enemy, he and Nephthys have a common goal. She will give him a chance to get close, to hear him out."

"I don't believe he would—" Tef started.

"You've got to admit," Dharr cut in, "that's a stretch."

Alyssa lifted the golden amulet. The Rathadi's eyes widened.

"Do you still think so?" she asked. "He left this for me. And he knew that I would find it after he was gone."

Understanding dawned in Dharr's face. "He wanted to make sure that whoever was passing the information to Nephthys would be convinced that he wanted to get you out of the way. That was the only way he could ensure he would be able to get close to her."

"And why would he go through all of this?" Paul asked, his mind still reeling, trying to process the information.

Alyssa looked him dead in the eyes. "Heru-pa is planning to kill Nephthys."

———

HERU-PA'S SKIN tingled as Nephthys circled behind his back once again. He clenched his fists, willing himself to stand still.

"You truly believe you could convince the Rathadi elders to give up Alyssa Morgan in exchange for the cure to the disease?" she asked, slowly moving in front of him.

Heru-pa nodded. "Since her arrival, she has been... troublesome. The elders would not make the decision in the open, but I can get them to agree to it."

"Even if I believed you could do that," Nephthys challenged. "Why would I think that you would want to? Why would I trust a traitor?"

Heru-pa squeezed his fingers into the soft flesh of his palms again, hard enough to draw blood. He felt the liquid pool under his fingernails.

"You don't need to trust me. We both get what we want," Heru-pa said, his tone even. He approached Nephthys, focusing on keeping his movements smooth.

A gleam sparked in Nephthys's eyes as she contemplated his words.

"She will be removed from the Rathadi," Heru-pa continued as he drew closer, "solving my problem, and you will get your—"

He launched himself at Nephthys. She stepped aside, even faster than he had anticipated, avoiding his first strike, but he stretched for her and his fingernails raked her face like talons.

Nephthys screamed and drove her fist into his stomach, dropping him to his knee. An instant later, half a dozen guards surged through the door. For several heartbeats, the room was frozen.

Nephthys stood motionless, her palm pressed against her right cheek. When she lifted it, blood covered her fingertips and four deep gashes marred her perfect face.

As one, the six Pureans rushed Heru-pa and threw him to the ground. He didn't fight as their fists and feet pummeled him. A kick broke his ribs. Another shattered his jaw. Stars blurred his vision.

"Enough!" Nephthys's cry broke through the red haze.

Heru-pa groaned. He drew in a breath and spit up blood. He forced himself to his knees and stared up at her and the four bright gashes in her cheek.

He cackled. Blood mingled with his spittle as it struck the floor beneath him. Nephthys stared at him, bewildered.

"You lost," Heru-pa sputtered, the pain shooting through his face and broken bones.

"You are mad," Nephthys seethed.

"That may be true, but you are already dying," he cackled again, hissing at the pain at the same time. His lungs tightened, and his laugh turned into a wheezing cough that sent hot needles through his broken ribs. He spat blood again. The new pain was a welcome relief to the burning he had been fighting from the poison that he had smuggled inside his own blood, and that had been coursing through his body since he arrived here. The same poison that now mixed with Nephthys's blood in her body.

Nephthys's eyes grew wide with realization. She stared at her palm, glistening with the fresh blood from the gashes in her cheek.

"The poison will continue to spread through your body until you perish in agony…" Heru-pa taunted.

Nephthys moved to him, lightning fast, and grasped a handful of his hair. "Tell me how to stop it," she commanded.

"You cannot," he rasped. "Your fate is sealed, as is mine."

"No," Nephthys breathed. "You wouldn't! You would not give up the Legacy."

Heru-pa gazed at her defiantly. "I lost the Legacy when you murdered my father."

Nephthys's face twisted. She dragged him to the chair. He hissed at the pain but would not give her the satisfaction of crying out.

She lifted the onyx dagger and yanked his head back. She pressed the dagger to the skin beneath his chin, hard enough to draw blood. "Tell me how to stop the poison, and I shall spare your life."

Heru-pa closed his eyes. A calmness washed over him, his body free from the pain.

I am Heru-pa.

Son of Horus and Ma'at.

"Tell me now!" Nephthys's cry was muffled in his ears.

He opened his eyes and met her gaze in silence, twin pairs of golden eyes burning into each other.

I shall know no fear.

Piercing pain. Stars exploded in his head. Then darkness.

PART 3

LEGACY

A FAMILIAR SCENT fills my nostrils. The softness of my mother's hands is a caress on my cheeks. The gold chain presses into my skin, and the new amulet weighs heavy against my chest. My father's palms grasp my head, and the power of the cartouche of protection fills me, its strength coursing through my body.

I open my eyes.

Set's icy-blue gaze stands out against his dark skin as a boyish smile fills his face. An onyx dagger rests in his palms. He holds it out to me. I grasp it.

Brothers forever.

Set's features age before me. He is a grown man. The boyish grin sours into a grimace. His eyes fill with venom.

Why do you hate me, Brother?

On its own, my hand thrusts forward, the dagger piercing his soft flesh. The hatred in his eyes turns to confusion, then agony. I pull the blade, and warm, red liquid spills over me.

I scream.

Amah!

My mother's face. She looks down at me, scared, but her feline eyes are full of love and kindness.

Amah…

This is a dream.

No…

It is a memory, my son.

My mother smiles at me. Her face transforms into the sacred Hybrid statue, half-animal, half-human, built to honor her and watch over me as I sleep beneath her sheltering arms.

I am weightless, soaring above the desert. I glide lower, effortlessly racing over the sand, into her arms, then into the sand below.

Unburdened by a body, I dive into the vast hall beneath the statue. The sacred pyramid stands tall, the sarcophagus, my resting place, lies at its peak.

I glide toward it, drawn by it.

The lid opens—

Alyssa's eyes snapped open. She gasped.

Hands on her shoulders, steadying her.

"You're safe," a soothing voice assured her.

Dharr.

She focused on her surroundings. A room. A ship's cabin. Familiar faces behind Dharr. Silent, unasked questions burning in their eyes.

She glanced down. She was on the floor, kneeling on a soft rug. A golden amulet rested in her palms. Slowly, her memory returned. Her mind filled in the gaps.

She gave Dharr a reassuring nod. "I'm okay."

"What did you see?" he asked.

She tried to collect her thoughts. "It… it was like when I

touched the amulet the first time. Except more details now, longer. I saw my mother... I mean Horus's mother, giving the amulet to him." She studied the amulet in her hands. "The memories, they aren't like before. Like with the crystal or when I was dreaming. They seem more like my own. I remember her smell, the way it made me feel."

"The memories. They have begun to reveal themselves," Tef whispered.

"What else did you see?" Dharr asked.

Alyssa's face darkened as the memories returned. "Set, as a boy, then..." She hesitated. "I killed him, then I fell... no—I soared."

"Like this morning?" Paul asked. "When we woke up—" He stopped dead in his tracks. He looked around the room and blushed daylily pink, a panicked expression on his face.

Dharr grinned. Clay's eyes grew before understanding spread through his face while Renley's lips curved up in the barest of smiles.

"I mean... uh... when Alyssa woke up," he stammered, "she said she had a dream about falling, then soaring, right?"

Alyssa tried to ignore the heat in her own cheeks. She stood as Dharr helped her to her feet.

"Yes," she said, eager to move on. "Except this morning I saw the *Valediction* and the amulet. Just now I saw the desert and the Sphinx. And the Hall of Records."

"The Hall of Records?" Dharr asked.

Alyssa nodded slowly. "I think I'm being called back to it," she said.

"How do you know?" Tef asked.

"I don't," Alyssa replied. "And I don't understand it, but this morning I was led to the amulet, somehow."

Dharr held out his hand, and Alyssa handed him the amulet. He held it up and studied it, peering through the triangular opening in its center.

"I don't understand it either, but we have to believe in it," he said.

"Getting into the hall will not be an easy task," Renley said, glancing at Alyssa, "given your current standing with the Egyptian authorities and the security precautions around the site."

"Not to mention the fact that we currently seem to be stranded on this ship since our only ride has been nabbed," Clay added.

Dharr gave him a sidelong glance.

"Hey, I'm not blaming anybody," he said, lifting his hands. "It could have happened to the best of us."

"Perhaps our new allies could help us?" Alyssa chimed in.

"They will probably be happy to be rid of us," Paul said.

"I'll talk to them." Alyssa stood and moved to the door.

Paul held up his hand. "You should rest," he said, then looked to Dharr.

Alyssa noticed the exchange between Dharr and Paul. Dharr nodded. "I agree. You should try to get some rest."

"I shall talk to Dr. Tibaldi," Renley offered, "and enquire about using their helicopter to transport us to an airport."

"I would have asked Sergeant Torin," Dharr said.

Renley inclined his head. "I believe Dr. Tibaldi is the senior decision maker."

"That may be true," Dharr said. "I would still prefer to talk to him. That woman terrifies me."

————

NEPHTHYS'S BODY was engulfed in flames. She screamed. She didn't know whether it was the rage or the searing pain that ripped the sound from her throat. She didn't care. The Purean healer stood over her. He finished injecting the medication and removed the syringe from her arm.

"This will stabilize the poison and ease the pain," he offered. "But the poison has already begun degrading your cellular structure."

Nephthys's lips were pressed into a tight line. She took a long, shuddering breath. "How long do I have?" she asked through clenched teeth.

The healer hesitated.

"How long?" Nephthys grabbed him by the collar of his robe and pulled him to her. The movement sent another wave of agony through her body.

"A day," he said, "perhaps two."

Nephthys roared and pushed him away, sending him tumbling to the ground.

She closed her eyes. She needed to think. The pain was subsiding, the burning in her body ebbing into a dull ache. Whatever medicine cocktail he gave her seemed to be working.

The healer collected himself from the floor and scurried to the door.

"Wait!" she called after him.

He cowered and turned to her, avoiding her eyes.

"Forgive my outburst," Nephthys said.

The man lifted his head, his face betraying his surprise, but only for an instant. He bowed to her. "I am at your command, my Queen."

"What are my options?" she asked.

He rubbed his chin, frowning, before clearing his throat. "I am afraid modern medicine does not provide an antidote to this poison," he said. "This body will fail."

Nephthys inhaled sharply as she processed his words. She simply nodded.

"We must focus on preserving your mind long enough to find a suitable vessel."

"We will never find a vessel with Rathadi blood in time," Nephthys challenged.

The healer's posture straightened. "There may be another possibility."

———

THE SOUND of the lock turning woke Tasha from her daze. The door opened, and she squinted at the bright light. She struggled to keep her head up while she half-stood, half-hung with her wrists shackled to the peg above her head.

One of the guards kept his weapon aimed at her while the other unshackled her restraints. As soon as her arms were free, she collapsed to the stone floor, striking it hard.

"Get up," the guard barked.

Tasha groaned and tried to pull herself up, but her legs refused to obey her will. She bit her lip to keep from crying out from the hundreds of pins and needles that seemed to be driving into her arms as the blood flowed through her limbs again. She had been shackled in this dark room with her arms above her head for God knows how long, deprived of food and water.

She willed herself to her knees then used the wall for support to gain her feet.

"Let's move," the guard said, motioning her forward.

"W-water…" Tasha croaked. She tried to swallow and winced. Her throat felt like it was lined with sandpaper. "Please…"

The guard eyed her, then he reached to his belt and pulled out a metal bottle. He opened it and passed it to her.

Tasha snatched it greedily and put it to her lips. The water burned like fire going down, and she spit it back up. A coughing fit shook her, torturing her parched throat.

"Easy," the guard said. "Slow down."

She forced herself to take a smaller sip. She swallowed it, then took another. Life returned to her with every precious mouthful of water. She hungrily gulped down the whole bottle.

"Thank you," she whispered to the guard.

He took the bottle back without a word. "Let's go," he said.

Tasha pushed off the floor and struggled to her feet. They stepped into the corridor, and a pair of guards flanked her as she followed him unsteadily along the hallway.

"Where are we going?" she asked, her voice slowly returning to her.

"Nephthys wants to see you."

Tasha's stomach roiled. She hugged her arms tightly around her body to prevent them from trembling, but her entire body shivered as the Purean led her to a door.

They entered the room. Tasha spotted a lifeless body,

strapped to a table. Terror washed over her when she recognized Heru-pa. His body was naked, save for a surgical drape that covered his hips. His face and body were covered with bruises and cuts, both of his eyes were swollen shut. His nose appeared to have been broken.

"Heru-pa..." Tasha whispered. "No..."

A Purean scientist in surgical scrubs stood over his body and removed a long, thick needle syringe from Heru-pa's hip.

"What are you doing to him?" Tasha demanded.

The Purean ignored her. He moved to a device that rested on a steel table at the far wall and inserted part of the fluid into the device. He studied the readout on the monitor. After several seconds he turned.

"It is as I had hoped," he said, directing his voice behind Tasha.

Tasha swiveled. A figure stood in the corner of the room, hidden in the shadow. She stepped out, and Tasha gasped when she recognized Nephthys. The Hybrid woman's flawless complexion had turned ashen, and four angry welts marred her right cheek, ruining her otherwise perfect features. She moved slowly, as if every step came with great exertion or pain.

"His bone marrow appears to be free of the poison," the scientist continued, his chin jutting out.

Nephthys approached Tasha. The guards tightened their grips on her arms. Nephthys moved closer until the woman's sickly sweet breath invaded her nostrils. She grabbed Tasha's hair and moved her head from one side to the other, appraising her. Tasha snarled and tried to pull away.

"So much fire," Nephthys said, her voice raspy. She gripped Tasha's hair tighter, sending waves of pain through her scalp before finally letting go. She turned to the scientist. "Will she survive the procedure?"

An icy surge of dread washed over Tasha. Her gaze darted between Nephthys and the scientist and Heru-pa's lifeless body. "What procedure?" she asked.

"She is young and strong," the scientist said, ignoring her. "But the outcome is uncertain."

"What procedure?" Tasha asked again.

"Assuming she survives," the scientist continued, unfazed, "to fully activate the Rathadi heritage, she must be exposed to Thoth's weapon. The original strain in the hall."

"And that will complete the transition?" Nephthys asked.

"As it did for Alyssa Morgan," he replied.

"What are you talking about?" Tasha pleaded.

The scientists offered a look to Nephthys, and she nodded. He turned to Tasha. "Your body will be used to generate pure Rathadi blood, which will serve to cure Nephthys," he said.

Tasha's mind reeled. "What?"

The scientist turned to the guards and pointed to an empty table. "Prepare the subject for the procedure," he said.

The guards dragged Tasha to the table.

"No!" Tasha sobbed. "Wait!" She strained and bucked against the guards.

Her flailing arm hit one of them in the face. He raised his arm to strike her. Tasha tensed and held her breath, anticipating the blow.

"Stop!" Nephthys commanded. "I do not want her damaged."

The guard lowered his hand and bowed to Nephthys.

The woman approached Tasha. "If you cooperate and the

procedure works, you will have performed a great service to me." She paused. "If both you and I survive this ordeal, I shall consider setting you free."

Tasha stood still as she processed Nephthys's words. She flinched when the guards grabbed her even tighter and secured her to the metal table.

Nephthys faced the scientist. "I will make the necessary arrangements for Cairo. We will leave as soon as you are finished," she said and left the room.

Terror coiled inside Tasha's chest like a snake as the Purean scientist approached her and inserted an IV line into her arm. Slowly, her vision began to fade, and her mind was consumed by blissful darkness.

————

ALYSSA RESTED on the wide bed in her lavish suite, her head propped up on two pillows, while Paul loafed in the oversized leather armchair.

"What is it like?" he asked.

Alyssa turned to him.

"You know," he said. "Remembering his memories. Are they... just like your own?"

Alyssa shook her head. "No. At least not yet. But I'm not sure what it will be like eventually. I can already feel the changes. Before, whenever I tried to go back to remember, I had this feeling of falling. All the time."

"And now?"

"Now it feels like I have more control. It's... It's... hard to explain," she fought her frustration. "It's almost like an out of body experience. Seeing things through somebody else's eyes. Soaring through the air."

"That sounds wicked," Paul said.

"It's exhilarating... and terrifying."

"How far back can you go?"

"I don't know. They are just disjointed bits and pieces right now. Some of them I can control, some I still can't... but I'm aware that they are memories, and I can probe deeper."

"Do you think—"

The door opened, and Clay came in. He grinned at Alyssa. "Well, it appears Lord Renley's skills of persuasion may rival your own. The Society has agreed to let you use the helicopter to get to mainland, and they have even arranged a transport to Cairo from there."

"That's fantastic," Alyssa said.

"They said you can leave as soon as—"

"Wait," Alyssa interrupted. "*You* can leave? Does that mean you're not coming with us?"

"The helicopter only seats four," Clay said. "Also, the Rathadi are still ignoring Dharr's attempts to contact them. He and Nel want to return to Indonesia and tell them in person what happened."

Alyssa sat up. "So that means Dharr won't be going to Egypt with us, either?" A painful tightness spread in her throat.

"Is it wise to head back," Paul asked, "given the circumstances of our departure?"

"I suppose that's one of the reasons he asked me to come with him," Clay said, unable to hide the excitement in his voice. "Dharr thinks that because of my role in helping to develop the treatment, the elders and the other Rathadi may be more likely to listen to him. And I can also help check on the status of the infection."

Alyssa mulled over his words. She could not argue with the logic. Still, not having Dharr and Clay with her... "What about Tef?"

"She will go to Cairo with you, Paul, and Lord Renley."

"She's going to... stand out," Paul said.

Alyssa thought for a moment. "I think we'll be all right," she said. "It's a good thing we're going to Egypt. We'll get her to blend in."

Paul looked at her quizzically.

"Trust me," Alyssa said. "We'll be good."

Clay drew near Alyssa and touched her arm. "How are you faring?" he asked.

"Better," she said. "Like I'm finally making real progress."

"Hmm..." Clay mused and cocked his head.

"What is it?" she asked.

"Nothing, really." Clay tried to keep the grin off his face. "It's just... all that training with Dharr and no progress. And now, bang!" He glanced at Paul. "It appears you simply needed a different type of stimu—"

He yelped when Alyssa punched him in the ribs and Paul smacked him on the head.

"Get out of here!" Alyssa yelled.

"Sure thing," Clay said, hopping to the door. He opened it, then looked over his shoulder, a toothy grin splitting his face. "The helicopter will be ready to take off in forty-five minutes. I suppose that should give you enough time for some private—"

"Go!" Alyssa yelled again and chucked a pillow at the door as Clay ducked out, chortling.

"I can't believe him," Paul said, shaking his head. He closed the door behind Clay. "Unbelievable—"

"Right," Alyssa cut in. "Like we'd spend any time thinking about *that*, with everything else going on."

"Really…" Paul said, moving closer to the bed.

Their gazes locked.

"I mean, does he really think all we think about is…" Paul leaned down, a wicked glint in his eyes.

"Seriously…" Alyssa said, her throat tightening. She felt Paul's breath tickle her neck as his mouth almost brushed her skin.

Alyssa swallowed. "Forty-five minutes?" she breathed.

Paul nodded. "Mmhhhmm."

"Shouldn't we lock the door?" she asked, her voice turning raspy.

Paul's lips creased into a devilish grin. "It's already locked," he whispered as his lips moved to hers.

———

FORTY-EIGHT MINUTES LATER, Alyssa stood with the others in the hangar, hiding a smile. The cleanup and repair work from Heru-pa's abrupt departure had been suspended, and the vast space was mostly empty, save for the helicopter and the small group of people and Rathadi saying their farewells. Renley and Paul shook hands and exchanged words with Dr. Tibaldi and Sergeant Torin before they boarded the helicopter sitting on the helipad platform. Xander leaned against the wall, chewing on his cigar. She smiled and gave him a wave, and he tipped his hat. The Society had invited him to stay and participate in an "intellectual exchange," as he put it.

His kind of folk, Alyssa thought wistfully when Dharr stepped up to her. The concern was etched in his face.

"You sure you'll be okay?" he asked.

"Tef and Paul will watch my back," Alyssa replied. "And if things get really bad, we'll have Lord Renley to sort things out," she added with a weak smile before turning serious again. "You're doing the right thing. The Rathadi must be apprised of what has happened."

"They have completely ignored any further attempts at communicating with them," Dharr said. "I can only hope that showing up in person will make them listen to us—if they don't throw me in the brig on sight—or worse."

Torin and Dr. Tibaldi joined them. "The second chopper is on the way," Torin said to Dharr. "It will be here within the hour. A jet will be waiting for you once you reach mainland to transport you to Indonesia."

"We are grateful for your assistance," Dharr said.

"It was my privilege," Torin replied.

Alyssa extended her hand. "Thank you for your help, Sergeant."

"Good luck," Torin said, accepting her hand.

"And thank you, Dr. Tibaldi," Alyssa said. "The Society's help will not be forgotten."

The Italian woman eyed her silently for several moments. "Please do not forget the *modus operandi* of the Society, Miss Morgan. Our role in this should be forgotten." Her lips curved into a graceful smile. "However, on a personal note, you have made the last two days more exciting and meaningful for me than I could have imagined." She gave a brief nod. "Until we meet again."

Alyssa returned the nod then faced Dharr. She put her arms around him and held him tight. "Thank you for believing in me," she whispered. "Do take care of yourself, and Clay." She blinked to fight back the tears before stepping back and wrapping her arms around Clay. "Be safe," she managed around the growing lump in her throat, then she turned to Nel and gave her a long hug.

Tef and Dharr stood together, Tef's palms resting on his forehead, her fingers shaped in the Rathadi blessing. She spoke softly to him in their tongue. When she lowered her hands, Dharr took her head in his palms and touched his forehead against hers. They stood in silence for several moments before they broke off and Tef headed for the chopper, her eyes glistening. Alyssa followed her.

"You keep her safe, too," Dharr called out after Alyssa. She swung around and nodded, her throat too tight to form words, then she stepped inside and pulled the door shut behind her.

She lifted her palm to Dharr and the others through the glass as the helipad lifted skyward. Her stomach was a hard knot, and her heart thudded inside her chest. A few days ago, the idea that she would feel safer aboard a Society yacht than returning home to Cairo would have been laughable.

How quickly things change.

She squinted as the view of the hangar was replaced by the brilliant sparkle of the sun against the glass structure. Her eyes blurred. Paul reached for her hand, and their fingers intertwined. She used the other to wipe her eyes as the rotors began to spin up.

KAMAL PACED through the well-manicured lawn of the Ministry of Antiquities. He entered the building, greeted the guard, and walked up two flights of stairs to the office suite of the minister. A middle-aged woman, her straw-colored hair cropped short, sat at a desk facing a tall oak door. She looked up from the computer screen, studying Kamal from behind the leopard-print rims of her glasses.

"Good afternoon, Dr. Khanna. May I help you?"

"Good afternoon, Nesrin, I would like a minute of the minister's time," Kamal said.

"Is the minister expecting you?"

Kamal lifted an eyebrow. "He is not, but it is quite important that I talk to him right away."

"My sincere apologies, Dr. Khanna, but I'm afraid this is not a good time." Nesrin's reply was polite, yet sharp. "The minister is busy packing and asked not to be disturbed."

"Packing?"

Nesrin adjusted her glasses. "The minister is about to leave to film his documentary at the Khuwy Tomb. I will be glad to take a message for you and deliver it to the minister as soon as he becomes—"

Kamal pasted on a smile. "Please listen to me carefully," he said through clenched teeth. "You have about three seconds to buzz the minister and tell him I'm here. I'm going to see him, one way or another."

Nesrin's eyes widened, and she pressed her lips into a grimace. She shifted uncomfortably in her seat, then pushed the intercom button.

"Thank you," Kamal breathed.

"Yes, what is it?" the minister's voice came over the speaker at her desk.

"My sincere apologies," Nesrin said. "I understand that you asked not to be disturbed, but Dr. Khanna is here. He says it's urgent."

A few seconds later, the office door opened, and the minister's broad face appeared.

"Dr. Khanna!" he boomed.

"Minister," Kamal said. "My apologies for the inconvenience."

"Nonsense," the minister waved his hand, his camera-ready smile never faltering. "Come in, come in!"

"Thank you, Minister," Kamal said and stepped inside the lavish office.

The minister pointed at an armchair. "Please sit down. May I offer you tea?"

"No, thank you," Kamal replied. "I'm afraid the matter is quite urgent."

The minister tensed at Kamal's tone. "Urgent? What is it?"

"I'm afraid the safety sensors around the hall have detected trace levels of the pathogen."

The minister's smile wilted. "We have a leak?" he asked. "How serious is the situation?"

"I believe it is contained, but with your permission, we need to close down the site until we've been able to ascertain the cause of the problem."

The minister ran his hand through his full head of hair, ruffling it. "This is going to create quite a spectacle. You are sure there is no other way?"

"I'm afraid so. And as a precaution, I advise we set up a guarded perimeter around it."

"A guarded perimeter?"

"Only as a precaution, of course. No unauthorized person should enter the site until we know what kind of threat we're dealing with."

The minister nodded thoughtfully. "Of course, of course," he said. "You have my full support. How long do you think it will take until we've... ascertained the cause?"

"I hesitate to speculate at this time, Minister. You have my assurance that I will check on the site myself as soon as it is secure."

"Very well," the minister said. He stood. "And thank you for your vigilance, Dr. Khanna."

"Thank you, Minister. And good luck with the filming."

"Ah, yes! Indeed!" The minister gave another grin.

Kamal turned to the door and left the office. *Pompous ass...* he thought. But he got what he needed.

Nephthys will be pleased.

A smile spread across his lips as he left the building and

paced to his car. His chauffeur opened the door, and Kamal settled into the leather seat as the car set off into the Cairo traffic.

His phone rang. He looked at the number but didn't recognize it. His finger hovered over the dismiss button for a second, but he changed his mind and answered it.

"Yes?"

"Kamal?"

He sat up when he recognized Alyssa's voice. "Alyssa," he managed. "How are you?"

"I'm fine. Any news from my father?"

"I'm afraid I haven't been able to get through to him since last time."

He heard her sigh.

"Are you safe?" he asked. "Where are you?"

"We're on our way to Cairo."

Kamal's jaw tightened. "You're coming back? This may not be the best—"

"We have to," she said. "And we'll be fine. We're arriving at a private terminal and everything has been arranged."

"Private terminal?"

"Yes, but that's not important," Alyssa said. "We need your help."

"Anything, if it's within my power."

"We need to get into the Hall of Records. Alone."

Kamal wrinkled his brow. *First Nephthys, now Alyssa?* "The Hall of Records?"

"Yes, can you get us inside?"

"How many of you?"

"Four."

"I will see what I can do."

"Thank you, Kamal."

She cut the connection.

Kamal rubbed his forehead. Nephthys would not be pleased with this new development, but he had to inform her. He leaned back in the seat and allowed himself a brief respite before he picked up the phone.

It's shaping up to be an intriguing day.

———

TASHA WOKE up to the hum of a jet. Her head was threatening to burst. She lifted her hand to massage her temple when it was jerked back by a restraint. She forced herself to open her eyes and craned her neck to look down. She regretted it immediately. Her head spun, and she felt like she was going to be ill. She closed her eyes and rested back against the pillow. She lay for several moments, taking deep breaths, waiting for the nausea to subside.

She tried again, slower this time. She cracked open her eyes and glanced down. Her skin tingled. She was dressed in fresh clothes and was all cleaned up. An IV line had been placed in her left arm, and her wrists were strapped to the fully reclined airplane seat.

She looked across the narrow isle. Nephthys reclined in another seat, facing her. Her skin looked even more ashen and her cheeks hollower than when Tasha last saw her.

"Congratulations," Nephthys said when she noticed Tasha's gaze. "You survived the procedure."

"Where are we going?" Tasha asked. Her throat was dry and

her voice hoarse. "And where is Heru-pa? What have you done to him?"

Nephthys sneered. "He got what he deserved."

Tasha's stomach clenched at her words.

The Purean scientist entered the cabin. "Ah, good, you're awake," he said. He inspected her with professional curiosity. "How do you feel?"

Tasha remained silent, her jaw clenched tight.

He offered her a cold smile and lifted her head then shined a penlight into her eyes. She cringed at the light, but continued staring at him defiantly.

"Strong and feisty," Nephthys said. "Your strength serves both of us, but do not press my patience."

Tasha lifted up in the chair. "I want to know—"

The plane spun wildly—*or was it her head?* The noise of the jet increased, as though somebody had turned up the volume on a pair of headphones. A second later, Tasha threw up violently.

Nephthys leaned back, her lips pinched. She raised an eyebrow at the scientist.

"Extreme nausea is a common symptom following a bone marrow transplantation," he said to Nephthys, looking unperturbed. "The Rathadi stem cells are embedding into her own bone marrow."

Tasha's mind reeled, from his words as much as the sudden vertigo. "Bone marrow transplantation?" she cried. "Stem cells? What did you do to me?"

"Your body is preparing to produce Rathadi blood," the scientist said.

Rathadi blood? Tasha took small breaths, fighting the queasiness and trying to make sense of all the information.

Nephthys's phone rang. She glanced down at the display. "Get her cleaned up," she said and stood. "I want her ready when we land." She answered the call.

"I hope you have a good reason to disturb me," she said into the phone.

Her lips pinched at the words she heard.

"Take care of it," she said, moving to the back of the plane. "I do not want the girl harmed. The others are expendable," she said before her voice blended in with the hum of the jet.

———

ALYSSA GLANCED at the screen embedded in the bulkhead. *One more hour.*

So far, the trip has gone about as smoothly as she could have hoped for. After the Society's helicopter had taken them to Marrakesh, they boarded this small jet that was transporting them to Cairo. They had made sure the flight didn't have any additional personnel other than the two pilots, who were in the cockpit, ready and waiting, when the four of them arrived.

Paul stirred next to her. His head drooped on her shoulder, snoozing contently. Across the narrow aisle, Renley and Tef reclined in their plushy seats with their eyes closed. Alyssa glanced at the bag at the Rathadi's feet. She had made the request before they left the *Valediction*, and it was waiting for them in the jet when they arrived.

So far, so good.

The few hours downtime in the plane were a welcome

reprieve from the pace of the last few days, but she couldn't shake the feeling that it was merely the calm before a massive hurricane. Still… at least the phone call with Kamal had eased her concern about getting inside the Hall of Records. After she practically had to be smuggled out of the country a few weeks ago, getting into the hall was going to be a challenge—especially without her dad to help them.

Her chest squeezed.

No, not her *dad*.

I am not Kade's daughter.

The sense of loss hit her again, overwhelming her other thoughts. The pressure in her chest built and threatened to crush her. She took small breaths and waited for it to go away. Slowly, it subsided, and she was able to breathe again normally.

She leaned her head back into the headrest. *Does he know?*

Of course. He had to know. Her mom must have told him. But if he did know, why had he kept it from her all this time?

She chewed her bottom lip and felt the heat grow behind her eyelids. She lifted her hand to press it to her eyes, to stop the tears before they started. Paul stirred beside her. He opened his eyes groggily. When their gazes met, he sat up, more awake.

"Hey," he whispered, his expression echoing the concern in his voice, "what's wrong?"

Alyssa gave him a soft smile. "I'm sorry," she whispered back. "I didn't mean to wake you."

"Wanna talk about it?" he asked.

Alyssa shrugged. She kept silent for several moments. "It's about Kade," she said.

"You're worried about him?" he asked. "I'm sure he's fine. You said his cell—"

"No, it's not about the jail." She sighed. "Of course, I'm worried about that too, but it's…" She paused, not knowing how to continue. "Does he even know I'm not his daughter?"

Paul looked at her, surprised.

"And if he doesn't know already. Once I tell him, will he feel the same about me? Love me the same?"

Paul moved his hand to her cheek. "A few days ago, Renley told me he would give up everything to make sure Tasha comes back safely. I have never seen him so upset. If he feels that strongly about the girl he adopted when she was ten…" He paused, leaving the implication hanging. "You will always be Kade's daughter. And he will always love you. And besides, he probably already knows the truth."

Alyssa sighed and squeezed his arm gratefully.

Renley stirred in his seat. His eyes were still closed, but his soft snoring had stopped, and his lips had curved into the hint of a smile.

"Lord Renley?" Alyssa asked.

He cracked open his eyes. "My apologies for overhearing your conversation. But I could not have put it any more elegantly than has Mr. Matthews."

Tef roused in the other seat. "Definitely."

"Look at you two dropping eaves," Alyssa muttered. "What if we had been talking about something truly private?"

"Why do you think we kept our eyes closed?" Tef teased.

"Very funny," Alyssa said. She pointed to the packet at Tef's feet. "Well, since you are up, why don't you try this on? We're getting close."

Tef sighed. "Serves me right…"

"Come on, it'll only be until we get out of the airport."

Tef picked up the bag and trotted to the bathroom in the rear of the plane. A couple minutes later she came out. She was dressed in a full-length black *burqa* that covered her from head to toe, and a set of matching gloves. Only the bridge of her nose and her reptilian eyes were visible.

She tugged at her sleeve. "Do I really have to wear this?"

"Unless you want to cause quite the commotion when we land in Cairo," Alyssa replied.

Tef exhaled sharply, causing the veil to flutter up and expose a sliver of the shimmering scales of her face.

"Uh, you may want to not do that," Alyssa said.

Tef gave her a look. "Seriously?"

"You'll be out of it soon enough. Until then—" Alyssa reached into the bag and handed her a pair of large sunglasses —"you may want to put these on."

Tef shook her head, but donned the glasses. With every part of her body covered, she looked like any other modest Muslim woman.

"Perfect," Alyssa said.

"And we're sure we'll be able to get through security without issues?" Paul asked.

Renley leaned forward. "Dr. Tibaldi assured me that the proper arrangements have been made for our arrival. Since we'll be going through passport inspection and customs at a private terminal, everything should be in good order."

"Any word from Dharr?" Alyssa asked Tef.

"Not yet," the Rathadi replied. "But with all that's happened, he may prefer radio silence."

"Makes sense," Paul said. "Last thing we need is Nephthys knowing what we're up to."

Nephthys... Alyssa shuddered. "Do you think Heru-pa—?"

Tef took off her sunglasses. "If Heru-pa had succeeded, we would know."

A long stretch of silence hovered, the muffled roar of the engines the only sound filling the cabin as they contemplated her words.

The pilot's voice on the intercom broke the silence. "Ladies and gentlemen, we have begun our descent into Cairo. We shall be on the ground in approximately fifty minutes."

Alyssa glanced out of the window, suddenly even more aware of the weight of the golden amulet in the inside pocket of her jacket as the pilot continued his instructions for their landing.

———

THE PLANE TOUCHED DOWN LESS than an hour later. Alyssa watched the runway rushing by beneath her as the plane decelerated smoothly.

Welcome home, she thought wryly.

The plane taxied past the commercial gates and entered a broad alley lined with dozens of private hangars. One of the wide hangar doors on their right lifted open, and the plane turned inside. They weaved between several other small jets before coming to a stop. Alyssa eyed the collection of Citations and Gulfstreams inside the space as the engines spun down and the large doors closed behind them.

The pilot's voice rang through the intercom. "Per our instructions, the copilot and I will remain in the cockpit until all of you have deplaned and left the hangar. I will now lower the door. Thank you for allowing us to fly you. I hope your flight was smooth and your visit to Cairo will be enjoyable."

Fat chance of that... Alyssa thought.

A moment later the cabin door lowered. Alyssa grabbed her backpack and slung it over her shoulder as Renley picked up his small travel bag and stepped out. She followed him down the stairs, with Paul and Tef trailing behind.

A white SUV with yellow airport markings approached. It stopped beside the jet, and two men dressed in gray suits exited. One of them carried a clipboard with papers, the other a hand radio. Alyssa tensed.

Renley seemed to notice her anxiety. He leaned over. "Please try not to worry. This is quite routine."

The man with the radio stepped forward. His beard was neatly trimmed and as black as his hair, which was the color of crude oil. "Welcome to Cairo," he said with accented English and a professional smile that seemed pasted onto his olive-skinned face.

"Thank you," Renley said. "I trust all of our paperwork has been pre-processed?"

"Yes, of course," the man replied. "We merely need to finalize the arrivals documents. It will only take a minute of your time." He nodded to his partner with the clipboard who stepped back to the car and got into the passenger seat.

The man with the radio said all the right words, but the tone of his voice made the hair on Alyssa's neck stand up. His lips curved into another smile when he met her gaze, but his fist clenched tightly around the radio.

"Something doesn't feel right," she whispered to Renley.

"I'm quite certain everything is fine," Renley replied. "We shall be on our way soon."

Alyssa glanced at Tef. Her expression was hidden behind the *burqa* and sunglasses, but her posture reminded Alyssa of a coiled viper ready to strike.

A moment later, a second, smaller gate on the far end of the hangar opened and a vehicle entered.

"Ah, this must be our ride," Renley said.

Alyssa sized up the white van as it approached. "Unless you requested a full-size van, I think not," she said.

She took a step back. The bearded man shouted into his radio, and the van accelerated abruptly at them.

"It's a setup!" Alyssa yelled. She shoved Renley back.

The man reached inside his jacket. A dark blur swept past Alyssa as Tef surged forward, *burqa* fluttering in the air. The Rathadi covered the ten feet to the bearded man in a single leap and kicked him in his chest, driving him to the ground.

Before he had a chance to recover, Tef pounced on him, slamming her knee into his gut.

He groaned, and his eyes bulged.

Tef slipped her hand inside the man's jacket and pulled out a pistol. She swung it on the van and fired.

Alyssa's eyes darted to the van as the staccato cracks of the gunshots reverberated through the metal hangar.

The driver's side wheel blew, and the van swerved sharply to the left. The wheels squealed on the pavement as the van fishtailed and skidded to a stop.

An instant later, the side door slid open, and four men dressed in black tactical gear leaped out, automatic weapons in hands.

Alyssa was on the move before the last man hit the ground. "The car!" she yelled.

The four men rushed for them.

She pushed Renley in front of her to the airport SUV with Tef and Paul trailing behind. She flung open the passenger door.

The second airport official sat in the passenger seat, frozen.

Tef pointed the pistol at him. "Get out!" she yelled.

All color drained from his face. He dived out.

Alyssa threw her backpack inside and squeezed through to the driver's seat. Tef climbed in beside her as Renley and Paul leaped into the back.

Alyssa threw the car into reverse and stepped on the gas. The car peeled backward, leaving two black lines on the pavement beneath it.

The men continued racing after them, but the car outpaced them. One of the men lifted his weapon to fire, but another pushed down the barrel.

Alyssa slammed on the brakes and whipped the steering wheel to the right. The front of the SUV swung around to the left, tires screeching. She threw it into drive and floored it, heading for the open hangar door.

They raced out onto the tarmac, and Alyssa stole a glance in the rearview mirror.

"Watch out!" Tef cried.

Alyssa turned the wheel on instinct, barely avoiding a luggage carrier.

The parked Gulfstream jet appeared out of nowhere.

Alyssa swerved sharply the other way, just missing it.

A loud *clonk* from the rear seat sounded distinctly like a

head smacking the window. The string of curses from Paul's mouth confirmed it.

"Sorry," she cringed, squinting in the bright sun as she wrestled the fishtailing SUV. She somehow managed to regain control and guide the vehicle back into a straight line between the planes sitting on the tarmac. "This thing handles like a cinder block on ice!"

"We've got to get out of here before we hit something!" Tef yelled.

"That way!" Renley pointed to the right, between a couple of concrete buildings. "It looks relatively empty."

Alyssa steered the car between the two buildings. She risked another glance back at the hangar.

Paul looked out of the back window, rubbing his head. "I don't think they're following us," he said.

Alyssa slowed down. "How do we get out?"

"There's a gate up ahead, on the right." He pointed.

"Won't they stop us at the gate? To check papers?" she asked.

"Keep moving," Paul said. "This is an airport vehicle, and the windows are tinted. They can't see inside. Just get ready to punch it if they don't lift the gate."

Alyssa steered the car to the gate. She slowed as they approached it.

"Keep going, Miss Morgan," Renley said, his voice as tight as Alyssa's grip on the steering wheel.

They moved closer.

Alyssa held her breath. Her right foot tensed over the accelerator, ready to—

The gate lifted. She exhaled. She passed slowly through the

open gate and pulled onto the street. She continued following the airport access road.

"Now what?" she asked.

"I suggest first we dispose of this vehicle and find something a bit less conspicuous," Renley said.

"The main terminal should have car rentals," Paul chimed in.

Alyssa turned onto the road for the main terminal buildings and headed for one of the large parking structures. She stopped at a gate and pressed a button for a ticket, then drove inside and pulled into a spot. She threw the SUV into park and killed the engine, gripping the steering wheel tight to keep her hands from trembling.

Paul patted her shoulder from the back seat. "Nice driving."

Alyssa barked a nervous laugh. "I almost crashed into a twenty million dollar plane!"

"But you didn't," he replied.

Renley leaned forward. He wiped his forehead with a handkerchief. Alyssa noted the tremor in his hands. "I couldn't agree more," he said, managing to keep his voice steady. He turned to Tef. "And that was a most impressive display of marksmanship," he added. "To hit the tire on a moving vehicle at that distance—"

"I was aiming for the engine," Tef cut in, her voice dry.

A moment of silence stretched before Paul snickered. Alyssa shot him a glance, then chuckled. Before long, Renley and Tef joined in, and they all burst out, giddy on the adrenaline and their narrow escape.

Alyssa rubbed her face, as if she could wash away the tension. "I suppose it's better to be lucky than—"

Her phone chimed. She pulled it out. "It's Kamal," she said, ready to answer.

"Wait." Paul put his hand on Alyssa's arm.

Alyssa blinked.

"Don't answer," he said.

"Why?"

"Kamal was the only one you've told we were coming."

Alyssa's mind reeled at the implication. "But it's Kamal!" she cried out. "And Torin and Claudia Tibaldi knew, too. So did the pilots!"

The phone chimed again.

"We can't take that risk," Paul said.

Alyssa pulled her hand back. "He's one of my dad's oldest friends. He's helped us countless times. You can't seriously suggest that he had anything to do with what just happened."

"What if his phone is tapped?" Paul said. "If that's the case, they'll be listening to everything."

Alyssa opened her mouth to reply but couldn't find any words.

The phone dimmed. Alyssa stared at the empty display, a sinking feeling in her chest. "How are we supposed to get inside the hall without Kamal?"

"We'll figure out something else," Paul said.

"How?" she asked. "And even if we get inside, what if things don't work?" Her voice quivered. "What if this whole thing is just a wild goose chase based on some stupid dream, despite what we all think or want to believe?"

Tef reached out and put a calming hand on her arm. Alyssa didn't realize it had been shaking. "I believe in you," the Rathadi said. "And so does Dharr, halfway around the world.

You are now our best hope against the threat of the infection, against Nephthys. I choose to believe there is more to this than just dreams."

"The visions and memories guided you to the amulet," Paul offered.

Alyssa sensed the weight of their gazes on her. She covered her face with her hands for a long, ragged breath, then lowered her arms. "Okay, so where do we start?"

"Let us arrange a transport first," Renley offered. "Then the hall."

"I agree," Tef said. "We can visit the site, do some recon, figure out what we're dealing with. If there is a way in, we'll find it."

Thirty minutes later, Alyssa navigated their gray rental Land Rover along the four-lane road that led from the city to the Giza Plateau. Renley occupied the seat next to her, and Paul and Tef shared the back bench. Alyssa squinted as she spotted the commotion ahead of them on the road, a few hundred meters short of the Great Pyramids.

"Uh… guys," she mumbled.

Renley perked up in the passenger seat. Tef and Paul leaned forward.

"I think things just got a bit more complicated." She pointed at the military checkpoint ahead. A makeshift gate blocked the road.

"What's that all about?" Paul asked.

"I don't know," Alyssa said. "Shall I turn around?"

"No," Renley said. "Keep going. Allow me to talk, please."

As they approached, a soldier stepped forward. He dropped a cigarette and ground it underfoot then lifted his palm, beckoning Alyssa to stop the car. His other hand rested lazily on the automatic rifle hanging from his shoulder. Alyssa gripped the steering wheel tight as she brought the car to a stop and rolled down the window.

"*As-salaam alaikum,*" the soldier said.

"Good afternoon," Alyssa replied.

"What is your business here?" he asked, switching into heavily accented English.

Renley leaned to the soldier. "Good afternoon, Corporal. I am Lord Renley IV. I'm a patron of your Ministry of Antiquities. My companions and I have arranged a private tour of the excavation site in two hours," he said. "What is the meaning of this?"

The soldier stood straighter. "My apologies, sir," he replied. "There has been an incident. No visits today."

Alyssa's stomach dropped. "This is really important—"

"There are to be no exceptions," the soldier said. "Please turn around and leave."

Alyssa stared at him, tensing. Renley gently touched her knee. Alyssa took a deep breath and nodded. "Of course," she said. "Thank you."

She rolled up the window and made a U-turn. She looked dejectedly at the Great Pyramids receding in her rearview mirror.

"How are we supposed to get in there now?" she cried out. "Without Kamal and Kade?"

Renley's lips were pressed into a tight line.

"Do you think Nephthys had something to do with this?" Paul asked.

Alyssa shrugged.

Paul leaned forward to Renley. "You mentioned the ministry. What about the Minister of Antiquities?"

"I was stretching the truth," Renley replied.

"In any case, what about him?" Alyssa asked.

"He might be able to get us in," Paul said.

"Kade couldn't stand that guy." Alyssa said. "He thought the minister was a—" She glanced at Renley and stopped herself. "Anyway, do you really think he would help us? After all the trouble I caused?"

Renley cleared his throat. "Regardless of Dr. Morgan's opinion of the minister—however well-founded it may be—he could be our only remaining option to get inside the Hall of Records," he said. "I know that he feels a certain obligation to you after your role in developing the cure to the Horus epidemic."

Alyssa drew back at the name. "How do we even know we can trust him?" she asked. "What if Nephthys got to him, too?"

"We don't know," Paul said, "but it's unlikely. As much as we may not like him, I don't think he's the enemy. And our options keep dropping like mayflies in June."

Alyssa chewed on her bottom lip. "Kamal did mention that he has been surprisingly helpful to my father." She glanced to Renley. "Let's give it a shot."

Renley pulled out his phone and dialed information.

"Good afternoon," he said. "The number for the Ministry of Antiquities in Cairo, please." He held for a few moments. "Yes, please connect me," he said.

A few moments later a soft ringtone sounded from the phone against Renley's ear, then a click.

"*Wa-alaikum as-salaam*," he replied. "Do you speak

English?" He waited for the response. "Ah, brilliant. This is Lord George Renley calling from the Royal Archaeological Society in Great Britain. May I speak with the minister?"

He held still for a moment. "No, he is not expecting my call."

Renley's face darkened. "Yes, madam, but—"

His expression pinched. "Could you just tell him—?"

"No... yes... I understand... yes... but this is quite the urgent matter."

"Are you quite certain?" He sighed. "Very well. Will you just please tell the minister that Lord George Renley called and have him contact me as soon as he can?"

Renley sighed again and ended the call.

"I guess that didn't go well," Alyssa said.

"Mrs. Faquid, the minister's assistant, informed me that the minister has just left for the field. He is meeting with his film crew at the Khuwy Tomb to shoot a documentary—and he is not to be disturbed until he returns tomorrow evening."

"Bloody hell," Paul grunted. "Now what?"

Alyssa perked up. "Tomb of Khuwy? In Saqqara?"

She pulled the car over and typed into the GPS. When the route map appeared on the screen, a small smile built on her lips.

"That's what I thought. It's less than an hour's drive from here. A couple of years ago, Kade and I did some field work around Djoser's step pyramid in that area." She eyed Renley and the others. "What do you say we pay the honorable minister a personal visit?"

Paul shot her a skeptical glance. "Do you really think we can find him?"

"It's the Minister of Antiquities. At a dig site. He'll stand out."

"There is still the nontrivial matter of convincing him to help us," Renley said.

Alyssa glanced at Tef before lifting a mischievous eyebrow to Renley. "Indeed, but we still have a secret weapon. And a wise man once told me that a picture is worth a thousand words —especially when it's a living and breathing picture."

Renley held her gaze, his eyes serious, but the corner of his mouth lifted into a smile. "Old age does not guarantee wisdom, Miss Morgan," he said, "but I do appreciate the sentiment."

ALYSSA TRUDGED along the winding path, leading her and Tef deeper into the ancient burial grounds. She slipped into the shade of the massive limestone wall to their right, trying to escape the searing sun beating down on them. She glanced through one of the open sections, past the inner courtyard, at the six stacked *mastabas* that formed the step pyramid—the staircase to the heavens for pharaoh Djoser.

To their left, smaller tombs lay scattered throughout the grounds. Though nowhere near as spectacular, they had been just as susceptible to the scourge of grave robbing that has ravaged the ancient necropolis of Saqqara throughout the millennia.

Alyssa sighed and threw a look back over her shoulder to the parking area. Paul and Renley had stayed behind as part of their plan.

Let's hope it works…

Alyssa spotted a collection of trailers and trucks ahead. "That must be it," she said, glancing at Tef.

The Rathadi had donned the full-length *burqa* and sunglasses again. She held a round cardboard box in her hands.

"Let's just get this over with so I can get out of this outfit," Tef grumbled.

They strode purposefully for the collection of equipment trucks and crew trailers parked near the entrance of the newly discovered tomb.

"Just look like we belong," Alyssa whispered, eying the dozen or so people bustling among the vehicles and equipment.

They passed a parked truck when a man hopped off the trailer and into their path. He looked to be in his mid-thirties with a thick brown mustache, matching hair, and sun-weathered skin. He held a tall, open-faced studio light in each hand.

The man sized them up them, furrowing his brow. "This is a closed set," he said gruffly.

Alyssa put on her most naïve smile. "Oh, hi! My name's Ally," she said, her voice half an octave higher than usual. "I'm a junior at Cairo International High School. I'm interning at the minister's office this semester. Mrs. Faquid, the minister's assistant, sent me. The minister forgot his hat." On cue, Tef flipped open the lid of the box she was holding, revealing a khaki brim hat. "It's the one he prefers for interior shots," Alyssa continued, "because it complements his complexion in artificial lighting, and—"

The man held up a calloused hand. "No doubt..." he muttered. He nodded to the trailer. "Just put it in the truck. I'll grab it next time around and will make sure he gets it."

Alyssa pinched her face. "I'm really sorry, sir, but I'm afraid Mrs. Faquid was quite specific. I was to make absolutely sure the minister received it."

"Ron!" a voice came from the set. "Where are the lights?"

"Coming!" the man yelled back. He eyed Alyssa again then pointed to a large trailer on the periphery of the set.

"Fine, you can put it in his trailer. They've just about wrapped up the intro footage, so he can get it when he changes between takes. Just don't touch anything."

"Thank you so much!" Alyssa beamed as the man rushed back to the set.

Alyssa and Tef headed for the trailer.

"You should have been an actress," Tef said.

Alyssa gave a quiet laugh. "When I was little, I always wanted to have my own archaeology program. Kade used to film me when we were on digs, pretending I was doing my own show. I took myself quite seriously—for a ten-year-old. He probably still has the clips somewhere."

"Maybe you should talk to the minister about it," Tef quipped. "I hear he's got connections."

"I'll keep that in mind," Alyssa said.

They arrived at the trailer, and Alyssa knocked at the door. No answer. She pushed down the handle. The door opened with a burst of cool air. She stuck her head inside. "Hello?" she called out, then glanced at Tef before slipping inside. Tef followed her and closed the door behind them.

The inside of the trailer resembled a modern luxury apartment. The living room area was wide enough for two sofas and a dining table for six. A large flat screen TV hung on one of the walls. A portrait of the minister, beaming in his trademark khaki on khaki, adorned the opposite wall.

"Is this guy for real?" Tef asked.

Alyssa sighed. "You'll soon find out."

Tef glanced out of the window. "Someone's coming!" She dashed to the rear of the trailer.

Alyssa barely had time to step away from the door and move back before it swung open.

The minister stepped inside and closed the door behind him. He took off his hat and tossed it on the sofa then shook out his coiffed salt-and-pepper hair. He turned and jumped when he spotted Alyssa. A panicked grimace flared through him before recognition set in. He stared at her in disbelief. "Miss Morgan?" he called out, his brow furrowed. "What in the world are you doing here?"

"Minister," Alyssa said, looking at him with what she hoped was a pleasant expression, "please forgive the intrusion."

The minister bristled. "What is the meaning of this?"

Tef stepped out of the back room.

He eyed her suspiciously. "And who are you?" He turned to Alyssa. "Who is this?"

"Minister, please," Alyssa said. "Allow us a moment of your time and we—"

"Have you any idea how much trouble you have caused? Or the consequences of your actions? And now you're breaking into my space?"

"The door was open," Tef said. Alyssa shot her a glance.

"What?" The minister's expression soured even further. He turned and moved to the door. "I don't have time for—"

Tef slid by him and blocked the door. She pulled the pistol from beneath her *burqa*.

The minister's eyes widened, but he stopped. His eyes dashed between the gun and Alyssa. Tef locked the door, keeping her eyes on the minister.

"Have you gone completely mad?" He glared at them both. "What do you want?"

"We do not wish you ill," Tef said calmly.

"Do you know who I am?" he fumed.

"Minister, please," Alyssa said. "You may want to sit down for this."

He remained standing, a defiant glare carved into his face.

"Very well," Alyssa said. She nodded to Tef.

Tef reached up and took off her sunglasses and the head scarf. Her Rathadi scales shimmered, reflecting the fading sunlight that entered through the wide, tinted windows.

The minister paled. He opened his mouth as if to say something, but no sound came out. He shuffled back until his legs hit the sofa, and he collapsed into it.

Tef lowered the weapon.

"We mean you absolutely no harm, Minister," Alyssa said. "But we do require your full attention… with all due respect."

The minister stared at Tef, pale and unblinking. "Who…?"

Alyssa moved one of the chairs in front of him and eased into it.

"Will you please listen to what I have to tell you?"

He nodded, his gaze glued to Tef's shimmering skin.

"Thank you," Alyssa breathed.

Ten minutes later, the minister continued staring at the Rathadi, absorbing Alyssa's words. He took another sip of his second glass of scotch. The color in his face had returned to the usual olive tone, but his eyes held the same awestruck expression.

Tef met his gaze calmly. She had put away the pistol and

taken off the *burqa*, exposing more of her shimmering serpentine skin.

The minister reached out to Tef. "Please, may I?"

She nodded and held out her arm to him.

He shuddered when he touched her skin. His eyes glistened. "All these years…"

A knock at the door snapped him back. "Minister! We're back on in five!" a voice from the outside called.

"Yes, yes," he shot back then turned to Alyssa. "And you truly believe that this woman, Nephthys, and Dr. Khanna somehow conspired—"

"Yes," Alyssa replied glumly.

"Dr. Khanna visited me this morning," the minister said. "He said there was a leak at the Hall of Records site. I ordered a lockdown at his recommendation… and the military-controlled perimeter around it."

Alyssa's stomach clenched. They had suspected it, but the confirmation still hit her hard. *Kamal… how could he?* She swallowed to gain her voice. "We think Nephthys is using Kamal to get to the hall."

"Why?"

"I don't know," Alyssa said.

"What do you need from me?"

"We need to get inside the hall," Alyssa said.

"When?"

Alyssa stared at the minister wordlessly.

His eyes widened. "Tonight?"

"Right now," she said.

The minister placed a palm to his forehead, resting for several moments. Finally, he looked up and cleared his throat. "Very well," he said, then he drained the glass in one throw and set it on the table. He stood and handed the *burqa* to Tef. "It seems like a sin to cover this up," he said, regret ringing in his voice.

———

TASHA SHIFTED between the two Pureans in the back seat of the large SUV. Despite the width of the cabin, she was squeezed like a sardine by their bulging shoulders. She wiggled, trying to get as comfortable as her position and the shackles on her wrists allowed. At least she didn't feel like she was going to lose her lunch anymore, and her headache was all but gone. Still, riding sandwiched between two hulks with her hands tied behind her back was definitely not her preferred mode of travel.

She studied the driver's face in the rearview mirror as his brown eyes scanned the road ahead. He had met them at their plane, and they had immediately set out for the Giza Plateau on the outskirts of the city. Tasha had heard about Kamal Khanna from Alyssa and the others but did not expect to meet him under these circumstances. Then again, she never expected these circumstances at all.

Nephthys reclined in the passenger seat next to Kamal. Her breathing came in short and labored breaths. Whatever had happened to the Hybrid woman was certainly taking its toll, and fast. She assumed she had Heru-pa to thank for that.

Why were they going to the hall? She was trying to recall what the Purean scientist and Nephthys had discussed before the procedure, but her mind was still cloudy. And what was Kamal's connection to Nephthys?

The car slowed down as they approached some kind of a checkpoint. She tensed. Maybe if she could—

Nephthys glanced over her shoulder. "Keep her quiet," she rasped to the Pureans, "whatever it takes."

Kamal pressed a button, and a privacy partition lifted between the front and rear seats.

Tasha's mind went on autopilot. She studied the partition. If she could get her foot up, perhaps she could kick it. Create enough noise that the guard would have to—

As if reading her thoughts, the Purean to her right stirred. He pressed his hand against her throat and squeezed hard. Tasha yelped at the pain and the sudden lack of air. She opened her mouth, eyes bulging.

"Don't even think about trying anything," he growled. "I am capable of causing you a great deal of discomfort—without damaging you permanently. Do not test me."

Tasha managed to nod. The Purean eased his grip, but kept his hand locked around her throat. Tasha sucked in the air hungrily around his vise-like palm. She barely noted the SUV coming to a smooth stop.

Kamal said something in Arabic, his voice muffled by the partition, and a man outside replied tersely. A few moments later the car accelerated and continued on its way. The partition lowered. The Purean removed his hand from her neck, but the lump in her throat remained as they continued.

They left the paved road and continued over the sand to a large white tent that stood halfway between the Great Pyramids and the Sphinx. A few moments later, they pulled to a stop, and the Purean on Tasha's right exited the car. He opened the passenger door and helped Nephthys out.

The guard on her left gave Tasha a push for the open door. "Move out," he said.

Tasha scooted across the seat and out of the car as gracefully as her cuffed hands allowed. She stretched her legs and let the cold desert air fill her lungs, then she studied the circular tent that enclosed the entrance to the tunnel. The last time she stepped foot into that tent and the Hall of Records, she was at William Drake's side—and she had almost died.

But I'm still here, she thought, pressing her lips into a fine line. She had no desire to let fate finish tonight what it hadn't been able to accomplish on her last visit here.

She turned at the rumble behind her. A heavy military-style transport truck approached them and pulled up behind the sedan. Nephthys and the two Pureans turned to the truck, their attention shifted momentarily.

Tasha spotted her opportunity. If she could get behind the tent and use the darkness to her advantage—

She broke into a dead sprint for the tent. Before she took her fourth step, a wave of searing pain passed through her wrists. It spread like wildfire to her forearms, through her shoulders, and down to her legs. She collapsed to the sand, twitching uncontrollably.

Through the haze of agony, Nephthys approached. The woman observed her silently as she writhed in the sand, consumed by the flames that raged inside her body. Each heartbeat stretched to eternity—

As quickly as it had started, the fire in her body stopped. The absence of the pain was a blessing. Tasha's muscles continued to spasm as her body recovered from the sudden onslaught.

Nephthys held a small silver device out to her. "That was the lowest setting—because I do not wish to damage you." She adjusted a dial on the device. "Would you like to find out what the highest setting feels like?"

Tasha took short, gasping breaths. Pure terror flooded through her at the thought. She shook her head.

"Good girl," Nephthys said. "And because I know you're foolish enough to think you may be able to get your hands on this—" she lifted the device—"you should know that each of my guards has one as well."

The engine of the heavy truck cut off, and the tailgate dropped down. The Purean scientist stepped out, followed by a dozen Purean soldiers clad in black gear. Kamal eyed the men quizzically, then turned to Nephthys.

"Your men let the girl slip through their fingers at the airport," Nephthys replied to his unspoken question. "My men are here to ensure she doesn't interfere—if she decides to join us."

Kamal pulled at his collar. "I didn't think—"

Nephthys silenced him with a look. "Another team of my men has just landed and will be arriving shortly. Make sure they can get through. I don't want any surprises." She turned to her guards and pointed at Tasha. "Get her up," she said then faced the scientist, "and bring the suits."

The Purean scientist scurried to the back of the truck and returned with three black biosuits. He handed one to each of the guards, keeping one for himself.

"Keep out anybody who tries to follow us," Nephthys said, and she set out for the tent, leaning heavily on the scientist. The guards grasped Tasha's arms and lifted her up before pushing her to the tent after the lumbering pair.

Tasha eyed the scientist and the two guards, each holding their own biosuit. "What about a suit for me?" she asked.

Nephthys stopped and threw a wearied glance over the shoulder, yellow eyes boring into her. "On this night, you shall experience the hall and *all* it has to offer," she said with a voice that froze the blood beneath Tasha's skin.

————

THE GREAT PYRAMIDS rose out of the sand in the dim moonlight as Alyssa guided the Land Rover toward the soldiers at the checkpoint. She came to a stop before the gate and lowered her window. The soldier glanced in and snapped to attention when he recognized the minister in the passenger seat.

"Good evening, Minister," the soldier said in Arabic. "We were not expecting your visit tonight. Are you meeting Dr. Khanna?"

The hair on the back of Alyssa's neck prickled at his words.

"Dr. Kamal Khanna?" the minister asked.

"Yes, Minister," the soldier replied. "He and his team passed through less than ten minutes ago."

"His team?" Alyssa asked in Arabic. "Who was with him?"

The soldier glanced to her, surprised. The minister nodded to him.

"They arrived in two vehicles. A sedan and an equipment truck. I only saw one woman next to him. My apologies, Minister, I had assumed that—"

"The woman," Alyssa interrupted, "what did she look like?"

"Tall, slender," the soldier replied, puzzled.

"Anything else? Anything out of the ordinary?" Alyssa pressed.

He hesitated. "She didn't look very well, and…"

"And what?"

"I thought it was just a trick of the light, but her eyes—they looked… just like yours… yellow."

Alyssa inhaled sharply.

"What's going on?" Paul asked from the back seat.

Alyssa turned. "Kamal is here," she breathed, "with Nephthys." She translated what the soldier said before she faced the minister. "I don't know what Nephthys is planning, but I can guarantee that nothing good will come out of it."

The minister ran his hand through his hair then turned to the soldier. "How many men do you have here?" he asked.

"Four squads. A total of forty-two men. Eight are monitoring the access points on the roads, the rest are guarding the perimeter around the site, per your request."

"You need to assemble them, now," the minister ordered.

"You want the men to abandon their posts?"

The minister looked the soldier dead in the eyes. "It appears that, through no fault of your own, the people that should have been kept out are already here," he said gravely.

The soldier's jaw tightened. "I understand, sir," he said. "I shall assemble the men."

———

TWENTY MINUTES LATER, Alyssa lay in the sand and lifted the binoculars to her eyes, struggling to keep her breathing steady.

Before her, the Great Sphinx cast a serene gaze over the plateau, oblivious to the churning in Alyssa's stomach as she focused the lenses on the white tent beneath it. In the dim exterior lights, she spotted a dozen black-clad Purean soldiers stationed around the tent's entrance. She panned the binoculars across the sand. She barely noticed the movement of the Egyptian soldiers as they crept toward the tent under the cover of the night.

The minister crouched in the sand next to her. His radio crackled softly.

"All squads in position and ready," the voice announced.

An instant later three blinding spotlights flooded the Pureans.

"This is the Egyptian Army," a voice from a high-powered speaker boomed. "You are trespassing on national property. You are completely surrounded. Surrender immediately."

The Pureans lifted their hands to shield their eyes from the sudden onslaught. Several raised their rifles. Instantly, dozens of weapons from the soldiers surrounding the tent rang out in short bursts, the bullets impacting the sand in front of the Pureans.

They froze and lowered their weapons, their hands still covering their eyes.

"Stand down!" the voice commanded. "There will be no further warning. Lay down your weapons."

The Pureans stood still for several moments, then complied, setting their weapons down on the sand. A moment later, the Egyptian soldiers swarmed them and rounded them up.

Alyssa and the others rushed to the tent entrance. She cautiously lifted the flap. A rush of memories flooded her mind at the sight of the deep excavation pit and the metal ramp, zigzagging its way down.

She entered the tent and approached the ramp. The floor of the pit and its thirty foot high walls had been covered in concrete, giving it the appearance of a drained swimming pool. Its far side had been completely enclosed by a glass chamber that was accessible through a sealed door on the bottom of the pit. Inside the chamber itself, the stone door that had protected the entrance to the tunnel had been removed and replaced by a heavy metal hatch. Alyssa's breath quickened. One hundred fifty meters beyond it lay the entrance to the Hall of Records.

The minister pointed to a wide glass cabinet to the right of the chamber. Inside it, several biocontainment suits hung suspended from metal hangers. "The Ministry of Health developed a new generation of biosuits to allow the researchers to move around more freely," he said. "The filters have been specifically designed to keep out the pathogen that was found in the tunnel. Shall I have the men suit up to accompany you inside?"

Alyssa shook her head. As much as she would have liked the additional protection, the soldiers were more important here. "You will need every man to guard the Pureans," she replied. "And we must limit the risk of exposure. Your men have done enough."

"Are you certain?" the minister asked. "You don't know what awaits you inside."

"Nephthys left enough of her soldiers to guard the entrance to ensure she won't be disturbed. She won't be expecting anybody. We will have surprise on our side."

The minister gave a somber nod. "As you wish." He

reached into his pocket and offered an electronic keycard to Alyssa. "The combination for the keypad on the outer door is 122603. The safety mechanism on the inner door will not allow the seal to be breached until the outer door has been closed and secured. To minimize the pathogen flow into the chamber, the inner door can remain open for only sixty seconds. If it is not resealed manually within that time, the safety override will close it automatically."

"I understand," Alyssa said.

"On your return, once you have secured the inner door again, you will undergo a decontamination process before you can exit the chamber."

"Decontamination process?"

"A ten minute ultraviolet blast designed to eradicate the pathogen within the glass chamber. It is triggered each time the seal on the inner door is breached before the outer door can be opened again," he explained.

Alyssa nodded. "Thank you, Minister."

He extended his hand and she grasped it. "Good luck, Miss Morgan."

Alyssa faced Renley. "Lord Renley, it may be safer for you to wait—"

Renley lifted his palm. "You have taken me on an adventure of which I could have only dreamed, Miss Morgan," he said. "I am not about to jump ship now."

Alyssa looked at Paul.

"Don't even think about trying to talk me out of going with you," he said.

Tef stepped forward. "Enough talking," she said, her skin

glowing with anticipation. "Nephthys has a big enough head start."

They moved down the ramp. Alyssa eyed the automatic weapon in Tef's hands.

"On loan from one of the soldiers," she replied. "Nephthys may not be expecting anybody to come after her, but we're not going in there unarmed."

Alyssa stepped up to the rack with the suits. The gear looked lighter and less bulky than the previous versions. She opened the rack and pulled out two outfits.

Tef grabbed one and helped Renley with it, while Alyssa held the other one open for Paul. He climbed inside, and she closed the zipper. She picked up a set of gloves, and he slipped his left hand into one. It locked magnetically to the suit, forming a seal, then she attached the right one to the suit. Paul lifted his right arm, a sullen expression rippling through him as he stared at the empty gloved hand. Their gazes caught, and he cleared his throat.

"Helmet?" he asked, his voice hollow.

Alyssa shook off her own thoughts and pulled a helmet from the rack. She lifted it over his head, and it locked in place.

"Wicked," Paul said. "There's a display inside the helmet that just turned on. Looks like the system is running a self-diagnostic. Suit integrity just turned green. Now communications… filter condition shows one hundred percent… the battery is full. Looks like I'm set to go."

Alyssa glanced at Renley.

"All green on my side, as well," Renley said, giving her a thumbs up.

She moved to the outer door and held the keycard against

the electronic reader then entered the code. A moment later the light above the door flashed green and the airtight seal released with a faint hiss. The locking mechanism on the door disengaged.

Alyssa grasped the handle and swung it open. "You first," she said to Tef.

The Rathadi took a tentative step into the glass chamber, her skin gleaming in the bright light of the fluorescent lamps above them. Paul and Renley followed.

Alyssa took a final glance to the top of the pit. The minister lifted his hand. She gave him a nod and stepped through the door.

The sounds of commotion outside the tent stopped her in her tracks. She swung around. The minister rushed to the entrance of the tent and looked out then wheeled around. "There's more of them!" he yelled. "Go! Go!" He waved his hands furiously.

Alyssa dashed through the outer door and locked it an instant before the stock of a rifle flashed through the tent flap and connected with the back of the minister's head. He dropped to the ground like a stone, and a Purean soldier stormed inside. He pointed the weapon at Alyssa.

"Stop!" he bellowed.

Alyssa leaped to the inner door and pressed the keycard to the scanner. The light in the chamber shifted to a red hue, and the seal of the inner door released.

The Purean's face tightened. He kept the weapon aimed at her. "Don't move!" he warned as two more Purean soldiers rushed inside.

The trio stalked down the ramp, keeping their weapons locked on Alyssa and the others.

"Seal the inner door and come out," the Purean said.

Alyssa met his gaze, unblinking. She didn't move.

"Get inside the tunnel," she said.

"Alyssa…" Paul started.

"If they shoot through the glass, they will break the containment and release Thoth's bioweapon," she said, trying to keep the tremor out of her voice. "They won't risk that. Get inside."

Renley grasped the handle of the inner door and swung it open.

"Stop!" the Purean soldier commanded again.

"Keep going," Alyssa said.

Renley stepped through the inner door. The Purean soldiers followed his movements with their weapons. Their faces were tense, but they didn't fire.

Paul stepped inside the tunnel after Renley, followed by Tef. Alyssa kept her eyes glued on the soldiers as she slipped through the inner door and backed into the tunnel. A pair of chained lights ran the entire length of the floor along each wall, bathing the tunnel in a soft white glow. She took three steps backward, then spun and took off down the corridor.

Thirty yards into the tunnel, she caught up to the others.

Paul stared at her, panting. "Did the minister say there were more?"

Alyssa stared at him silently, her mind reeling at the implication.

"Where did they come from?" Paul cried.

"I… I don't know," Alyssa said, dazed. She allowed herself a moment of panic then forced it back. They had a job to do.

She glanced at her watch then back to the open door at the entrance. "We bought ourselves some time, but in less than eleven minutes they will all be coming after us," she said. "We need to find Nephthys before then."

Tef stared into the long corridor with a faraway look.

"Tef?" Alyssa asked.

"I've imagined being here so many times," she said.

Alyssa eyed the weapon in Tef's hands ruefully. "But never with a rifle in your hand."

———

Tasha took another deep breath, letting the ancient smell fill her nostrils as she continued climbing the stairs of the stone pyramid. Her terror at entering the tunnel without a protective biosuit had ebbed when she hadn't felt any ill effects. Soon after, the apprehension had turned to awe when her body appeared to feed on the ancient air, gaining strength from it with every passing minute. Even with her hands cuffed behind her back, she climbed the steep stairs nimbly and surefooted. Her mind was clearer and her senses sharper than they had been in days.

A few steps ahead, Nephthys leaned heavily on the Purean scientist, her labored breathing and shuffling steps echoing through the vast cavern. They had been forced to stop three times already to allow her to catch her breath, and she looked like she needed another rest, but the Hybrid woman kept her gaze locked on the summit of the pyramid and continued, one heavy stride in front of the other.

Behind Tasha, the pair of Purean guards flanked her. Aware

of the change in her, they had stepped back, their fingers hovering over the buttons that controlled the stun handcuffs around her wrists. There was no way she could reach both guards and Nephthys before at least one of them had time to activate the device, so she continued the ascent in sullen silence, her jaw set tight.

She snapped out of her thoughts when Nephthys reached the summit. The woman stepped away from the scientist and moved haltingly to the sarcophagus that rose up in the center of the platform. She straightened her back, the simple movement seeming to drain the last remaining ounces of strength from her.

"I am running out of time," Nephthys breathed. The scientist took hold of Tasha's arm and pulled her toward Nephthys.

"Kneel," Nephthys commanded.

Tasha shook off his hand. "Why? You said we needed to get inside. We're here. What else do you need from me?"

Nephthys took a shuddering breath. "A final ritual, necessary to fully activate the Rathadi blood inside you, so it can be used to cure me."

"You never mentioned that," Tasha scoffed.

"Do not question me, girl, for I am out of strength and time."

Tasha continued glaring at her defiantly. Nephthys reached for the silver activator. Tasha tensed and held her breath, bracing herself for the searing pain. Nephthys sighed and dropped it to the ground. "I do not have time for games," she said.

The guards lifted their weapons.

Nephthys's voice was labored, but her golden eyes burned fiercely when she spoke. "You can submit to the ritual and let us harvest your blood willingly. When we are finished, you will be free. Or we can ensure your cooperation through less civilized means, harvest your blood, and leave you up here to bleed to death." She motioned to the guards. "If the girl is not on her knees in three seconds, shoot her legs."

The guards aimed their weapons at Tasha's legs.

"One..." she counted. "Two..."

Tasha sank to her knees before Nephthys, the defiant gaze never faltering.

The woman regarded Tasha. "Strong and stubborn to the end."

The guards lowered their weapons and moved to Nephthys, helping her ease to her knees across from Tasha. Nephthys lifted her arms, shaping her palms into a triangle, then pressed them against Tasha's head. Her golden eyes locked onto Tasha's. "Open your mind to me," she whispered.

Tasha's skin glowed warmer at the woman's touch.

She heard the voice again, but this time Nephthys's lips didn't move. *Open your mind to me.*

Tasha's skin tingled. A rush of heat coursed over her, spreading from her head into the pyramid beneath her. She tensed, fighting every instinct to shake free of the woman's touch.

Nephthys's face hardened, and her eyes glowed with an ethereal radiance. The heat beneath her palms hovered at the edge of pain. Tasha bit her lip to stifle a groan.

The woman's eyes flared, and her hands seared with heat. Tasha shrieked. She flung herself back, away from Nephthys, away from the scalding agony. A bolt of panic went through her when she realized that her body refused her commands. She hadn't moved, and nothing but a silent scream had passed through her lips.

Terror washed over her.

What's happening?

She cried out, but her mouth was hers no longer. The cavern remained silent, save for the sound of her own heartbeat thrashing in her ears. Her vision narrowed to a point, and acid rose up in the back her throat.

Stop resisting, Nephthys's voice rang through her head.

Tasha's wail tore through her mind. *Let me go!*

Nephthys's grip on her tightened, and Tasha felt like the air in the room was being sucked away from her.

You will never be scared again, the voice rang in her head, teasing, tempting. *You will never be anybody's puppet again. You will finally be free.*

Tasha strength ebbed from her. *Please...* she whimpered silently.

Without warning, images flooded her, taking hold of her mind like a thousand flashbulbs exploding all at once. More and more cracked across her vision, drowning her in a sea of stars. Tasha's mind froze in terror as realization struck.

No!

I will not let you take me!

A ghost of her own memory flashed through her mind. Tasha clung to it desperately.

A barefooted girl in a snow-covered alley... an old plastic doll... The girl reaches for it...

The doll dissolves like ashes scattered by the wind. Horror suffocates the girl as her fingers shimmer then fade away, one by one, her hand dwindling into air until—

Nephthys's golden eyes pierced through Tasha, and her lips curled into the barest hint of a smile.

You are already mine.

———

ALYSSA SLOWED as she neared the end of the tunnel. A vast subterranean hall opened below her, illuminated by a faint glow.

The Hall of Records.

She motioned the others to stay behind and laid down on the tunnel floor. She inched forward. As her vision adjusted to the dim light of the cavern, she made out the stone pyramid that rose from the fog-covered ground beneath her. Brought here brick by brick from Horus's home island, each side of the pyramid's base stretched more than two hundred feet, and over three hundred steps led to its summit.

Tef crawled next to her and peered inside the cavern. She inhaled sharply. "The sacred monument," she whispered.

Alyssa spotted figures on the summit. Three of them wore black biosuits and surrounded a pair kneeling on the ground.

"Nephthys," she whispered when she recognized one of the kneeling figures. The other's back was facing Alyssa.

No suit… Another Rathadi? It had to be to survive here without a biosuit. *Heru-pa?*

She furrowed her brow when she realized the weapons of the two black-clad figures were pointed at the Rathadi kneeling across from Nephthys.

Renley scooted next to them. He squinted as he studied the

scene before them. "Can you make out anybody?" he asked Alyssa, keeping his voice low.

"Nephthys, three others in biosuits, and one more without a suit."

"Another Hybrid?" Paul asked as he moved beside them. "Heru-pa?"

Alyssa shrugged.

"What are they doing?" Paul asked.

Alyssa concentrated, and the image became sharper, but they were still too far to make out details. She sighed. "I can't tell."

Renley eyed the rifle in Tef's hands. "Can you hit Nephthys from here?" he asked.

Tef glanced at him, blinking at the bluntness of his question.

"She has to be stopped," Renley said, his jaw set. "And we do not have time. The other Pureans are not far behind."

Tef looked to the summit. She shook her head. "And if I miss, we lose the element of surprise."

"Then we have to get closer," Renley said.

"The two with the weapons seem to be paying attention to the kneeling Rathadi," Alyssa said. She rose and crept to the stairs carved into the wall. The others followed. They descended quietly, trying to blend into the shadows of the wall, until they reached the mist-covered ground.

They crossed the cavern to the stairs of the pyramid and began their ascent. Alyssa and Tef first, followed by Paul and Renley who moved as quietly and quickly as the protective gear allowed.

As they drew close to the summit, Alyssa crouched. She crept up the last few stairs then peaked over the edge.

She stifled a gasp when she caught sight of Nephthys. The Hybrid woman's elegant face had withered, now resembling a skull with skin stretched paper-thin over the once delicate features. Dark rings formed around her closed eyes. Alyssa froze when she noticed Nephthys's hands on the other figure's head.

The Bond of Legacy!

She beckoned to Tef. When the Rathadi scooted up beside her, Alyssa eyed the rifle and pointed to Nephthys. Tef gave a brief nod. She raised the weapon and aimed.

Before the gunshot rang out, Nephthys slumped to the stone floor. Tef lowered the rifle. A baffled expression rippled through her.

Alyssa's skin tingled when the other kneeling figure rose. Her lithe form teetered as she gained her feet, her legs quivering like a newborn calf's. Recognition struck and awareness rose inside Alyssa's chest like fire, burning everything in its path.

No... God, no...

"What's happening?" Renley asked from below.

"Please... no..." Alyssa whimpered, her body frozen to the stone pyramid, the understanding paralyzing her.

Renley moved up and lifted his head above the summit. "Tasha!" he cried out.

Tasha turned to them, wavering.

Renley leaped up and rushed for her.

The Purean guards at her side lifted their weapons, but she pushed them down. She leaned over Nephthys and pulled a slim object from beneath Nephthys's robe.

"Lord Renley!" Alyssa called out, finally finding her voice. "Don't!" She turned to Tef. "Stay here, shoot her if you must," she instructed, ignoring Tef's perplexed look, before she bolted after Renley across the summit.

Tasha tilted her head as Renley approached, her features as cold and expressionless as a slab of granite. Renley slowed, hesitating, and stopped short. Tasha took a tentative step forward, closing the distance between them.

"Lord Renley!" Alyssa called out again. "It's not—"

Tasha's hand shot forward. Renley rose up as if snapping to attention, then slumped.

The scream died on Alyssa's lips as Tasha pulled a black dagger from his chest.

Alyssa reached him, and he collapsed into her arms.

Renley's mouth fell open. He stared at the white fabric, blood seeping through his gloved fingers. He coughed, and red spittle covered his lips and the visor of his suit. He lifted his head past Alyssa.

"Tasha…" he groaned. "Why?"

Alyssa turned. Tasha's irises smoldered in deep amber, rimmed by a band of violet. Alyssa's breath hitched. Disbelief rang within, even as she stared at the proof right in front of her.

The face and body were Tasha's, but the mind belonged to another.

"Nephthys!" she spat, fighting a wave of nausea that washed over her.

The guards moved in on Alyssa, but Nephthys motioned them to stay. She ran languishing fingers through the long, auburn hair and stretched out her arms like a butterfly unfurling its wings for the first time. She seemed to mold into her new body, her stance and posture growing steadier with every passing second. "I think this body will serve me well… until I find a more suitable vessel," she taunted Alyssa in Tasha's voice.

"How did you…?" Alyssa breathed.

"Not all vessels are as willing as Horus's offspring," Nephthys said. "Reaping a mind to control a vessel has been a necessary part of my existence…" She studied her hands, her lips curving into a smile that did not reach her eyes. "It gets easier with practice."

Alyssa glared at her, frozen into stillness, but every fiber within her shook with rage.

That could have been me. My body.

She caught movement at the edge of the platform.

Tef raised the rifle.

Lightning quick, the Purean guard closest to Nephthys surged forward and wrapped his arms around her, shielding her slender frame with his body.

Shots rang out, impacting his back as they fell to the ground.

The second guard lifted his rifle over Alyssa's head to return fire.

Alyssa roared, her rage fueling her. She charged into him, slamming him to the ground.

The Purean regained his composure almost instantly. Muscles bulged under the biosuit as he flipped Alyssa to her back and dived on top of her. Alyssa struggled, but he was fast despite his size. His gloved hands locked around her throat.

He snarled, spittle flying like venom through his clenched teeth, covering the inside of his visor.

Alyssa fought for breath, wriggling like a fish, but he held tight.

She gasped for air, clawing at his head, but the helmet and the armored biosuit protected him from her blows.

His eyes shone down in triumph.

She reached up and locked her hands around his helmet and twisted it. His face froze when the airtight seal released. Alyssa yanked the helmet off his head and smashed it into his face. He gasped, and the ancient air filled his lungs. His body writhed, the scuffle forgotten as the bioweapon ravaged his body.

Alyssa squirmed out from beneath him.

A haze streaked through her vision as the other guard leaped off the ground and charged Tef. She continued firing, but the armored suit absorbed her bullets, and he rushed her like an avalanche made out of flesh. He tackled her, pinning her beneath him.

The weapon flew out of her hand, sliding to the edge of the platform.

The guard pulled a long knife from a sheath on his calf and lifted it, ready to plunge it into Tef's chest.

A shot rang out, and the Purean's visor burst into a hundred fragments. He slumped to the ground lifelessly beside Tef. Alyssa snapped her head to the source of the shot.

Paul held the rifle in his left hand, his eyes hard as flint, as he balanced the barrel with the stump of his right arm.

"Shoot Nephthys!" Tef cried.

Paul swung the weapon at Nephthys. She lay on the ground, struggling to gain her feet, her body new and not yet familiar. Paul's expression shifted, and his eyes softened. He blinked, hesitating.

"Shoot her!" Tef yelled again.

"Tasha…" Paul mouthed.

"It's not Tasha!" Tef screamed.

"Paul... no," Renley's voice came in a rasp. "Please... remember your promise."

Paul lowered the weapon. A triumphant smile stretched across Nephthys's face.

"You fool!" Tef screamed.

Nephthys leaped to her feet, faster than Alyssa thought possible. Paul lifted the weapon again, but it was too late. She covered the distance to Paul in the blink of an eye and ripped the rifle from his grasp by the barrel. He lunged for her, but she danced aside and smashed the stock of the rifle into the back of his neck. Paul crumpled to the ground.

Alyssa rushed Nephthys, but Tef arrived first. Nephthys sidestepped Tef's attack, turned, and drove the butt of the rifle into her face. Tef lurched back, stunned, blood bursting from her nose.

Nephthys spun the rifle, pointed it at Tef, and fired.

Tef's head jerked back as if dragged by invisible strings, and she collapsed to the ground lifelessly.

Alyssa screamed. Her balance faltered, her attack turning sloppy.

Nephthys slid aside, and Alyssa stumbled forward, her momentum carrying her past her opponent.

Nephthys kicked the back of Alyssa's knee, dropping her to the ground.

Searing pain passed through her scalp when Nephthys grabbed her hair and pulled it back. Nephthys swung the rifle around her neck and pressed it against her throat. Alyssa fought for breath, her arms flailing. Her vision clouded, closing to a single point, as dozens of Purean soldiers swarmed the summit of the pyramid.

The soldiers surrounded them, pointing their weapons at Nephthys and Alyssa.

Nephthys drew herself tall, her slender frame seeming to grow larger. She stared them down, golden eyes burning into them.

"I am Nephthys, Queen of Atlantis and rightful heir to the throne," Tasha's voice sounded in Alyssa's ears as if through a haze. "I have taken a new vessel. You shall continue to obey me as you have. If you point a weapon at me again, you shall die where you stand."

As one, all weapons trained on Alyssa.

Without warning, a Purean soldier dropped, his visor shattered, as a series of cracks reverberated through the cavern. An instant later, another fell beside him. Alyssa twisted her head to the stairs. A familiar figure rushed onto the summit, dressed in black body armor, firing his weapon on the run.

Dharr?

Alyssa's mind swam, and her vision compressed to a point. Then—nothing.

THE SACRED MONUMENT grows cold beneath my feet. The sarcophagus, my resting place, beckons. Slowly, I step to it and peer inside.

A crystal in the shape of a pyramid. A mind gem.

My thoughts fall away and my mind reaches out for it, unbidden. My hand follows. The mind gem glows, first white, then a blood crimson.

The floor dissolves into darkness. The crystal falls and I with it. I reach after it, but it is beyond my grasp. The red light grows more intense, blinding—

Alyssa jerked up. The chaos of gunfire and shouting washed over her. A hand latched on from behind, pulling her back down. She strained against the hold. *Let me—!*

"Alyssa, stop!" She pivoted at Paul's hushed voice. "Stay down," he said, his voice taut. Staccato sounds of gunfire echoed off the cavern walls as muzzle flashes broke above them through the dim illumination.

She took in her surroundings. They huddled at the foot of

the pyramid, hidden in the mist that covered the ground, on the far side of the cavern from the entrance.

"Wh-what's happening?" she stammered.

"It's Dharr! And other Rathadi," Paul said. "They're here!"

"Dharr?"

"They caught the Pureans off guard. Bought us time to get you down from the summit."

The summit... The memory hit her like a bolt of lightning.

"Tef?" she muttered, dread rising up in her chest.

Paul shook his head despondently.

"No..." Alyssa whimpered.

"I... I should have taken the shot..." Paul stammered. "I thought..." His face withered, and his words crumbled. "She looks like Tasha." His voice broke when he finally spoke again. "She *is* Tasha."

"No," Alyssa said. "She is not." She sucked in air and tried to choke back the anger swirling inside her, threatening to break free. "What about Renley?"

"I... I don't know." Paul ducked deeper into the mist as a stray round pinged into the side of the structure, pelting them with stone fragments.

A slim figure dashed across the cavern and skidded to a stop near them. She was dressed in black body armor and a full-face helmet. The visor lightened, revealing a piercing feline gaze beneath a set of blond curls.

"Nel!" Alyssa called out.

The Rathadi kept her automatic rifle at the ready as she crouched beside them amid the chaos. "We need to get you out of here, now!" she said between heavy breaths. "We managed to surprise them, but we're outnumbered. They are regrouping."

"No," Alyssa shook her head. "I am not leaving."

"We have to keep you safe!" Nel urged. "The elders want you back. The ceremony—"

"I have to get inside," Alyssa said.

Paul and Nel stared at her. "Inside where?" Paul asked.

Alyssa patted the structure beside them.

"Inside the pyramid?" he asked. "How?"

They dropped down as another salvo strafed their makeshift cover, sending stinging shards at their heads. Alyssa pointed to the top of the pyramid. "From the summit."

"Seriously?" Paul called out. "We have to go back up there to get inside?"

"Another memory?" Nel asked Alyssa.

Alyssa nodded.

"The elders tell of Rathadi legends about a power hidden inside the sacred monument," Nel said, "a power that draws its strength from all the Rathadi." She grasped Paul's shoulder. "Go with Alyssa. We will cover you and will hold them off as long as we can."

"Thank you," Alyssa managed. She grabbed Paul's hand and took off. They raced up the stairs, three at a time, with Nel at their heels.

"We need to get to the sarcophagus!" she yelled.

"And then what?" Paul asked.

"Just keep up!" she called back, continuing the ascent at a full sprint.

A Purean soldier appeared on the stairs above. Alyssa and Paul dived down and flattened themselves against the stairs. A shot rang out behind them, and the Purean collapsed. "Keep going!" Nel yelled, lowering her rifle. They sprang up and continued to the top.

They reached the summit, breathing hard, and hunkered down at the sarcophagus. Four other Rathadi in body armor rallied to their position and formed a ring around them, shielding them from the Purean fire.

"Now what?" Paul yelled.

Alyssa pulled up her sleeve. She ripped off the bandage that covered the cut on her arm. She winced as she squeezed her wound, and the blood pooled at the top of her sutures.

"What are you doing?" Paul cried out.

Alyssa ran her palm over the wound, then brushed it along the side of the sarcophagus, coating it in her blood.

Paul stared at her open-mouthed as the seconds ticked by. "Is something supposed to—?"

The next word stuck in his throat when the sarcophagus began to descend.

"How did you?" he asked, baffled, then he stopped. "The memories…"

The sarcophagus slowly sank into the pyramid. When its top disappeared below the floor, a stone slab began to slide over the opening. Alyssa reached for Paul's hand again. "Let's go!" she yelled and leaped inside the descending sarcophagus, pulling him with her through the opening.

"Hold them off until it's sealed!" Nel's command rang as they lowered into the pyramid, and the gunfire intensified above them.

They hunkered down inside the sarcophagus as it lowered down a vertical shaft. Cool air drafted up from below and washed over them as the shaft opened up into a cavernous space that seemed to grow larger as they descended. Its triangular walls were sloped, their highest points merging into the shaft that led to the summit of the pyramid above them.

Alyssa struggled to remember the vision. "There was a crystal… it was red…"

"A red crystal?"

"I… I think so… I think it is the key—"

A shadow passed above. Alyssa glanced up. An instant before the shaft completely sealed, a figure dived through the gap and plummeted down.

"Watch out!" she cried out and reached for Paul, but it was too late. Nephthys landed behind him and flung him over the side of the sarcophagus.

"Paul!" Alyssa screamed as he tumbled into the darkness.

Nephthys thrust at her head. Alyssa raised her arm, just barely blocking the strike. She felt the bite of a blade as it drew blood along the back of her hand, and she hissed out in pain.

Nephthys struck out again, but Alyssa managed to trap her wrist. Nephthys didn't pull back. Instead, she pressed the dagger forward. It took every ounce of Alyssa's strength to keep the blade away from her throat.

Nephthys snarled at her from behind Tasha's features, the yellow eyes burning brightly. Alyssa hissed, pushing hard against the charge. Without warning, Nephthys pulled back. Alyssa staggered forward, her balance upset. Nephthys twisted and plunged down on top of Alyssa.

Alyssa gasped at the sting. She looked down and blinked in confusion. A black hilt jutted out from her chest, and a bright red patch blossomed around the blade. The dull burn spread like fire, rising into red-hot torment. Shadows danced in her vision. Darkness crept into her eyes.

Pain. Shooting, searing pain.

And then nothing.

———

PAUL FELL INTO THE DARKNESS, a scream frozen in his throat. He extended his left hand to the sarcophagus, clawing at its side as he rushed past. His fingers brushed a stone ledge at the bottom, and he latched onto it, pure terror turning his grip into a vise. The jerk sent waves of torment through his arm and shoulder, but he managed to hang on, dangling from his arm. He wrangled down the panic welling inside him and tried to swing his right arm up, fumbling for purchase, but his stump slipped off the narrow ledge.

Paul willed himself to hold on, the muscles in his left forearm growing tired, stretched to the breaking point. With every passing second, he was getting closer to the ground. He grunted with the effort, unable to control the tremors in his left arm.

Hold on!

His fingers gave out, and he slipped. He inhaled to scream —then his legs hit the ground, and he smashed to the floor, his terror temporarily forgotten, replaced by the shock to his ankles and knees. He fell forward, just managing to turn his head and avoiding smashing his visor into the stone.

He lay dazed as his battered body and mind sluggishly recouped, then he forced himself to his back with a groan.

The sarcophagus continued its descent, perched on a tall

stone column that sank into the floor beneath him. High above
the sarcophagus, a rectangular band of lights ignited, bathing
the top of the huge chamber in a soft, golden glow. A moment
later, a larger band below it illuminated a horizontal slice of the
sloping walls. Then another, and another. Each second, one
more section of the vast pyramid-shaped chamber was revealed
by a rectangular band of light, each band larger than the previous, traversing down the four walls toward the floor.

Paul gasped. The sloping walls were made up of great tiles
layered in pure gold, as if forged from a mountain of the
precious metal and molded into place inside this chamber. The
bands of lights reflected off the gold carvings, bathing their
strange panoramas in an alien yellow hue, from grassy
meadows brimming with exotic flowers to tree-covered mountains towering over boundless waters. Amid the landscapes,
countless scenes depicted the Rathadi, their hybrid bodies
carved meticulously into the vast golden canvas.

The last band lit up, illuminating the floor with a pale glow.
Paul's breath hitched. Even the fantastic carved murals could
not compare with the scene that enveloped him. Hundreds—
no, *thousands*—of life-sized Rathadi statues lined up in precise
row after row like ancient sentinels, covering the entire floor of
the immense chamber. He thought the Terracotta Army in
China had been mind boggling, but this… Each statue, lifelike
in its unique detail, rose amid its neighbors with its hands
extended forward, one hand resting atop the other, as if
forming an altar for the triangular crystal perched on the
open palms.

The sarcophagus reached the floor of the chamber, the
sound of stone against stone snapping Paul back. He pushed

himself to his knees, gritting his teeth and ignoring the protestations from his bruised body.

He spotted Tasha—*Nephthys*—hunched over inside the sarcophagus. She slowly rose, her back still to him.

He shuffled backward across the floor until his back touched a statue, then he crawled behind it, finding cover in the dim light.

Dread rippled through him. *Where is Alyssa…?*

He peeked out. Nephthys scanned the floor around the sarcophagus. She tilted her head, a vexed expression on her face. She stepped out of the sarcophagus and peered into the room, surveying the chamber. He spotted the black dagger in her hand and ducked behind the statue again, clenching his fists. *Alyssa…*

"Come out, come out, wherever you are…" Nephthys's mocking words in Tasha's voice rang through the cavern.

Her steps approached. Paul pressed his back against the cold stone, making himself as small as he could manage. He held his breath.

The footsteps stopped, then moved away.

Paul exhaled. He waited two more seconds then scampered to the next row, away from the sarcophagus and Nephthys, and crouched behind another statue.

He risked another glance. Nephthys had moved to the opposite side of the sarcophagus, circling it slowly. He popped up and dashed to the next row. He stayed low, keeping the sarcophagus between him and Nephthys as she stalked the chamber. They looped the chamber in a deadly round of hide-and-seek.

"I am not amused by this game," Nephthys's voice rang out.

Paul dashed back another row. A red glimmer in his peripheral vision caught his attention. He turned—and shrank under the piercing gaze of the statue before him. For a brief moment, time stood still as he stared into the lifelike eyes of the stone sentinel. He forced himself out of the trance.

The magnificent Rathadi before him was unlike any of the other sculptures, not only in the detail of the craftsmanship, but also the pose of its hands. Its arms were raised high into the air, palms forming a triangle in the Rathadi blessing. Draped around the neck of the statue hung a perfect stone carving of the sacred amulet. Inside its triangular opening rested a fist-sized triangular crystal, smoldering with a faint red glow.

Paul gasped as comprehension dawned, and Alyssa's words echoed through his mind. *The red crystal is the key...*

The key!

He wrapped his fingers around the gem and pulled on it, to no avail. He pulled harder.

Come on, you bloody—

A memory flashed across his mind. Paul used his left hand to shape his two gloves into the Rathadi blessing and pressed them along the perimeter of the crystal, just as Alyssa had done to unlock the Hall of Records. The crystal pulsed once, as if roused back to life, then slid out without resistance and dimmed. Paul released a breath he didn't know he had been holding and slipped the crystal into his pocket.

He took a steeling breath and straightened his shoulders, standing tall. He turned and faced Nephthys.

"You want me?" he growled. "Come get me, you maniacal shrew."

NEL'S EARS RANG. She pressed her palm to her brow, trying to stem the flow of the blood that caked the thick strands of hair falling to her face. She had been forced down to her knees, but her eyes were fierce as she glowered at the garrison of black-clad Pureans that surrounded her and the two dozen Rathadi. They kneeled, huddled in a circle, with their helmets removed and their hands held above their heads. They had been able to buy Alyssa time, but in the end the Pureans' numbers over-whelmed them. Dharr kneeled beside her, grimacing as he stared at Tef's lifeless body near the sarcophagus. Nel took in the score of Purean and Rathadi bodies that lay scattered at the summit and at the base of the pyramid. She clenched her jaw at the grief and senseless killing.

The sounds of stone grinding on stone filled the cavern and drew her back. The platform slid open. The Pureans aimed their weapons at the open shaft.

Nel held her breath.

She slumped when she recognized Nephthys, in Tasha's body, standing tall inside the sarcophagus as it raised from within the pyramid. The Pureans lowered their weapons.

Nephthys loomed over Paul who kneeled next to her, skin pale behind the visor of his helmet. Then Nel spotted Alyssa. She lay lifelessly on the floor of the sarcophagus, blood spilling from a wound in her chest. The sarcophagus stopped. Nephthys lifted Alyssa's lifeless body by her collar and threw her to the ground.

Dread surged through Nel's veins, each heartbeat hurling icy daggers into her heart. She crumpled. Perfect silence stretched through the cavern. The Rathadi held still as statues, their faces frozen with disbelief. Nel searched out Dharr's gaze in hopes for a bright spark against the darkness that had gripped her, but his face was a mask of pain, his eyes mirroring her own anguish and despondence.

"Horus's Legacy is over!" Nephthys's voice thundered through the cavern.

Paul stirred, and Nel caught his glance. He leaned forward on his knees, pressing against the side of the sarcophagus. He lifted his left hand just barely above the rim. A glint of red shone from between his gloved fingers. Her breath hitched.

Paul's eyes moved to Alyssa. He brought his right arm to his body and drew an outline of a necklace on his chest. His eyes moved to Alyssa again.

Nel's thoughts raced then understanding struck.

A distraction… He needs a distraction.

She evened her breathing, keeping it shallow and silent, and curled her palms into tight fists. She slowly rose to her feet.

"No," she said, defiantly. "Horus's Legacy will never be—"

Nephthys surged forward and grasped Nel by her throat. She lifted her up like a ragdoll.

Paul dived on top of Alyssa and ripped open her vest, revealing the golden amulet. He pressed the red crystal into the triangular opening.

For an unimaginably long second nothing happened, then the crystal pulsed—and again—like an ancient heart waking from an age-old slumber. With each pulse, a brighter wave of light rippled to the walls and into the shaft beneath the sarcophagus, before the entire pyramid erupted into a blinding red blaze.

Nephthys dropped Nel and stared at Alyssa's body as it

seemed to surge with electricity. It rose into the air, carried by invisible currents.

Alyssa's body jolted and contorted into a back-breaking arch. She gasped.

DARKNESS.

For a fleeting eternity, she was the focus, the convergence.

The light burst out, rushing away in a thousand streams of brilliance. The lights slowed and stopped, hovering, surrounding the girl like stars against the jet-black of a night sky.

No... not stars.

One point of light brightened then closed in—slowly at first, then faster, gathering speed before it slammed into her, ripping her breath away. It shattered into images and voices that swarmed her mind.

She reeled.

Another point pulsed and advanced.

She cowered.

I'm not ready!

It rushed at her. Then another.

The girl screamed as the lights flooded her consciousness, drowning her in a relentless storm—

There... a familiar warmth. A pinprick in the distance. Slowly, through the onslaught and haze she reached for it.

Amah...

The light grew and took shape. She clung to the familiar contours of the face, focusing.

Gradually, the storm inside her ebbed, swirling into a tight vortex, carving order out of chaos. She became the whirlwind that raged within her, controlling it and bending it to her will.

A pair of eyes gazed down, two green orbs, glinting, feline, ever aware. *Amah* smiled, her serenity and confidence filling Alyssa with strength.

You shall know no fear.

Amah's face shimmered then faded away.

No, don't leave... the girl pleaded. She reached out, but new lights flooded into her like an ocean pouring into a cup. The ripple of energy surged over her, singeing the nerves on her skin as she struggled to control it and guide each piece into its place.

She was engulfed by a blaze that raged endlessly within her body, and she recoiled beneath each light as if it were a whip on her bare skin. A thousand voices filled her mind, threatening to burst her open.

After an eternity, she stared out into the darkness. A single light remained, red and foreboding.

I am inception.

The words echoed in the girl's head as the light expanded and surged into her. It raged through her flesh, her mind and vision, bathing everything in a burning red glow, growing hotter with every heartbeat.

She screamed.

———

PAUL'S MOUTH gaped open as the feeling in his chest threatened to tear him from the inside. Alyssa's body seemed to shimmer, her long brown hair stirring in the electric currents that streamed through the air. The pyramid blazed red, like a star coming alive, flooding the vast cavern in a crimson fire.

She's alive...

The light stopped as abruptly as it had exploded.

Alyssa opened her eyes and gleaming red pupils flared at him. Paul gasped, and the Rathadi and Pureans stood still like the statues beneath their feet, mesmerized by the sight before them.

Nephthys lunged at Alyssa, lighting fast, the onyx dagger driving for Alyssa's chest.

Alyssa's motion seemed unhurried, but her hand lashed out faster than Paul's eye could track, and she wrapped her palm around Nephthys's wrist.

Nephthys's face twisted in disbelief, then pain, as Alyssa held her at arm's length then forced her to her knees.

Nephthys snarled, fighting to escape the grasp, but Alyssa held her motionless. Their gazes locked. Nephthys stared into Alyssa's eyes, as if unable to break the fiery spell. Her struggling slowed before it ceased completely.

Alyssa moved her palm to Nephthys's forehead. She bent down to her, lips brushing against Nephthys's ear, and whispered a word.

Nephthys sank to the floor.

The silence that stretched through the cavern was complete. Then, as if a spell broke, the Pureans rushed Alyssa as one. She raised her head, and red eyes burned into the soldiers like twin flames, stopping them in their tracks.

"It is over," Alyssa said.

Paul flinched at the sound. Her words rang not with the sound of a single throat, but as if uttered by countless voices.

The Pureans stood motionless, held by an invisible force.

Alyssa lifted her hand. "Your fight is over," she said, and the Purean soldiers lowered their weapons.

Dharr leaped up and barked a command, and the Rathadi surged to their feet. The Pureans stood in a trance and did not resist as the Rathadi disarmed them.

Alyssa faced Paul again. Her lips curved into a small, familiar smile. The red glow in her eyes faded, and she slumped to the floor.

Paul rushed to her side. Alyssa's skin was pale and clammy, and her eyes shone a dull gray. He cradled her head.

"Ally..." he muttered, unable to put any strength in his words.

Dharr kneeled at her side across from Paul, his eyes boring into her. "The voices?" he asked, his voice trembling. "Who...?"

Alyssa swiveled to him, and a confused expression rippled through her face. "The Rathadi..." she answered weakly, gazing out beyond him.

"What Rathadi?" Paul asked.

"The Rathadi," Alyssa repeated. "The crystals... their lives... their ancient power."

Dharr inhaled sharply. "The ancient power? Is that how you defeated Nephthys?"

Alyssa nodded slowly, holding him in the same unfocused gaze.

Paul's skin prickled with a sense of foreboding. He grasped her head between his palms and leaned over her. Alyssa looked through him as if lost in a far-away thought. The realization slowly dawned.

"Your eyes," he said, dread rising in his chest.

"It came at a price," she replied.

"You... you're blind..." Paul's voice faltered.

"Alyssa! Paul!" Nel's voice rang from the edge of the summit.

He swung around. Nel kneeled over George Renley's body.

Paul squeezed Alyssa's arm. "It's Renley."

"Take me to him," she said.

The Rathadi and Pureans parted as Paul led her to Renley. He lay on the ground, his gloved hands pressed against the red spot that stained the front of his suit. Alyssa kneeled beside him.

Renley moved his hands to his helmet. Nel reached out and held them back. "The bioweapon..." she said.

"I am already dead," Renley replied, his voice weak. "I wish to taste the ancient air, as my grandfather did before me."

Nel's face darkened, but she released his arms, and Renley removed his helmet. Paul guided Alyssa's hands to Renley's face.

"Did you...?" Renley asked. "Did you stop them?"

Alyssa nodded. "I did. We all did."

"And Tasha? Is she gone... forever?"

Alyssa remained silent, her gray eyes mirroring Renley's anguish.

Renley gripped Alyssa's hands. "Bring her back," he pleaded. "Promise me you will bring her back." Blood mixed with tears and traced his sharp features in crimson rivulets before weeping to the ground. He stared into the empty space above them. "Thank you for... for showing me..."

His voice faded, his breathing turning to slow, rattling

gasps. He shuddered, his face knotting in a grimace. Renley inhaled one more time, then his chest stood still.

Alyssa joined her palms in the Rathadi blessing and placed them on Renley's head.

"You are George Renley," she whispered. "Son of George Renley. You shall know no fear."

Alyssa seemed to gather all her remaining strength. She leaned on Paul and Dharr as she gained her feet.

"The time of war is over," she said to the Rathadi and Pureans before her. Her voice was pitched low, but it carried full of authority and reproach. "There has been enough blood shed between our people. Because of my weakness, countless Pureans have perished on our home island. Thousands more have died through the millennia as we brought this senseless war to other worlds. Ages ago, I counseled peace, but Horus did not listen. Though we may never be united as one people, there shall be truce. The time for conflict has come to an end."

Silence spread through the cavern as her words sank in.

Paul stared at her. "Who are you?" he asked.

"Thoth?" Dharr muttered reverently.

She tightened her grip on Paul's arm. "He lives inside me, as do countless Rathadi beside him," Alyssa said. "As does our first ancestor."

A cold wash swept through Paul, raising goose bumps on his arms. "Ra...?" he said, wonder filling his voice.

Alyssa crumpled.

ALYSSA SHIFTED on the thin mattress. She inhaled and felt her ribs expand. Stretching, she tested her arms and legs. She ached in every muscle, but she was whole and alive. She rubbed her eyes and took a moment to shed the sleep from her brain and allow the visions of the night to give way to the day. She blinked, closed her eyes, and blinked again. The darkness remained.

The memories swept through her like a sandstorm, and she felt as choked as if she had swallowed dust. The sense of loss squeezed her gut.

She pressed her cheek to the meager lump that passed as a pillow and forced herself to breathe. In and out. And again. Slowly, the panicky daze cleared. She kept her breaths shallow and silent.

A palm touched her arm.

"Ally?"

Alyssa's heart seemed to freeze, then it began to pound. "Dad?"

Kade wrapped his arms around her, and she took in the familiar scent that came with him. The scent of home.

In another lifetime…

A muffled sob racked him as he pulled her into his arms.

"Oh, Ally…"

Her tears came, desolate and endless. He held her in silence, rocking her slowly as she pressed her wet eyes into his shoulder.

She swallowed, tasting salt. "You're here… How?"

Kade pushed her back gently and held her at arm's length. She could feel his gaze on her, soaking in the sight of her body. "It seems the minister called in some major favors."

"Where are we?" Alyssa asked.

"The El Aini."

"And Paul? Is he…?"

"He is fine," Kade said. "He's been at your side, checking in on you."

Alyssa heaved a sigh of relief. "The others?"

"They are fine, Ally. Don't you worry about it right now."

She lifted her hand to her eyes to wipe them. She stopped. "My eyes… Is there anything…?"

She felt his palms tense on her arms. "The doctors say there is no physical damage, but…"

"But what?"

"They don't know if you will ever regain your sight," he said, his voice on the verge of cracking.

Alyssa stayed silent as she processed the words.

He squeezed her arm again. "Ally—" he started.

"Dad—" she said at the same time.

"You go," Kade said.

She took a deep breath, looking for a place to start. "When I was with the Rathadi," she finally said, "I found out that my Hybrid blood… is not from my mother."

Kade sighed. "I suspected you would find out… eventually."

"So you knew?" Alyssa's voice hardened. "That you were not my father?"

Kade eased down on the bed beside her and wrapped her hands between his palms. His fingers were rough from years in the field, and warm against her skin. "I have always been and will always be your father, Ally," he said. "I have raised you as my own daughter. Your mom was pregnant when we met. I didn't care whose child she carried. I loved her more than life itself, and I knew I would love the child she carried inside her like it was my own." He pulled up her hands and kissed them. "I never thought of you as anybody but my own daughter from the moment I first saw you born."

Alyssa felt heat behind her eyelids again. She blinked to stop the tears.

"Horus is my father…" she whispered.

His hands wavered for a heartbeat. "And that woman… Nephthys—" he started.

Alyssa bolted up at the name. Dozens of images flooded her, cracking across her mind's eye.

"Ally!" Kade cried out. "Are you all right?"

Alyssa tried to control the onslaught, make sense of the images. The ghost of a memory stirred. She pressed her fists to her temples, willing herself to remember. There… swimming in her memory like the shadow of a fish out of sight, beneath the surface of a lake. She willed the image closer. The recollection flashed across her mind, the jagged pieces falling together.

"The Pureans! They have the cure!" she cried out.

"What? Slow down. What are you talking about?"

The words flooded from Alyssa. She dared not stop for fear of losing them if they didn't spill out. "You must tell Paul. Tell him that the cure is on the Purean truck. That Nephthys brought treatment for her soldiers in case they were exposed!"

"How do you know?"

"Nephthys... before I put her to sleep, our minds touched and..." Her head swam.

"Ally, you have to rest."

"You have to tell them!" Alyssa cried as the nausea crept from her stomach to her head. "Promise me!"

"I will, of course," Kade said. "For now, rest."

Alyssa didn't fight him when he held her close and guided her head down to the pillow.

———

ALYSSA OPENED HER EYES.

"I was wondering when you'd come around," Paul said. His face shone in the bright overhead lights.

"Paul?" Alyssa blinked and reached up to her eyes. "I can see!"

Paul looked at her quizzically. "Xander did mention complications from the procedure, but I didn't think blindness was—"

"Xander's procedure?" Alyssa cut in. She glanced around, taking in the familiar features of the medical bay of the *Valediction*. "Where...? I... I thought I was at the El Aini."

"The El Aini?"

"Where is Kade?"

Paul lifted his brow. "Kade? He's in Cairo… in jail." He leaned forward. "Alyssa—"

Alyssa's mind reeled. "What about Nephthys? And the Hall of Records? The battle with the Pureans?"

Paul reached out and grasped her hands between his palms. "Alyssa, remember Xander's procedure earlier today? He said that the side effects may induce some false memories… that they may feel absolutely real."

Alyssa pulled back. "No! It *was* real! I—"

Paul reached out again. "Don't you fret," he said. "I'm here. Everything is going to be all—"

His face twisted. He stared down at the blade that protruded from his chest. Behind him, Nephthys snarled, yellow eyes glowing madly.

All sound disappeared, and time slowed to a standstill. Paul slumped to his knees. His eyes locked onto Alyssa's in a silent embrace before they glassed over, and he crumbled to the ground.

Nephthys loomed over Alyssa and raised the blade again. She slashed down—

Alyssa woke at the edge of a scream, breathless, surrounded by darkness. She shuddered and pressed her fists against her temples.

It was a dream… Just a dream… She grasped at the vestiges of the memories, turning in nonsensical ways.

Is it still night?

From the carousel of visions came some order—a slow

awareness. The dry coolness of the air and the smell of antiseptic.

The hospital.

My eyes…

Alyssa blinked and strained into the darkness.

Nothing.

The tears came unbidden, welling up from somewhere deep inside. She pressed her hands against her eyes as if trying to stop them, hide them. Wetness seeped between her fingers, until her mind dragged her into the oblivion of sleep once again.

———

ALYSSA WOKE at the sound of the door opening. For a brief moment, a thought hovered at the edge of a memory… a dream… It buzzed at the fringe of her senses before disappearing like grains of sand in the wind, transforming into a familiar shuffle of feet.

Alyssa sat up. "Hi Dad," she said.

Kade moved to the bed and gave her a hug, letting out a soft chuckle. "For years you've called me by my first name. Now that you know I'm not your biological father, you insist on calling me Dad. You may be the Legacy of all the Rathadi, but you're still acting like a teenager."

A knock rasped against the door.

"Am I interrupting something?" Paul's voice rang into the room.

"Paul!" Alyssa called out.

He stepped inside the room and wrapped his arms around her. She took in his scent, its intensity stirring up images of his body next to her, surrounded by a red glow. She pushed those thoughts aside.

"How are you feeling?" he asked.

"Fantastic," she lied. "Did you get the message about the cure?"

"Yes," Paul said. "I contacted the minister. He was quite helpful in recovering the vials from the vehicle. He sent samples to the WHO and to the Rathadi, and has prioritized the research in the facility here."

"Who would have thought?" Kade quipped. "Turns out the minister also provided quite the cover story for what happened in the hall. *'The test of the emergency procedures around the site has been a complete success,'* " Kade said in his best impression of the minister's voice. "He even managed to convince everybody that the weapons fire people reported was part of an emergency military scenario the army was practicing. If he keeps this up, I may have to rethink my opinion of him." He paused. "He did ask me to tell you to just knock next time," he said. "What's that all about?"

Alyssa gave a soft smile. "I'll tell you some other time."

"Can't wait," Kade replied.

"What about Kamal? Any word on where he may be?" Alyssa asked.

"Nothing so far." Kade's voice grew serious again. "He has disappeared completely."

Paul put his hand on her arm. "The information about the cure," he said. "How did you know?"

"In the hall, when Nephthys and I... connected," Alyssa replied. "Her mind was still vulnerable, so soon after she reaped…" She trailed off, her stomach clenching at the word. "Where is she now?"

"She is being held aboard the *Valediction*."

"The *Valediction*?"

"Yes," Paul said. "Dharr is there, too, working with Xander to figure out some way to keep her contained and under control —and to prevent her from doing additional harm." He paused. "What you did to her in the hall… Can you do it again?"

"I don't know," Alyssa said. "But even if I could, it wouldn't last. She will recover again, and she will continue to get stronger—if we allow her to."

"Well, I for one am glad I never met her," Kade said, "but based on everything I've heard, she sounds too dangerous to keep alive."

Paul's palm tensed on Alyssa's arm at Kade's words.

Kade cleared his throat. "I'm sorry, I know you and Tasha went through—"

"You're right," Alyssa cut in. "Nephthys is too dangerous. I need to talk with Dharr and Xander."

She couldn't see Paul's face, but she heard the change in his voice, the deliberate calm. "I will set up a call," he said.

"No, not a call. I need to talk to them in person."

"I'm not sure it's wise for them to leave the *Valediction*," Paul said.

"I need to go back there," Alyssa said.

"Ally, I think you need more time to recover," Kade said.

Alyssa's limbs tingled with fatigue as exhaustion came over her in waves, starting in her muscles and sinking into her bones. She reached out and grasped Kade's arm. "I don't have time to recover," she said, her voice tight.

ALYSSA NESTLED AGAINST PAUL, curled up on the plushy sofa in her suite on the *Valediction*. The warmth of his body went a long way toward helping her forget about the sixteen-hour journey that had brought them here. After learning about Alyssa's request, Claudia Tibaldi had personally arranged transportation for her and Paul, and less than a day later, they were once again aboard the Society's megayacht. After a brief, but decidedly warmer welcome than she had received on the previous visit, she was ushered to her suite and told that Clay and Xander were on their way.

The knock at the door stirred her. The smell of unburned tobacco filled her nostrils before the door opened completely, and Xander entered the room. Alyssa recognized Clay's shuffling gait behind him. She beamed.

"Hi Clay," she said. She held out her arms as he approached her, and he wrapped her in a warm hug. She smiled at the familiar feeling of the stubble on his chin as it gently scratched against her cheek.

"Mr. Hart," Alyssa said after releasing Clay's embrace. "Thank you for coming."

"Miss Morgan," Xander's drawl filled her ears, seeming even thicker in the dark, "it is a real pleasure to see you again." He coughed. "I mean... my apologies for the choice of words..." She heard the familiar sound of him chewing the cigar with renewed vigor.

"Has there been any news on the treatment for the Rathadi?" she asked Clay.

"The WHO have completed the preliminary tests," Clay replied. "So far, the results have been encouraging"

Alyssa breathed a sigh of relief. "That's good news. What about Nephthys? Where is she now?"

"Sedated and restrained in a cell with four Rathadi guards around it," Clay said. "And another four stationed outside in the corridor."

"I must admit, your message was a bit cryptic," Xander interjected.

"What I'm about to ask you is... sensitive," Alyssa said.

"You certainly do know how to make it intriguing," Xander chuckled.

"What have you been able to find out about Nephthys?" Alyssa asked.

"Not much, unfortunately," Xander replied, the mirth fading from his voice. "We have kept her sedated for security reasons, but that limits what we can find out about her."

Alyssa chewed on her bottom lip, suddenly hesitant about her plan. As if sensing her internal battle, Paul reached out and took her hand in his palm. She had shared her scheme with him. To her surprise, he fully supported it. She took a deep breath.

"You said that if things don't go as planned, your procedure has the risk of erasing somebody's memories completely. Is that correct?" she asked.

"Indeed," Xander replied.

"Can you make it happen on purpose?"

"Wipe out somebody's memories on purpose?" Xander asked, taken aback. "Do you realize what you're asking."

"Completely," Alyssa replied. "Can you do it?"

"I suppose it's possible," Xander answered cautiously.

"What will happen to that person? Will they be able to learn?" Alyssa asked.

"Possibly," Xander said. "But it could also leave them permanently brain damaged."

"Alyssa," Clay said, "what you're proposing is—"

"I know what I'm proposing," Alyssa interrupted, a measure sharper than she intended. She turned back to Xander. "So you're saying this is possible."

"Yes," he replied, unable to hide the apprehension from his voice. "Assuming we want to move forward, did you have a time frame in mind for this procedure?"

"The sooner, the better," Paul chimed in before Alyssa could reply. "Believe me, Tasha would rather be dead than be a puppet for that woman."

———

THE MOIST AIR coated Alyssa's eyelashes in salt and tousled her long hair. Like the ocean that stirred within her, the breeze was a mere hint of the power of the sea, a power that when roused could toss whole ships like toys. She savored the smell of the brine, drawing the salty air into her nose and mouth, as she stood on the terrace of her suite facing the water beneath her.

She shifted her hand from the banister and found Dharr's arm. The texture of his skin was rough beneath her palm, his muscles tense, as he absorbed her words.

"Have you told Paul yet?" Dharr asked.

"No," Alyssa said softly, with a trace of guilt.

Silence stretched between them.

"The Rathadi scientists confirmed it," he finally said, breaking the silence. "The cure we recovered appears to be working."

Alyssa's heart quaked, relief flooding through her. She squeezed his arm tighter.

"And the minister informed me that he was able to obtain diplomatic credentials for the Rathadi," he added.

"Have the Rathadi agreed?" she asked.

"They will be there," he said.

Another silence stretched between them.

"Dharr… I'm so sorry about Tef," Alyssa said.

"Tef was a soldier first," he said. "She knew the risk." His voice was strong, but he could not hide the anguish that embittered it.

"We would never have succeeded without her. Without all of you."

"Succeeded?" Dharr scoffed. "Is that what we did? At what cost?"

They remained quiet for a long time, each lost in their own thoughts.

"Paul deserves to know," Dharr said, finally.

"I will tell him, I promise. After we know about Tasha."

———

ALYSSA STEPPED ALONG THE CORRIDOR, her hand on Paul's arm. The sound of a heavy door opening filled the hallway before Paul moved again. Alyssa heard the door lock behind them.

"We just passed a couple of Rathadi guards," Paul said. "She is still being kept under tight security until Xander confirms the results of the procedure."

They stopped again. "We're here," Paul said.

Alyssa's skin tingled with anticipation. She heard Clay's footsteps approach.

"How is she doing?" Alyssa asked when Clay stopped in front of them.

"She woke up a little while ago," Clay replied. "She's in bed, resting, under constant surveillance. Xander is reviewing the data, but from what we've seen so far, things could not have gone better."

"What does that mean?" Alyssa asked.

"Based on the preliminary results, she has the intellectual capability of a six-year-old," Clay said.

"Can she learn new things?" Paul asked.

Clay snickered. "Not only that, but she scored off the charts on the IQ test Xander administered. It's too early to be certain, but Xander believes her ability to form new short- and long-term memories is completely intact."

"Who would have thought we had another genius in our midst?" Paul quipped.

Clay chuckled again, then his voice turned serious. "Are you ready to meet Tasha 2.0?"

"Let's do this," Alyssa said.

"I'll be out here with the guards to give you and Paul some time alone with her," Clay said as he unlocked the door and opened it.

Alyssa took in the smell of the room. It smelled like... bubblegum and crayons.

"She's on the bed," Paul said. "And she seems fascinated by her hands."

They stepped inside, and the door closed behind them. Alyssa heard a stir from the bed, sounding as if Tasha sat up. Paul gasped.

"What is it?" Alyssa asked.

"Her eyes," Paul said. "They aren't yellow anymore. They're violet again."

Paul pulled up a chair for Alyssa and helped her down, then pointed her in Tasha's direction. He pulled another chair for himself and eased into it.

"Hi," Alyssa said softly.

"Who are you?"

The voice startled Alyssa. It was Tasha's, but rather than carrying Tasha's usual sarcasm, or Nephthys's bitterness, this voice was filled with the innocence and curiosity of a young child.

"My name is Alyssa," she said. "And this is Paul."

"What's wrong with your eyes?" Tasha asked.

Alyssa winced. *How many more times will I hear this question?* "I can't see," she replied.

"Aww... I'm sorry," Tasha said. "Will you play with me?"

"Sure!" Paul chimed in eagerly. He scooted his chair closer to the bed.

Tasha giggled, making her sound like a little girl.

Paul pressed a stuffed animal into Alyssa's hand. She took it and pointed it at Tasha, shaking it.

Tasha giggled again. "Will you be my friends?" she asked.

Alyssa froze, a shadow of a smile dimmed the raw edge of her emotions. "Always," she replied softly.

"Renley left his entire estate and wealth to Tasha," Paul said, as they continued playing with her. "It will be more than sufficient to guarantee her a comfortable life and the best care."

Alyssa smiled absentmindedly.

"She'll be okay," Paul said. "We will make sure of it, right?"

"I know he would rest well knowing that you are taking care of her," Alyssa said.

"You?" Paul asked. Tasha squealed with delight at something he did. "Not *we*?"

Alyssa tried not to react, wanting to draw out this time. She pressed her lips together, forcing them into a smile.

"Hey… what's going on?" Paul stopped, his voice betraying his concern.

"More!" Tasha giggled.

"Can we talk?" Alyssa asked. "Alone?"

"Awww…" Tasha sniffed.

"Yeah, sure," Paul said, his voice tight. He helped Alyssa stand, and she took his arm.

"Where are you going?" Tasha asked.

"Don't worry, we'll be back before you know it!" Paul said.

"Okay, bye!" Tasha called after them.

They knocked on the door.

It swung open. "So what do you think—?" Clay started.

"In a minute, Clay," Alyssa said. "Sorry…" she muttered as they moved past him.

Paul guided her to another section of the hallway before they stopped. Alyssa took Paul's arms in her hands and faced him. She steeled herself, more for Paul's sake than her own.

"I'm dying," she said.

"Wh-what?" Paul stammered.

Alyssa regarded him through her unseeing eyes, wordlessly and unblinking.

"But… you… you are the Legacy! You're the Daughter of Ra!"

"Paul…" Alyssa said. "I need you." She moved closer.

"No," Paul said, his voice crumbling. He held her off. "No, you can't. Not after everything… that's not fair!"

"What happened in the hall… I told you there was a price."

Paul pulled his arms from her palms. "Your eyes!" he cried. "Losing your sight isn't a high enough price?"

Alyssa reached out and touched his cheek. Paul took a deep, shuddering breath, but did not move away.

"The others? Do they know?" he asked.

Alyssa nodded.

"So I'm the last to find out?"

"I dreaded this the most…" Alyssa said, her voice finally failing her. "More than telling Kade… More than anything…"

He sobbed and pulled her into his arms, holding her close. "Isn't there anything that can be done?" he asked, tears frosting his voice.

Alyssa gently pushed him away and held him at arm's length.

"There is," she said.

THE THIN LAYER of fog lingered against Alyssa's feet and clung to the delicate robe, pasting it against her bare skin. She inhaled deeply, letting the scent of the moist air flood her nostrils and its bitter taste fill her mouth. The energy quivered within her like an ocean of power.

Alyssa stepped onto the cold, smooth stone of the sacred monument, and the cloth shifted and fluttered gently against her skin, stirring memories, ancient and new, and sending them rippling through her mind...

Amah places her hands on my head, her thumbs and forefingers shaping a triangle in the blessing of our people, representing the rays of the sun that give life to us. "Horus, my son, you are worthy of that name, and of the animal companion you have chosen," she says.

Seven levels of forty-nine stairs separate me from my new beginning. Each of the seven levels symbolizes a year of my life. A year lived without the animal gift. A life incomplete. I take the first step, counting the stairs silently—

The command bracelet that circled Alyssa's left forearm brushed against Kade's biosuit as he strode at her side together with Paul, guiding her ascent. Dharr's steady breaths echoed behind Alyssa, blending in with Nel's soft footsteps beside him. They continued climbing the stairs of the ancient structure...

Horemheb, my loyal general, strides beside me as we ascend the hallowed structure, pain carved into his strong features. I have lived with the blood of the falcon for more than eight decades, bestowed with the gifts of his magnificent sight, his strength and speed, his intuition. I move my hand to the ornate patch that covers my left eye. How close I came to losing these gifts completely—

The chanting from hundreds of Rathadi throats drew Alyssa back as it reverberated through the cavern, filling her ears. The Egyptian military had arranged transportation and privacy for their sojourn to this hall, which had remained undisturbed for millennia until they trespassed into it less than a year ago...

I climb the pyramid wordlessly, unable to ignore William Drake's triumphant stare burning into my back and the pistol aimed at my head. Paul's shuddering breaths fill my ears as he trudges beside me, his wounded arm in a sling... Drake's eyes glint in the dim light of the cavern, then his face contorts... My body begins to throb as Thoth's ancient weapon surges into every cell, awakening my Hybrid consciousness for the first time—

The chanting drew to a crescendo and stopped when they reached the summit.

"We're here," Paul said. Alyssa cleared her mind of the memories and came about, sensing the gazes of the Rathadi that have gathered beneath them. Kade and Paul took their places at each side of her as Dharr and Nel turned on the step below, ready to address the Rathadi.

"A month ago, Horus was taken from us," Dharr began, his strong voice reverberating through the vast chamber, "killed in a malicious plan devised by Nephthys. That night marked the death of many of our family, our friends. Those of us who survived were left on the brink of extinction. But perish we shall not. For though Horus was taken from us on that night, his Legacy continued. Before he left to become one with our ancestors, he joined in the sacred Bond of Legacy with his daughter, Alyssa Morgan, who had been raised by Kade Morgan as his own." He paused. "Many of you questioned whether this... *human half-breed* was a fit vessel for Horus, and fit to be his true Legacy. On this day we stand before her, united, questioning it no longer." He swiveled to Alyssa. "Behold the one true Legacy, Alyssa Morgan, Daughter of Horus and Anja."

Alyssa lowered her head, and Dharr placed the golden chain over her head. The weight of the heavy amulet around her neck felt familiar, and warmth spread through her body. A gentle memory stirred the hairs on the back of her neck.

"The Rathadi are offering their blessing," Paul whispered from behind her.

Alyssa envisioned the hall and the Rathadi surrounding the sacred pyramid, lifting their hands in the blessing of their people—of *her* people. She straightened her shoulders and swallowed to gain her voice.

"Let us remember those without whose sacrifice we would not stand here today," Alyssa said. "Heru-pa will live inside each of us forever, as will all the Rathadi who have perished in this war." She paused as the image of Tef's shimmering face flashed through her mind. "Nephthys is no more. The Pureans have vowed to honor the truce between our people. The time of war has passed." She gathered herself, struggling to keep her voice steady for her next words. "The time of Nephthys has passed... and the time of Horus has passed."

The Rathadi chanting began anew as she turned. Kade and Paul guided her to the sarcophagus. Every step had her heart thudding faster, louder. She placed her hand on the stone, and dread added to the cold lump in her belly. She summoned all her strength and entered the sarcophagus then lay down. The cold glass beneath her that formed the base of the new cryochamber woke shivers under her skin.

Horemheb's dark eyes glisten. "My Lord, I do not understand. Why?"

My single eye meets his pair as I place my right hand on his shoulder, his posture rigid like a carving under my touch.

"One day, I shall be unearthed by my descendants, and I will live again," I tell him. "But today, my final memory shall be written."

Kade pressed his gloved hand against Alyssa's cheek. "I refuse to think of you as gone," he said, his voice cracking under his own words.

Alyssa did not try to blink back her tears. "Goodbye, Dad," she said.

Another gloved hand touched her cheek.

Paul...

"This isn't right..." he whispered.

Dharr stepped forward. "Are you ready?"

Alyssa's throat went dry, as if it had never known moisture. "Yes," she whispered.

A sob escaped Paul's lips. "Remember, the cryosleep will be activated when the glass lid closes," he said. "If anything goes wrong, you can open it from the inside. You can also use the command bracelet... And we have installed sensors and will be monitoring—"

Alyssa squeezed his hand. "Paul... we've been through this."

He choked back another sob.

"It is time," Alyssa said.

The Rathadi chanting carried through the cavern, its strangeness hauntingly beautiful in its richness and simplicity. Dharr pressed a button, and the glass lid slid over the sarcophagus's glass chamber.

Alyssa felt the tremor in her hands and fought to still it.

I am Alyssa Sarah Morgan.

The lid closed, and the Rathadi voices and echoes of the hall were reduced to complete silence.

Daughter of Horus and Anja.

A hiss of air. Cold. Freezing. Alyssa shuddered. Coldness coursed through her body.

Blood of Ra.

I close my eyes. *Amah* gazes down at me, her feline eyes smiling, calming, and full of love. A warmth fills me, radiating into my limbs as the ancient power courses through me again.

I know no fear.

PAUL WAS SQUEEZED into a tiny chair in the brightly colored room. He picked up one of the cards with his right hand. He lifted it up and turned it around. He flipped it through his fingers. The little gears and servo motors in his prosthesis whirled softly beneath its skin-like texture. He was still getting used to this technological marvel that Clay and Xander developed in collaboration with the Rathadi, but it felt more a part of himself every single day.

"Come on!" Tasha poked his arm impatiently, snapping him out of his thoughts.

"Sorry," Paul said. He smiled a distracted smile and laid the card on the table in front of her.

"This one's a circle," he said, tracing the red circle on the card. "See?" He looked at Tasha. "Now you try."

Tasha pointed to the card, tracing the circle. "Cir-cle," she repeated.

"Strong work!" Paul said. "I'd better watch out. You'll catch up to me at Oxford before long!"

Tasha beamed at his tone as he picked out another card.

"And this one?" he asked, tracing the three lines of the triangle. "You remember this shape?"

Tasha stared at it, scrunching her face.

"This one's called a triangle," Paul said.

"R... R... ian..." Tasha stuttered.

"Close," Paul said, laughing. "I know it's harder. It starts with a *T* not *R*. Tri-an-gle."

Tasha looked at him, a puzzled expression on her face.

Paul's phone rang.

"Sorry," he said, fishing for it in his pocket. He glanced at the caller ID. "School... figures..." He stood and answered it, turning away from the table.

Tasha studied the card. Her eyes tightened. She followed the contours of the triangle with her finger. Slowly her hands came together, and she joined her thumbs and forefingers, forming a triangle between her palms over the card. She cocked her head then lifted her palms to the window and into the sun. She stared through her palms at the light, her pupils widening despite the glare, a hint of golden amber breaking through the deep violet.

"R... R... *Ra,*" she whispered.

THE END

Continue the story with:

DAWN OF RA
Book One of the Blood of Ra Prequel

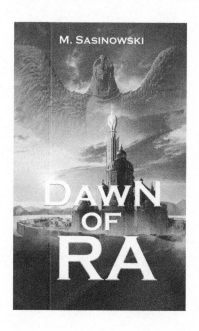

Millennia before Alyssa, Paul, and Tasha…
One island, two ancient races.
A young boy, exiled to a distant land, rises to become
worshipped as the falcon-headed god.

This is how it all began.

CHAPTER 1

The boy stalked through the tall grass, noiseless as a shadow, eyes glued to his mark. The afternoon sun caught the smooth scales in the brush ahead, sprinkling the vines with dancing sparks. The two-foot-long reptile seemed oblivious to the boy's presence as it raked leaves from the sinewy branches of the brittlebush with its powerful jaws.

He braved another step, rolling his foot in the soft soil from heel to ball. The lizard lifted its head and flicked its forked tongue in and out of its mouth, tasting the moist summer air. The crest around its neck flared then fluttered nervously, displaying a brilliant green.

The boy froze mid-step and held his breath. This was as close as he had ever stood to a Malachite Lizard. It was an immature male, the neck crest half-grown and still almost translucent, but the boy knew that what this razor-toothed menace lacked in size it made up for in speed—and wicked temper.

For several heartbeats neither moved. Then the boy pounced.

The reptile twisted and scurried for the undergrowth. For a moment it looked like it might escape, but the boy leaped in the air and stretched—

He landed on the lizard with a grunt and snatched it around the midsection with both hands, pinning it to the ground.

The beast hissed, its neck crest on full display. The boy pressed down, mindful of the reptile's claws and the twin rows of sharp teeth that lined its jaw. He slid up and pinned the animal's neck to the ground while he used his free hand to reach behind him and pull the large canvas sack from his belt.

He shook the sack open with his left while he slid his right palm along the body of the reptile until he reached its thrashing tail, then grasped it firmly. With a grunt, he lifted it off the ground, keeping the snapping jaws as far away from his body as he could manage. A triumphant smile spread across his face as he moved the bag under the squirming beast.

Abruptly, the lizard dropped to the ground and scurried away. The boy blinked, staring at his right fist, still clenched around the writhing tail. His mind struggled to catch up with what just happened.

The snickering behind him snapped him back.

"Behold, Heru-pa, mighty conqueror of lizard tails!" the young voice called out.

Heru-pa whirled. Set's ice-blue eyes crinkled with barely concealed amusement. He scrutinized the tail in Heru-pa's hand with exaggerated curiosity, revealing the gleam of white teeth against the dark of his face. "What a magnificent specimen you've ensnared. Mia is going to be so impressed."

Heru-pa flung the wiggling appendage at his friend. "I forgot they did that."

Set dodged the flying tail with annoying nimbleness, still grinning shamelessly.

"You could have helped, you know," Heru-pa grumbled, his shoulders sagging. He pointed to the dagger at Set's hip. "Could have put your heirloom to good use."

"And miss all the fun? Not for Ra's wings!" Set replied, struggling to keep his composure. He slipped the dagger from its scabbard and lifted it theatrically. "This noble blade was not forged to slay fledgling lizards. It was made to drink of the blood of ancient draccans."

Heru-pa glanced at the onyx blade enviously. He leveled his friend with a withering stare, but could not contain the laughter bubbling up in his throat. "Go kiss a joltfish. Next time, you can play the lizard wrangler, and I'll be looking out for his mom."

"I wouldn't dare!" Set cackled. "It seems like you need all the time you can get to sharpen those trapping skills. You'll be putting them to use soon enough."

Heru-pa's face darkened. "I won't be trapping lizards." He glanced south, beyond the highlands. It seemed like only yesterday that the hybrid nature of the Rathadi was unveiled to him during the Ceremony of Revelation. At that time, his sojourn to find his own sentinel had seemed a lifetime away.

"I know," Set said, the mirth fading from his voice. He slipped the blade back into the scabbard and clasped Heru-pa's shoulder. "You will find a mighty sentinel that is worthy of you. And you of him."

Heru-pa gave his friend a grateful smile.

"Still," Set said, an impish grin spreading across his face

again. "It's a good thing there's plenty of time left before your Rite of Valediction."

Heru-pa smacked Set's hand off his shoulder and punched him in the arm.

Set yelped and rubbed his sore limb. "You may be stronger, but I'll always be faster. Not even joining with your sentinel will change that."

"Only in your visions," Heru-pa shot back.

"Well, then it's as good as true," Set replied smugly.

Heru-pa sighed and picked a shoot of honey grass before plopping onto the meadow that extended over the valley below them. He nibbled on the stem, letting the sweet juice coat his mouth as he peered northward across the grass, past the coastline of the Inner Ring, and to the Center Island beyond the water. The sprawling terrain of the Inner Ring, the home of the Rathadi, stretched out to the east and west, before curving north and connecting again on the far side of the island. The contours of the Ring rose and dipped in concentric layers, from low-lying prairies at its edges to the soaring highlands at its interior, as the landmass completely encircled the island metropolis that rose from the water: the city of Amun.

The Purean capital was completely enclosed by an immense defensive wall that towered one hundred feet above the shimmering, turquoise water of the channel that separated it from the Inner Ring. Every hundred paces, bastion towers rose another one hundred feet into the sky. Yet even the bastions were dwarfed by the single alabaster spire that jutted out into the blue sky from the palace grounds in the center of the island.

"We should head back soon," Set said, drawing Heru-pa back, "before they catch on we snuck out again."

Heru-pa extended his arm toward the western horizon and used his palm to measure out the distance between the sun and the highlands below. It stood two hand spans above the horizon. "Let's stay another half span," he said absent-mindedly.

Set gave him a playful shove. "You daydreaming about Mia again?"

Heru-pa spit out the honey grass, his somber expression reflecting his spirit.

Set noticed the shift in his friend's mood. He eyed Heru-pa quizzically. "Why the glum face?"

"My Rite of Valediction," Heru-pa started, then stopped, unsure of how to continue.

Set sighed. "You know I was just having fun with you. If anybody is worthy of Ra's sentinel, it is you. He will seek you out, and you will—"

"It's not that," Heru-pa cut in.

Set raised his eyebrows. "It's not?"

"Will you…" Heru-pa swallowed. "Will you join my mother and father during the ceremony, and complete the Triad?"

Set opened and closed his mouth, but no sound came out. Finally, he managed to stammer, "M-me? The Third Pillar? But… but I'm not Rathadi. And besides, shouldn't your grandfather—"

"I talked to Grandfather," Heru-pa said. "And to my parents."

"And they agreed?"

"You know how they feel about you. Besides, they think that it would be good for our people."

"A Pure One? As a Pillar?" Set shook his head. "Have they talked to my parents?"

Heru-pa hesitated. "Not yet, I... I wanted to talk to you first."

Set rose and stood as proud and tall as his five-foot frame allowed. "Heru-pa, son of Isis and Osiris, it shall be my honor."

Heru-pa allowed a smile to spread over his lips. He got up and extended his arm to his friend. "Brothers forever."

Set clasped his forearm. "Brothers forever," he replied. "So, have you thought about your adult name?"

Heru-pa nodded.

"And?" Set asked.

"You know I can't tell you."

"Not fair!" Set groaned. "Not even now that I'm going to be—"

A cacophony of bells froze the next word on his lips. Heru-pa's thoughts spun at hearing the sound.

"Th-the alarm?" Set's face mirrored Heru-pa's own disbelief.

Heru-pa returned his friend's bewildered gaze. "We have not been attacked since…"

"Maybe it's a military exercise?"

Heru-pa shook his head.

Blood drained from Set's face as realization struck. "I need to get back to the capital!"

Heru-pa glanced to the temple on the east side of the Ring. It would take them the better part of a span running at break-neck pace to get there. They would then have to cross the long bridge over the channel to the Center Island. He turned and looked south to the highlands.

"No," Heru-pa said.

"No?" Set croaked.

"It will take too long to get to the temple, let alone across the bridge to the capital. And what if we don't make it in time? We could be trapped on the bridge during an attack."

"We could take the sky carriage when we get to the temple." Set pointed to the tethered gondolas shuttling between the Rathadi temple and the Purean palace.

"And risk being fried by the Eye while we're dangling in the air?" Heru-pa shot back. "We'll be safe in the highlands. If we head for Shadow's Beak, we'll get a better view of the Outer Ring and what is happening."

"You want to get closer to the Brim?" Set's voice shrieked into a falsetto. "Are you crazy?"

"Don't you want to see what's going on?"

"Our parents are going to kill us when they find out!"

"We'll just tell them we thought we'd be safer hiding in the highlands, rather than risk racing across the bridge," Heru-pa replied, a mischievous look on his face.

Set stared at him, as if unable to believe what he was about to say. "I am so going to regret this."

Heru-pa whooped and took off, racing for the high ground.

"Wait, slow down!" Set yelled before rushing after him.

"We're not going to miss it!" Heru-pa yelled back, trying to carry his voice over the ringing of the alarm bells. He continued racing at full speed, weaving his way between branches as they made their way up the small mountain.

A quarter span later, they arrived at a steep cliff, panting hard.

"Why'd you stop?" Set asked. He pointed right. "Serpent's Pass is that way."

"The path will take too long," Heru-pa replied. "Besides, we want to get up as high as we can, not just cut across the highlands."

Set gaped at the cliff before them. He gave Heru-pa a pleading look. "Please tell me you're not thinking what I think you're thinking."

"It's less than fifty feet. And it's an easy climb, just like going up a ladder."

"Maybe for you," Set said. "My mom told me—"

"Don't be a craven. Mia could do this climb in her sleep."

Set's jaw tightened at the mention of the girl's name.

"I'll lead the way. Just do what I do." Heru-pa studied the cliff face. A route seemed to appear in his head as if sketched by an invisible hand. He stepped to the wall and reached for the first handhold then grinned over his shoulder. "See you on top."

The surest handholds seemed to seek out his fingers all by themselves as Heru-pa scaled the wall, and before long, he was halfway up the cliff. He glanced down. Set was a dozen feet below him, clinging to the rock with white-knuckled fingers.

"You're doing great. Just keep doing what you're doing," Heru-pa called down.

Set grunted a reply that sounded like a reference to a foot and Heru-pa's backside, but he pressed on.

A short while later, Heru-pa crested the ridge. He reached down and helped Set over the edge.

"Told you that you could—*Ow!*" he yelped when Set smacked him in the head.

"I can't believe I let you talk me into this!" Set called out between ragged breaths. "This has got to be the most stupid thing that you've ever—" He looked to the sea, and his jaw dropped.

Heru-pa followed Set's gaze south. Beyond the Inner Ring, separated by another, wider, circular basin of water, stood the vast Outer Ring, known as the Brim, which completely encircled the Inner Ring and served as the first defense of their island home. Past the Brim, in the open waters of the South Sea, six massive black warships held station, their red, rectangular sails billowing in the wind.

"It *is* an attack!" Set called out, the words frosted with fear.

Heru-pa took in their surroundings. They were on the edge of a cliff, a sheer drop of at least two hundred feet on the side facing the Brim. He recalled his grandfather's lessons about the formidable natural defenses of the island. The ringed outer and inner landmasses and the two circular bodies of water formed a defensive perimeter that had repelled assaults on the island for millennia. Thousands of treacherous rocks hidden from view just beneath the water that surrounded the Brim made a night attack impossible, forcing any fleet to attack by day and exposing them to the terrifying power of the sun weapon.

"Calm down," Heru-pa said, trying to keep his voice steady. "We're safe here."

"What are they waiting for?"

Heru-pa reached into the bag he had strapped around his back and pulled out a metal cylinder. Set's eyes widened.

"A farseeker? Where did you—"

"I borrowed it from *Amah's* observatory," Heru-pa said, expanding the device and lifting it to his eye.

"You what?"

Heru-pa ignored him and aimed the farseeker north, back to the Center Island and the massive bowl-shaped mirror that crowned the tall spire in the heart of the capital. The Eye of Amun was designed by his grandfather and used the power of the sun to keep the island safe. A dozen Purean and Rathadi soldiers, the Guard of the Eye, stood in position on the platform, their own farseekers trained on the ships.

"Why aren't they using the Eye?" Set asked.

Heru-pa swung the glass out to the sea again. "The ships are still too far. At that range it won't be strong enough."

"They're going for the gate!" Set cried out. Heru-pa watched with morbid fascination as five of the six ships broke off and steered for the massive water gate that protected the single entrance from the open sea to the Brim Basin, the circular body of water between the Brim and the Inner Ring. The ships formed a wedge, picking up speed as they drew closer. Huge battering rams at the bows of the ships skimmed just over the surface of the water.

The warships collided with the gate. A blinding light then a huge explosion swept over the island. The shockwave traveled across Heru-pa's skin and through his body, stealing his breath. He gasped, almost losing hold of the farseeker.

"Amun's grace," Set muttered.

Heru-pa blinked through the flickering spots that assaulted his vision. His heart plummeted as the smoke cleared, revealing a gaping hole in the outer gate.

The air stilled, and perfect silence hung in the air, then the ringing of the alarm bells intensified and changed pitch.

"The breach alert!" Set gasped.

The sixth ship changed course and targeted the remnants of the massive gate hanging from its vast hinges.

Heru-pa focused the farseeker at the Eye of Amun. The Guard moved in a coordinated bustle, and the huge mirror tilted down and toward the ship, preparing to unleash the energy of the sun upon it.

"They are doomed," Heru-pa whispered.

The air grew still and heavy, and the chatter of birds hushed. A chill rolled in, as if bearing the threat of a storm, swallowing the sultry day. The landscape dimmed, but not into the dull gray of a cloud-covered sky. Instead, a faint yellow engulfed the island, like the glow cast by a fading torch.

Set raised his head and pointed at the sun. "Look!"

Heru-pa squinted, shielding his eyes with his hand. A dark disk moved in front of the sun.

"A black sun!" Set exclaimed.

An eclipse? A cold shock rippled through Heru-pa. *The Eye...* He honed in on the spire. The soldiers on the platform stood frozen, their gazes raised to the skies.

The warmth ebbed, and the sky darkened while the black disk swallowed the sun. Fireflies winked on as a chorus of crickets began their twilight song. A star materialized, then another. A few final ripples of light rushed over the ground before darkness descended on them.

Heru-pa forced his gaze back to the sea, just in time to see the black ship break through the battered gate and enter the narrow channel that led into the Brim Basin.

"It... it got through..." Set moaned. An instant later the batteries of catapults on both sides of the narrow channel sprang to life.

The first volley of the boulders missed its mark, and the ship continued its course untouched.

"Come on!" Set pleaded.

A second volley took to the air. Most of the projectiles splashed harmlessly into the water again, but one of the giant rocks scored a hit, turning the ship's center mast into a rain of splinters. Heru-pa stared mesmerized as the huge beam pitched and collapsed onto the deck, crushing everything in its path.

"Take that!" Set hollered.

A glimmer of light appeared in the sky, then the sun brightened, returning daylight to the island.

A moment later the ship erupted in flames. The screams from dozens of throats reached Heru-pa's ears. He blinked to dim the flashes of light inside his eyes then pointed the farseeker at the ship again. The sailors scurried around the deck to keep the ship on course, even as the searing heat from the Eye continued to burn and consume them. Heru-pa zeroed in on the men's faces. Their skin was covered by strange, swirling markings.

"Why aren't they jumping off?" Heru-pa cried out. "Why aren't they saving themselves?" A figure caught his gaze. He focused the farseeker. A woman stood on the bridge of the ship, seemingly unaffected by the blaze. Even though the sky was bright, and the ship was alight with flames, shadow pooled around her like smoke. Fire lapped at the wood surrounding her, but no flicker of its light reached the woman's form. She lifted a wooden staff in her right hand.

No, not wood.

Heru-pa blinked. The staff coiled around her hand like a serpent. She moved her arms and her mouth, barely visible beneath the dark hood, as if in a chant or incantation. Before her, sinuous shapes that looked like thick ropes coiled together began moving, their jet-black scales shimmering in the flames. Heru-pa's chest tightened, and dread pooled in his stomach.

Serpents?

"Set—!" he called out when another salvo of stone projectiles took to the air. This time three of them scored direct hits, gouging huge chunks of wood from the deck and port side of the vessel. The hooded figure stood still as a statue, surrounded by the smoke, yet seemingly unscathed by the flames. She turned her head and fixed Heru-pa with a piercing gaze, her eyes burning into him with spellbinding intensity.

Heru-pa gasped and reeled back. He yanked the farseeker from his eyes as if it were on fire.

"What happened?" Set asked. "What did you see?"

"I… I…"

A hand grasped Heru-pa's shoulder. He screamed and whirled—and stared into a pair of reptilian eyes peering down at him.

"Q-Qar?" Heru-pa stammered.

CHAPTER 2

Heru-pa and Set stood shoulder to shoulder, heads bowed. Qar's even breathing echoed behind them as the fading sunlight streamed into the vaulted interior of the elegantly appointed chamber, shining across the gilded columns and the silk tapestries suspended between them.

A tall, regal woman rested in an exquisite chair against the far wall that was covered by a blanketing mural painted by the Pure One's master artisans. The woman wore a deep-blue robe that left one shoulder bare. Her slender jawline and prominent cheekbones looked carved out of dark marble, and her almond-shaped eyes glinted like polished sapphires, matching the stones in the slim crown that adorned her head. A dozen Purean guards and twice as many court attendants lingered against the other three walls of the hall.

Heru-pa rocked from one foot to the other, doing all he could to prevent himself from fidgeting with his tunic. After what seemed like an eternity, the woman turned to Set. "Are you hurt?" she asked.

Set shook his head without looking up.

"Have you any idea what you put me through?"

"Mother—" Set began.

"Don't you 'mother' me!" she interrupted. "Instead, explain to me why the crown prince of the Pure Ones is roaming around the Ring during an attack, instead of being safely behind city walls?" She leaned forward, her palms digging into the armrests. "And why, of all the souls in Amun's realm, it is the Rathadi weapons master who finds him and brings him home?"

Heru-pa and Set flinched at her tone. The woman stood and approached.

"Where were they?" she asked Qar.

"Shadow's Beak, Your Majesty," the weapons master replied. "Fortunately, one of our lookouts spotted them, and I was able to reach them quickly."

"Shadow's Beak?" the queen's voice went up an octave. "How did you get up there?"

Set shuffled his feet. "We… we climbed."

"You what?"

"I…" Set started but stopped under her glare.

"You are the crown prince to the Pure Ones," the queen said. "You must learn to act like one."

"Yes, Mother," Set said meekly.

Heru-pa stirred. "Your Majesty, it was all my fault. I—"

"Hold your tongue, boy!" the Purean queen snapped at him. "I shall get to you in good time. You may be a Rathadi princeling, but never forget that Set is the crown prince of the Kingdom Island of Atlantis, the heir to the ruling family. You are not his equal. Have you any idea of the risk to which you exposed him?"

Heru-pa flinched again. He felt heat rising behind his eyelids.

The queen waved one of the attendants over.

"Take the prince to his chambers. He is not to leave until I have spoken with him again."

"Yes, Your Majesty," the attendant said, and scurried to Set. She grasped his arm and nudged him along. Set shot Heru-pa a dejected look over his shoulder as he followed the woman out.

"Now to you, Rathling," the queen said to Heru-pa. "You have endangered the prince's wellbeing and his life, and once again brought discontent to me. We shall make certain that this is the last time. One night in the castle cells should make you think twice before you decide to endanger the crown prince's life again."

"The castle cells?" Heru-pa whimpered, unsure he heard right. Behind him, Qar's steady breathing hitched for the first time since they had entered the queen's chamber.

She nodded to one of her royal guards. "Captain Nebet, take this miscreant below."

Heru-pa tensed as the captain approached him. His lower lip began to tremble.

Qar stepped in front of Heru-pa. "Your Majesty…" he began. The guard stopped and hesitated.

The queen's eyes narrowed. "You dare to defy my order, Weapons Master? In my own palace? You have my gratitude for bringing my son to me unharmed, but you forget yourself." She addressed the guard again. "Take him, Captain."

Nebet reached for Heru-pa.

The huge door to the throne room opened loudly, and a

quiet voice filled the chamber. "If you lay your hand on my boy, Captain, it will be the last thing it will ever touch."

The guard froze.

Heru-pa whirled. "Grandfather!" he sobbed.

"Silence, boy," Thoth directed a burning glance at him.

Queen Nuit glared at the old Rathadi. "You dare to come into my hall and threaten my captain?"

"I will take care of the boy, Your Highness," Thoth said, and approached Heru-pa.

"Your *Majesty!*" Queen Nuit bristled. "You will address me properly in my own palace, and you will learn your place, Archsage!"

"Enough!" another voice called out from behind Heru-pa's grandfather. All the soldiers in the room snapped to attention and sank to one knee.

Geb, the High King of Atlantis, entered the hall. His bronzed face was all angles and hard corners, sharpened further by a carefully trimmed beard that was streaked with fingers of silver. He crossed the chamber, his white and gold cloak rippling around him.

Qar took a knee and pulled Heru-pa down to the cold stone.

"Thoth, take your grandson to his parents," King Geb said. "And tell King Osiris I have need of his council. Return with him soon as you can."

Thoth bowed. "As you wish, Your Majesty." He glanced to Heru-pa. "Let's go, boy."

The queen opened her mouth, but the king cut her off with a raised hand. "My Queen, I understand your displeasure, but we have more important things to worry about than two runaway princelings."

Heru-pa tried to keep a stoic face as he hurried after his grandfather. Qar bowed low to the king and queen and followed them out.

They left the throne room and stepped through a vaulted gateway into a corridor. A thick red carpet lined the marble floor beneath their feet, muting their footsteps as they aimed for the stairs to the sky carriage terminus that would take them across the channel to the Temple of Ra. Arched supports held up walkways that encircled the high walls overhead.

"Your mother is displeased," Thoth said. "What in Amun-Ra's name were you thinking?"

"We just wanted to explore the Ring, Grandfather. Soon I will have to go out and—"

"Soon, but not yet," Thoth interrupted gently.

"When the alarm rang, we thought it would be safer to stay where we were, rather than to head back." Heru-pa pulled at his collar. "And… and we thought maybe we could see Amun's gaze," he added, with a trace of guilt. "We didn't mean to upset anybody."

Thoth stopped at the bottom of the wide stairs that led to the terminus. He faced Heru-pa and took a knee. His gray lupine pupils shone with an intensity that stirred the fine hairs on the back of Heru-pa's neck.

"Do not rush to know destruction and death," Thoth said. "Both will seek you out of their own volition, and before you know it, you will wish they had never found you." He paused. "I understand your youthful fascination, but the relationship between the Rathadi and Pure Ones is strained, at best. We can ill afford your childish games complicating matters further. You and Set are old enough and wise enough to know better. You are both princes. Learn to act like them."

Heru-pa winced at his grandfather's words.

"Do you understand the importance of what I am telling you?"

Heru-pa nodded.

"Good," the old Rathadi said, and stood. "No doubt your mother and father will attempt to convey the same message. Perhaps not quite as calmly."

Qar chuckled softly, and Heru-pa shot him a glare.

They climbed the stairs in silence and reached an expansive terrace on the east side of the palace that served as the entry point onto the sky carriage. Two Purean guards greeted them. Manned by Pureans on this end and Rathadi on the side of the temple, the thick tethers that held the moving gondolas spanned the channel and connected the Purean palace and the Temple of Ra. Constructed to provide a quick way for the Rathadi and Purean royals to interact, it was yet another marvel of engineering that had been conceived and developed by his grandfather.

They entered one of the gondolas, and Qar latched the door behind them. Heru-pa felt the slight lurch as the cables engaged, and the carriage began its journey to the temple. Soon they had left the grounds of the Center Island and were traveling over water. The trio sat in silence as Heru-pa watched the channel beneath them. The view of the dark water stirred memories of the burning ship.

"Who attacked us, Grandfather?" he asked.

Thoth regarded him silently before replying. "We do not know."

"They knew about the eclipse, didn't they?"

Thoth nodded. "Even we have not been able to master the overlapping cycles of the moon and the sun, despite years of trials and observations."

"*Amah* told me she was close to understanding it." Heru-pa gave his grandfather a timid smile. "I'm sure the two of you will figure it out soon."

Thoth's lips curved up whimsically. "Your words in Ra's ears, my boy."

They continued in silence as they approached the vast rooftop of the temple. Surrounded by four spires that rose up from its roof, the Temple of Ra was capped by the most revered symbol of the Rathadi, their sacred monument: an enormous pyramid.

The gondola stopped on the high terrace, the Rathadi terminus of the sky carriage. As they exited, they were greeted by a pair of guards. Heru-pa smiled, savoring the feeling of being back home. Even though only the narrow channel separated the Purean city and the temple, they could not have been more different. Unlike the Pureans and their monolithic and urban architecture, the Rathadi preferred spacious designs and open ranges. The temple and the sacred monument were the only substantial structures in the Inner Ring and were home to the royal family and the few who worked in the temple. Most of the Rathadi lived in smaller settlements surrounding it and in the eastern part of the Inner Ring.

They descended the stairs into the high gardens. Heru-pa found his mouth going dry, unable to forget the images burned into his mind through the farseeker. He swallowed to gain his voice. "Grandfather?"

"Yes, my boy?"

"When I watched the ship through the farseeker, I saw the men's faces… They were covered by strange ink."

"Like the Purean truth-seer?"

"Yes—" Heru-pa considered—"and no. They were different patterns."

"What kind of patterns?" Thoth asked.

Heru-pa chewed on his bottom lip, pondering how to best describe the swirling lines that covered the men's faces.

Thoth stopped and picked up a fallen branch. "Could you draw it for me?" He broke it in half and handed a piece to Heru-pa.

"I… I think so," Heru-pa said, and took the stick.

He stepped off the walkway and cleared a patch in the dirt, forcing himself to recall the details of the serpentine lines that covered the faces of the men on the ship. One particular shape came to mind. Two concentric circles, bisected with another swirling line. He squatted and drew the design as best he could.

His grandfather bent down and studied the drawing, stroking the gray fur of his jaw. "Are you certain?" he asked.

Heru-pa nodded. "What—?"

"Did you see anything else?"

"When I watched the ships, I thought I saw…" He stopped, unsure of how—or whether—to continue.

"Go on, boy," the old Rathadi urged.

"A woman," Heru-pa said.

"On the ship that broke through?"

Heru-pa nodded again.

"Was there anything you noticed about the woman?"

"She wore a dark robe. And seemed unaffected by the

flames. And… she had a staff." Heru-pa hesitated. "It may have been a trick of the light, but it looked like the staff was moving… coiling… like a serpent. I know that sounds—"

"Coiling like a serpent?" Thoth interrupted, his voice hardening. "Are you certain?"

"Y-yes," Heru-pa stuttered, flustered by his grandfather's shift in demeanor. "I… I think so."

Thoth stood and faced Qar. "Take the boy home. And tell King Osiris that the Purean king requires his presence." He used his foot to erase the drawing. "You must not speak of this to anybody," he said to Heru-pa. "Neither of you," he added, then turned and rushed back across the gardens before either of them could muster a reply.

"Wait," Heru-pa called after him when he found his voice. "Where are you going?"

"I must consult the royal archives," Thoth replied without slowing down.

Heru-pa flicked a questioning glance at Qar. The weapons master met his gaze halfway and shrugged.

"Who do you think they were?" Heru-pa asked.

"I do not know," Qar said. "I do not have your grandfather's wisdom, but few goals are worthy of sacrificing a small flotilla." The weapons master placed a palm on Heru-pa's shoulder and nudged him on. "Let's get you home."

They continued on wordlessly. Heru-pa's trepidation grew with every step.

"Is *Amah* really mad?" he asked.

"She is not too pleased."

"I really messed up this time, didn't I?"

"It is not for me to judge the actions of a prince," Qar said.

"But I would advocate a downcast gaze and multiple instances of the use of the words 'I'm sorry.'"

Heru-pa's shoulders sagged. "That bad?"

They turned the corner into the corridor for the royal living quarters, and the two guards that stood at the end of the corridor nodded when they spotted them. Qar raised his arm in greeting as they approached.

"The majesties are expecting you, Prince Heru-pa," one of the guards said.

Heru-pa sighed woefully as Qar knocked on the tall double doors.

"Enter," came a voice from within.

Qar opened the door. "Good luck," he said, and patted him on the back as they entered the chamber.

Fading sunlight poured into the spacious, vaulted interior through a west-facing wall that consisted of nothing more than a row of arched windows and a tall doorway that opened onto a sprawling terrace. Long, flowing curtains danced in the warm evening breeze as Heru-pa's parents stood on the sunbathed platform overlooking the channel and the Purean capital.

His father turned. "The adventurer returns," he said, his voice carrying the subtle confidence of one shaped from birth to lead. King Osiris wore his customary black trousers, but his chest and feet were bare. As one of the few Rathadi ever to live with the gift of the scorpion, he preferred the feel of the sun on his onyx skin. He appraised Heru-pa with vertical pupils, their deep black splitting an amber, rich as the sun rising over the Eastern Sea. "I heard you gave the Purean queen a sour stomach today."

Before Heru-pa could think of a reply, his mother

approached. At first glance Queen Isis could not have appeared more different from her husband. Flowing hair framed an elegant, bronzed face. A long, white robe covered a body that was petite and slender enough to almost seem delicate. At a second glance, a subtle edge of threat shined through her features, and watching her move was like witnessing a panther stalking prey in a tree. She embraced him tightly, then held him at arms-length. Her deep, feline eyes seemed to look through him as she studied him with an equal measure of relief and scorn. "Are you alright?"

He simply nodded.

"What were you thinking?" she asked.

"I'm sorry, *Amah.*"

"You have to be more responsible. I heard the queen was very upset," she said.

Osiris gave a chuckle. "I do wish I could have seen the look on her face."

Heru-pa turned to his father, mouth agape. Instead of the anger he expected, his father's scaly lips curved into a hint of a smile. The fading sunlight behind his tall form caught his skin at just the right angle, and the scales on his broad shoulders shimmered a trace of blue and green.

Isis frowned. "Truly? You are not helping."

"The boy was curious. That is a worthy quality in a future leader."

"His *quality* was going to land him in a Purean cell for the night!"

"I doubt the queen had any intentions of following through. She was vexed and wanted to give him a scare," Osiris said, and chuckled again. He quickly raised his hands when he saw his wife's glare, worthy of the Eye of Amun. "But I am certainly not saying he did not deserve it," he added.

"I'm just glad they were spotted, and Qar got to them when he did, before anything else happened during this assault."

"A handful of ships, My Love," Osiris replied. "That hardly qualifies as an assault."

"One of the ships breached the outer gate," Isis countered.

Qar, who had been standing by the door quietly, cleared his throat. "Majesties," he chimed in hesitantly with a bow. "My apologies for intruding, but King Geb kindly requested King Osiris's presence."

"He is calling the King's Council?" Osiris asked.

The weapons master nodded.

Osiris sighed. "The fearless ruler of the Pure Ones beckons." He reached for his black cloak that hung draped over a tall sofa then ruffled Heru-pa's hair. "Take care of your mother while I'm gone."

"Yes, *Tato*," Heru-pa said.

The king gave Isis a tender embrace. "Don't be too hard on the boy," he said before stepping through the door.

Qar bowed to the queen and followed him out. When the door closed behind them, Heru-pa's mother eyed him seriously. "Your valediction ceremony will take place in less than two months' time. You must make certain that you are worthy of your adult name."

"Yes, *Amah*," he said.

"I was worried about you."

"I know, *Amah*. I'm sorry." He stood in silence for several moments before he began trembling. He blinked to keep the tears from his eyes.

"It is alright," his mother said. "I am sure the queen was not that upset with you."

Heru-pa shook his head. "It's not that."

"What is it?" she asked gently.

"When I saw the men. On the ship. They... they just stood there as they... burned. As they burned alive."

Isis pulled him close. Heru-pa closed his eyes and took in the familiar scent of jasmine in her hair and the metopion oil on her skin. The images of the men burning and screaming on the ship slowly dissolved, draining the tension from him.

"Try not to think about that. Let us find something more enjoyable to discuss, shall we?" his mother offered.

Heru-pa swallowed and nodded.

"Did you ask Set about your valediction ceremony?"

A small smile flickered across Heru-pa's lips. "Yes."

"And?"

"He agreed!"

"Did you really expect anything else?"

"No," Heru-pa replied. His face grew somber. "It's just... with what happened today, I don't think that the king and queen will give their consent."

"Give them a few days. Unity Day is coming up. And your grandfather can be very persuasive," Isis said. "Sometimes a little too much for his own good," she added. "You know the king values his council, and I'm sure he can help sway both of them to allow Set to participate."

"If you think so," Heru-pa said, not quite convinced.

"I do." Isis pulled him in again, crinkled her nose, and shoved him away playfully. "You definitely need a bath before sleeping."

"But, *Amah*..."

"No arguments," she said. "I will have a bath drawn for you. Wash up and put your night clothes on. I will see you afterward."

Heru-pa nodded meekly and lumbered to the bath chamber.

Half a span later, he laid in his bed. Isis came in and eased down on the side.

Heru-pa reached for her hand. "I'm sorry, *Amah*, I didn't mean to worry you, or make the queen angry."

"I know," Isis replied.

He scooted over. "Will you stay with me? For a little while?"

Isis nodded and laid down beside him, holding him in her arms. Heru-pa closed his eyes and listened to his mother's breathing until he fell into an uneasy sleep.

In his sleep, the boy did not see his mother as she rose and blew out the candle, casting the room into complete darkness to all but those blessed by the gift of the sacred cat. Isis kissed him gently on his forehead then placed her palms on his head, her thumbs and forefingers shaped into the triangle that represented the rays of the sun bathing the earth.

In his sleep, the boy did not hear his mother when she leaned in and softly whispered, "You are Horus, son of Isis and Osiris. You shall know no fear."

ACKNOWLEDGMENTS

As always, my first words of thanks must go to my family who keep me grounded in the things that truly matter, provide unconditional support, and are an always-accessible sounding board for all those outlandish ideas that, with their help, somehow manage to evolve into a decent story. To Vera, Sarah, Heather and Misha—thank you. Your love, patience and support cannot be overstated.

Sarah deserves a special shout-out for once again writing the author bio. Thank you for giving the readers a glimpse into my life through your eyes.

My valiant group of beta readers for finding time in their busy lives to read and dissect the manuscript: Calais Fitzmaurice, Scott George, Patti Grayson, Elizabeth Hager, Amber Hodges, Nicole Lopez, Matt Paauw, Mike Snodgrass, and Ornina Yousef. On behalf of all the readers for whom you made Legacy of Ra a better book, thank you for lending your considerable talents and gifts to the world of my writing.

A big thank you to my editor, Phil Athans, for his constructive criticism and astute advice.

The hugely talented artist, Igor Voloshin, for providing his skills and creating yet another piece of art to grace my book. His gorgeous covers make my books look way cooler than any author deserves.

To the bloggers, booktubers, and instagrammers, for the wonderful reviews and for spreading the word about Alyssa's world.

My wife and greatest champion, Vera, who continues to support me more than I deserve and can ever thank her for. You are my rock and have my love and endless gratitude.

My final thought of appreciation is, as always, reserved for you, my amazing readers. All of this hard work and effort would have been pointless if it wasn't for you. Thank you from the bottom of my heart for continuing to allow me to share my imagination with you.

Hello, dear Reader,

Congratulations! You have finished the Blood of Ra Trilogy! I hope you liked it; Dad worked really hard on it. Are you sad? I teared up when I finished the last chapter of Legacy of Ra. Dad seemed pleased with himself about that.

This is a bit of a melancholic moment for me, writing the last 'author bio' of the trilogy. I could continue to go on about my dad, about everything he's done to deserve a book of his own. But I'm not going to. This is not about what Dad did, or what he does, but about what he will do. His own legacy.

There are a hundred things my father has done, and a hundred more he may do. As he continues to write, maybe he will do a sequel series, or pull a Star Wars and do a prequel series on Horus and his story first. Perhaps, he will leave the rest of what happens to Tasha, Paul, Clay, and Alyssa to your imagination and begin work on a whole new speculative fiction book.

His legacy will be the lives of the people he has touched. His students, banging their heads against the wall as they solved physics problems. His friends from med school, texting about apocalyptic-ready trucks one of them bought (Don't ask... Dad even based one of the characters on him). The lives of those he ameliorated and saved when he worked as a doctor. The dozens of people employed at the company he started. His daughter, forever touched by the countless acts of love he has committed for her. His legacy are the readers of the Blood of Ra series that made this all possible: you.

What will your legacy be? Will you be proud of that? Will you continue to read? Will you be inspired by what you read to make a difference? Will you try your best to be the best you can be? I hope you do.

It has been a wild ride. Thank you for being a part of it.

Sarah

———

———

———